VEGAS GOLD

THE VEGAS TRILOGY
BOOK 1

DALLAS BARNES

ROUGH
EDGES
PRESS

Vegas Gold
Paperback Edition
Copyright © 2025 Dallas Barnes

Rough Edges Press
An Imprint of Wolfpack Publishing
1707 E. Diana Street
Tampa, FL 33610

roughedgespress.com

Paperback ISBN 978-1-68549-617-3
eBook ISBN 978-1-68549-616-6
LCCN 2024951018

AUTHOR'S NOTE

Although based on the writer's experience as Director of Security & Surveillance in Resort & Casino operations, the characters, locations, and events herein are the product of the writer's imagination and used fictitiously.

Any resemblance to real persons, living or dead, is purely coincidental. All references to Resort & Casino operations, locations, protocols, and procedures are fictional presentations in an effort to protect the integrity of actual operations, the safety of staff, support personnel, and those who make Las Vegas real, our guests.

This book is dedicated to the men and women you don't see. Serving behind the scenes in resort and casino operations, they protect the lives and safety of guests and employees as well as the integrity of gaming. Their standards and qualifications are set by state gaming commissions. The challenges they face are not an easy task in an environment where emotions, money, alcohol, and nudity seem the norm. Many times, money is mixed with blood. It takes more than luck to protect Vegas Gold.

VEGAS GOLD

ONE
SATURDAY NIGHT LIVE

Balancing awkwardly, arms swinging, the shapely nude woman stood barefoot on the balcony railing above the main entrance of The Silver Palace in the glow of nighttime Las Vegas. The nude glanced at the crowd gathering below in the harsh night lighting. She hadn't gone unnoticed. The faces below stared up in awe. A worried valet attendant was on his cell with casino security. A middle-aged tourist from Buffalo climbing from a cab joined the faces staring into the night. He spotted the nude and dug in a pocket to remove bills and wave them in the air. "I'll bet a hundred she won't jump."

"Make it five hundred and you got a bet," a voice in the crowd answered quickly.

Her name was Jill Rogers. She was an attractive thirty-four-year-old nurse from San Diego. She had been married now for seven hours. It was her third. Elvis sang at her wedding. Her new husband, a surgeon, passed on her offer to make love after she appeared nude from their luxury suite bathroom. "Let's make it official," she suggested with a seductive smile, gesturing to the king-size bed.

Sixty-year-old Dr. Saul Ritter pushed from his chair to take his bride by the shoulders. Jill was his fourth wife, third nurse. He kissed her on the cheek and glanced at his five-thousand-dollar watch. "Dinner at nine, curtain for *The Beatles* at eleven. Let's save this for later."

The doctor was now down in the casino playing blackjack. It was Jill's telephone call to her seventeen-year-old son in La Mesa, coupled with the rejection by her new husband, which pushed her to the edge. "Tommy, honey, I'm in Las Vegas. You've got a new dad." She smiled into her iPhone.

"I don't want a new dad," the adolescent voice on her cell phone answered. "I already have two. Maybe I should try a new mom?"

A dial tone told her the call was over. Jill wept. Her new husband's literal kiss-off and her son's insult tore at her heart. All the men in her life, past and present, had rejected her. None wanted her. She was nude in every sense of the word. If nothing else, her pain-filled mind reasoned that with her death, she would have their pity. She moved for the balcony.

The crowd in the valet entrance watching the nude on the balcony high above grew quickly. Cars, cabs, limos, and a sea of cell phones waved in the night air as the growing crush of awe-filled faces stared skyward. Noisy shouts and insults filled the air. "Jump…come on, do it! You got no balls!" A burst of laughter followed.

———

LUKE MITCHEL WAS SITTING in the room directly above the nude woman on the balcony. Luke wasn't in Vegas to get married. Barbara Nichols, a friend and sometimes lover, was with him. The attraction for most people drawn to Las Vegas was to see and be seen. The excitement of wearing their best, or sometimes nothing at all, plus gambling and drinking, mixed with star-filled stages, was a powerful allure. Most visitors were drawn to the flame of the bright lights, but Luke Mitchel was different. He was in Las Vegas hiding. Not the usual situation for Vegas, but Luke Mitchel wasn't usual in many ways. He was hiding from the dark side of his life. He had been hiding from it for a long time. Barbara Nichols was downstairs shopping for an outfit for Lady Gaga's show.

As day turned to night, Luke sat in a comfortable chair, waiting, drink in hand, growing irritated with the noise from what he guessed was a crowd outside. He decided he'd look when he got up out of his chair, but he was in no hurry.

Luke was no stranger to casinos. He worked in one. He was the *Acting Director of Security and Surveillance* at the Wild River Resort in Rio Vista, Arizona. The hundred and seventy miles from Vegas to Wild River Casino was measured in more than miles. Although minor league in the world of gaming work, the Wild River Casino had become a disaster for Luke. The death of his mentor and boss—director of security, Jim Todd— had brought back a flood of painful memories he hoped were no longer part of his life, but they were.

A refugee from nine years with the LAPD, thirty-six-year-old Luke was no stranger to death. While working narcotics with the LAPD, his partner was shot and killed after walking into an armed robbery at a liquor store.

Sitting in an unmarked car outside, Luke heard the gunfire.

He scrambled out of the car to shoot and kill the sixteen-year-old running from the store, gun in hand. The video from the liquor store was graphic and convincing. The LAPD's *Use of Force Unit* and the *Shooting Review Board* found the shooting justified, but as weeks turned to months, Luke found little relief from the painful and haunting grief. His days and nights were filled with a never-ending string of *what-ifs*.

The LAPD provided counseling, a new assignment, and encouragement, but the waves of guilt grew worse. Most police officers losing a partner or having to shoot and kill in the line of duty found peace and went on. Luke wasn't one of them. The *ifs* were suffocating him. *If* he hadn't been the one to suggest he and his partner stop at the liquor store after their stakeout, *if* he hadn't picked that store, *if* he had gone in? He'd offered, but his partner, Rich Carson, just smiled and said, "Next time you're buying, pinhead." Carson opened the car door and was gone. Never to return.

The nagging ripples from the pebble in the pond were back. In Afghanistan, Corporal Luke Mitchel was on duty in the darkness when he found the mounting hours of nature's call could no longer be ignored. He reached out to a friend, another Marine, and asked him to cover his spot on the shadowy line for a few minutes. John Dillon smiled, cocking his weapon. "Ten minutes is all you get," he said. Luke hurried away.

It was only four minutes until the explosion and gunfire turned night to day. The firefight lasted six minutes. Two Marines and nine Afghans died. John Dillon was one of them. After the incident, the *ifs* had ambushed Luke for the first time. *If* only he hadn't asked

Dillon to take his place. *If* only he hadn't needed to relieve himself.

After the officer-involved shooting, the post-traumatic stress he'd suffered in Afghanistan was back and taking another toll. Day and night, it held him in a tight grip. Seven months after his police partner was shot to death, Luke came home to a quiet, empty house. He wasn't the only one suffering. His wife and three-year-old daughter were gone. He had lost more than a partner. He'd lost his wife, his child, and his heart. Two days later, Luke turned in his badge and gun and walked away.

The desert offered Luke a place to hide. He headed for it as fast as he could get out of LA. The searing heat, star-filled nights, and the vast panoramas offered haunting comfort. After combat in Afghanistan, the desert had somehow welcomed him home. His hunger for it could have been explained by a psychologist, but he wasn't interested in yet another outside opinion, he just wanted to be lost in the desert. Los Angeles—a desert in its own way—was now hundreds of miles behind him.

Now, weary of cars with smiling kids, motor homes, eighteen-wheelers, and three hours of driving, Luke looked for an exit. He found one and turned off the busy interstate.

Traffic on the two-lane, straight-arrow road he now drove along was light. Luke kept his speed at eighty-five miles an hour, flashing by slower cars, campers, and cars towing boats. It was more speeding *from* something, than *to* something. Another hour took him to an abandoned gas station, a car with broken windows and flat tires, and a sign saying *Rio Vista, Arizona, 8 Miles*.

Luke welcomed the sign. He was thirsty and wanted out of the car. He bumped his speed even higher, but the powerful Mustang joined in the conspiracy to make him miserable. It overheated. Condensation billowed from beneath the hood, clouding the windshield. "Son-of-a-bitch," he said before asking God to keep the car running until he reached something somewhere.

Luke drove across a bridge where the Colorado River separated California from Arizona with a red light on the dash staring at him. A sign on the bridge welcomed him to Arizona while another at the end welcomed him to Rio Vista, population: 3,406. The town, spread over a mile along Arizona 95, sizzled in a noontime temperature of one hundred and two degrees. Luke thought the place looked like a ghost town. He drove slower, still praying, finally spotting a repair shop. It was good news and bad news.

A gloved mechanic walked out to greet Luke and the steaming Mustang. "Overheated, ain't she," the mechanic said, stating the obvious. They raised the hood. "Looks like the pump may have given up. You speeding or something?"

"Can you fix it?" Luke asked.

The mechanic nodded. "Might take a couple days to get parts."

"You accept Visa?"

The mechanic spit. "Sorry, me and the Border Patrol, neither of us take visas."

Luke walked to a nearby motel. After a sleepless night and a bottle of coffee from a vending machine, he grew weary of the TV and a noisy, less-than-efficient air conditioner. He was reluctant to admit it, but the desert brought more worry.

Repair on the Mustang was going to take a serious bite out of the cash he had and after that, life was going to get grim. The car belonged to the LAPD credit union, and his wife would rightfully expect support. Reality was out of the shadows. Before leaving LA, he cashed out his police pension and mailed a cashier's check to his wife. He didn't know where she was, but he knew the check would be forwarded to her. The money would keep her comfortable for a while, but now he wished he hadn't been so generous. Grief had taken its toll, but the reality of the day, and the days to come, had hefty price tags hanging on them. He needed money.

Luke masked his worries and asked a motel clerk where he could find a drink.

"Try the bar at the casino," the clerk suggested.

"Casino?"

"Half mile up 95. On the left."

The walk was long and hot. Cars flashed by on the narrow roadway leaving Luke swarming in dust, but the casino wasn't difficult to find. Its towering glass façade glistened in the desert sun. Manicured palms lined the entrance, casting long shadows. Guest rooms with patios stretched high above the main entrance. The sprawling parking lot was dotted with cars, trucks, motor homes, and more. The casino supposedly belonged to the local Indian tribe, but Luke was sure they had a lot of help, and the profits were also going into other pockets. Still, it looked inviting, and all Luke cared about was that the air conditioning worked. A uniformed valet offered a smile as he opened the front door. Luke didn't think the man looked much like an Indian. A front desk, a dining room, chimes drifting from rows of slots crowded with seniors and an active card room with busy tables, added to the resort's atmosphere.

Luke's surprise grew even more when he found an indoor pool with twin waterfalls beneath a glass canopy and a view of the sky. There were no swimmers. A sign pointed to a lounge. Luke wanted a drink. Maybe two or three.

A whiteboard on a wall near the dim light of the bar had a message: *$25,000 Jackpot—Saturday Night.* Beneath the announcement, Luke read more: *Opportunities, Waitress, Cashier, Cook, Room Attendant, Night Desk Clerk, Security Officer—Experience Preferred.*

The seed took root. *Security*, hell, he could do that.

What kind of experience did they want and what was required? Was he qualified?

The casino was big, modern, and alive, even on a hot day in the middle of nowhere. The clatter and chime from slots filled the air. Players sat at a card table with an attentive dealer. Luke found the lounge, crossed to a padded bar, and slid onto a soft, cushioned chair. He was one of three at the bar. The bartender, a young, attractive female, wore faded jeans and a tight-fitting white blouse. Luke ordered a Jack Daniels and Coke.

"You a native of Rio Vista," Luke asked when the girl returned with his drink.

"I'm from Pittsburgh. The only natives here are Mojaves."

"Pittsburgh. You're a long way from home."

"Pittsburgh isn't home anymore. This is home now." She smiled.

Luke nodded. "So, you must like it here?"

The girl studied him for a moment before she reached beneath the bar to lift a telephone. She set the aging black telephone in front of Luke. "Security's number is 616."

Luke was surprised. "It shows that much?"

"It does." The girl moved away as another customer pushed onto a chair down the bar.

Luke took a swallow from his glass before setting it

aside. "What the hell," he said under his breath as he turned the telephone toward himself. He dialed *616*.

A male voice answered. Luke asked about employment.

"Yeah, we're looking," the voice said. "Stay put. I'll be out."

A tired-looking man in sunglasses, wearing a casual shirt and jeans arrived. He gestured for Luke to join him at a table. As they shook hands, Luke smelled alcohol on the man's breath. Luke guessed the man was in his fifties or early sixties.

"You want another one?" The man waved at the girl behind the bar. "I'm Jim Todd, director of security. Who you are?"

Luke later learned Todd had been fired from three casinos in Las Vegas and another in Loughlin. All after being drunk on the job. But the Mojaves seemed more concerned with Todd's skillset than his drinking habits. Todd was a *know-it-all* in every sense. He could read cards, knew the games, traditional and electronic. He could spot markings, short decks, counterfeits, corrupt dealers, dishonest employees, keyboards in the slots controlling the payouts, and cheaters when they sat down at a table. More important, however, was Todd's instinctive ability to read character. It had earned him his spot in charge of security.

Todd listened carefully when Luke spoke candidly about why he was looking for a job. Todd read Luke's face and hands. They said much about a man. Luke's words came out painfully, bit by bit. He searched for ones that somehow might soften reality. They didn't. When Luke finished, he looked to the floor, the wall, anywhere. Jim Todd saw that, too.

Todd took a final drink from his third glass. Then reached a hand across the table. "Welcome aboard, Luke."

"I've got to warn you, I don't know much about gambling," Luke said.

"Makes it easier," Todd replied.

In the days and weeks that followed, Luke thanked the bartender, whose name he learned was Barbara Nichols. He not only thanked her, he bought her dinner. They became friends. Very good friends.

———

THREE YEARS PASSED as Luke built a new life. He almost allowed himself to believe he was happy until he found Jim Todd dead in his car in the casino parking lot. There was an empty bottle of liquor in his calloused hands. Todd had taught Luke everything he knew about casino security—which was a lot. Luke was a quick study and had quickly become Todd's second in command.

After finding Jim Todd dead, Luke felt as if he had lost another partner. He knew the man was drinking himself to death, but he did nothing about it. Death was back, and the reminder lanced through him.

In the months following, Luke found becoming the acting director was more than challenging. It was both demanding and time-consuming. His cell phone never stopped ringing.

Now in charge, Luke supervised fifty-six men and women who covered the Wild River's four hundred and fifty slots, a card room, three dining rooms, four snack bars, valet, front desk, eight floors of guest rooms, boat docks, and a hundred other places where anything and everything could go wrong—but he loved it. If it happened at Wild River, good, bad, or ugly, a camera would see it, a CD would save it, and Luke Mitchel would have to make another call.

Luke knew with Todd's death, the Mojaves were watching him. They would decide his fate. Death was back, and Luke knew he had to get a grip on it. Why was it those closest to him died? Where was the logic?

He needed the job, but he was worried, shaken, and sleepless. The soul-crushing *ifs* were back. *If* he didn't get the job, *if* he didn't provide for his daughter, *if* he didn't…

The Marines, the LAPD, and now the Wild River Casino. What was it? Why was it? He needed to get away. To think, to decide, even to pray? Hell, how could he find a way out of this? Was there a way?

He needed some time, some space, some quiet. A commercial on television gave birth to an idea—*Wanna get away from it all? Try Vegas*. He hadn't had a day off in two months.

A second television commercial an hour later sealed the deal. This one was for The Silver Palace, a towering new casino, glistening in the Las Vegas sun. This image turned his idea into a reality. On the TV, a montage of the busy casino was followed by glimpses of inviting, comfortable guest rooms, restaurants, and shapely near-naked bodies surrounding pools.

Luke was tired and weary, but he was ready for it. He'd been to Las Vegas with his ex. They stayed in a comfortable room, saw great shows, got silly drinking, and won a couple of bucks. Hell, perhaps Vegas was the answer. The idea of walking into a crowded casino and not caring about who was doing what was appealing.

Luke called and made a reservation at The Silver Palace. No one went to Las Vegas by themselves unless there were gay, whore hunting, or intent on playing the latest winning scam just seen on *YouTube*, so Luke's next call was to Barbara Nichols.

She was surprised and hesitant, but finally accepted. The next morning, he told his number two man, Calvin Many-Coats, a savvy twenty-seven-year-old Mojave, he was going away, but didn't say where.

"The weekend and I'll be back. I'll have my cell, but don't call me."

"What's she look like?" Many-Coats asked.

During the drive to Las Vegas the next day, Luke tried avoiding little more than small talk with the green-eyed blonde, but Barbara was much more than an attractive woman. She was his lover, his confidant, and a seasoned, experienced bartender. She knew moods, attitudes, and perhaps most importantly, she knew bullshit when she heard it.

"Do you want to tell me the real reason we're going to Vegas?" Barbara asked after an hour of driving.

"Lady Gaga," Luke answered with a glance from the highway to the green-eyed blond beside him. "We've got reservations for her show tomorrow night."

"And which Gaga song do you like best?" Barbara pressed.

Luke considered lying. He hesitated. Truth was, and he knew it, he wasn't driving *to* somewhere, he was driving *away*, again. He was following a compulsion he didn't really understand. How could he put that in words? Barbara saw his reluctance and saved him from it.

"I know the feeling," Barb said. "Sometimes you just have to go. Where doesn't really matter. Just find a place, any place, as long as it's different. I call it getting lost in the crowd."

Luke nodded agreement. "Glad I invited you."

Luke expected to feel anxious when they reached Las Vegas, but he surprised himself when he found comfort in the bumper-to-bumper traffic. The Strip was crowded with cars, cabs, buses, and pedestrians. Most were in shorts or jeans sunk low on their asses. They were carrying shopping bags as they stared at the digital skyline, taking selfies, moving like lost sheep.

"Wow," Barbara said, watching the crowded sidewalks and the array of colorful casinos and resorts. "We're not in Kansas anymore."

Luke followed the traffic until The Silver Palace came into view. The towering façade stole their breath.

"You're absolutely right, Dorothy."

Luke followed a cab to the valet where they surrendered the car along with a ten-dollar tip to an eager uniformed attendant. The valet welcomed them and offered to check their bags. Luke added another ten to the tip.

It was hot. No surprise there, but stepping inside the automatic door to be swallowed by a rush of The Silver Palace's cool, conditioned air was a pleasant change. Barbara clung to Luke's arm as they moved through the crush of people.

The voices from the crowd mixed with chimes from an ocean of two thousand slots. Seated at the slots, there were shaved heads, beards, piercings, tattoos, big breasts, and makeup—way too much makeup. The sitters were young, old, White, and Black.

Luke paused and took Barbara's hand in his. This was raw Vegas. The towering ceiling was filled with chandeliers, the floor was polished and hosted a line of busy card tables as well as a circular bar with cushioned chairs and music.

Luke and Barbara were both experienced casino

employees, but they were lost in this. They were awestruck. The Silver Palace was comfortable, relaxing, and over-the-top awesome. Luke knew they were on camera. His eyes searched for them. There had to be many, but he found none. He knew they had walked through facial recognition, but he hadn't seen it. He looked for security officers. Saw none. The work the *invisibles* were doing was making the face of Las Vegas glow.

Here they were just another couple in the crowd. Here he wasn't a candidate for anything because someone died with a bottle in their hand. Here, he wasn't a Marine or an ex-LAPD cop. Here he was a guest. A guest with a beautiful woman holding on to his arm. This was Vegas. This was what he hoped for. With Barbara at his side, they moved to the front desk.

"The name is Mitchel," Luke said to a smartly dressed brunette behind the counter.

The girl offered a smile. "Welcome to The Silver Palace, Mr. Mitchel." Her fingers worked on a keyboard. She smiled again. "We have a Strip view suite waiting for you." The brunette pushed a flat silver electronic room key toward Luke. "One or two keys, sir?"

"One will be fine," Luke said. He thanked her with a nod before he and Barbara headed for the elevators. Both had worked late the night before. They were tired after the drive, but the Strip view suite drew them to the wide floor-to-ceiling sliding glass doors like bugs to a bright light.

The panorama of sprawling, colorful lights and endless lines of traffic, coupled with the fashionable two-room suite comfort, filled them with wonderment.

Barbara found the deep bathtub in the master bedroom. "Luke, come see this. It's big enough for two."

They ordered dinner from room service before Barbara filled the tub. Luke nearly fell asleep when she massaged his back with hot water and an aromatic sponge. He woke up when she moved the sponge to his lower stomach.

After making love and drinking more than they should, Luke and Barbara not only slept late the next morning, they slept most of the day.

"You know I can't drink at work," Barbara complained after they finished their breakfast in bed provided by room service.

"Must be difficult," Luke said.

"You try pouring all night and not drinking."

"Security is much easier," Luke said, as he searched the channels of the bedroom's big-screen TV until he found a football game.

Barbara dressed and announced her need for a new outfit for Lady Gaga's show. She kissed Luke and went shopping, leaving Luke to move to the big-screen in the living room where he watched the Buffalo Bills meet Kansas City.

His cell phone, as Many-Coats had promised, stayed silent. Las Vegas, Luke decided, no matter what the world thought, could be relaxing. He was eating cold french fries and watching a post-game show when a hovering drone appeared outside his balcony window.

At first Luke was surprised, then he realized it had to be linked to the din of crowd noise he was hearing outside. Barefoot, shirtless, and dressed in sweatpants, he pushed out of his chair and walked to the sliding glass door of the balcony. Hot night air engulfed him as he opened the slider.

The crowd noise was louder now. The drone hummed, hanging motionless in the night air thirty feet from his balcony. Luke studied it as he moved to the edge of the balcony and looked down.

He gave a muffled cry of surprise, his heart shooting up into his throat. He was standing one floor above a naked woman balanced awkwardly on the balcony railing. Luke stared. He could see her hair, breasts, a naked leg, and a bare foot.

––––––––

THE DRONE PILOT sat in The Silver Palace's dimly lit surveillance suite in front of large video monitors displaying a variety of images of the naked woman on the railing. The valet had called to alert them to the drama on the balcony. The drone was launched less than two minutes later.

Surveillance officers, along with Gayle Turner, the thirty-four-year-old surveillance director, crowded around the drone pilot to watch the drama unfold. On another monitor, two uniformed officers stepped off an elevator. The surveillance team, along with the director, collectively held their breath as they watched the monitors in silence.

The two uniformed security officers moved down the carpeted guest hallway to the door of the room. Their orders were simple. Get in and get the woman before she jumped. They hesitated at the door.

"What the hell are they waiting on?" Gayle Turner said aloud in the surveillance room as she simultaneously watched the hall camera showing the security guards and the drone camera aimed at the naked woman who nearly lost her balance.

––––––––

EIGHT MILES AWAY, in a private room at the Sun & Fun Spa, fifty-two-year-old Blake Mancini was enjoying a hot oil massage. Mancini was naked, overweight, and on his stomach on the padded table. The attractive therapist, twenty-four years younger, knew Mancini well. He was a generous tipper. Especially if her work included an oiled hand job.

"Time to turn over," the girl whispered, gently squeezing his glistening oily buttocks.

"My pleasure," Mancini said. He grunted with effort as he turned over with a growing erection. The chirp of his cell phone on a nearby table stopped his effort.

The girl looked to him. "Do you need to answer?"

The electronic chirping continued. Mancini gave her an annoyed nod. The therapist wiped a hand on a towel and handed him the cell phone.

"Mancini," he said as he sat up. The girl smiled and laid a towel over his fading erection.

"Blake," a female voice said in his ear. It was Gayle Turner. While she was the surveillance watch commander at The Silver Palace, Mancini was Director of Security. "We've got a jumper. On a balcony above the valet station and she's naked."

"Damn it," Mancini growled. His frustration was more disappointment than sympathy for the would-be-jumper.

"We've got a crowd of about a hundred and growing watching," Gayle added. "Lots of cells recording it."

Mancini knew it could not be ignored. A nude woman jumping to her death in Vegas on a Saturday night. Hell, the videos would be on TV before the blood was cleaned up. "You call the GM yet?"

"Not before you," Gayle assured him.

"All right, call him. Be brief. Tell him I'm on my way." He gave the therapist a look and pointed to his clothes.

————

AT THE SILVER PALACE, the two security officers were still standing in front of the door to the guest room. They knew cameras were watching, but they also knew no one could hear them.

"You know, if we use a master key and go in, if she jumps—everyone's gonna say we caused it."

"I heard about this guy at the Grand," the other officer agreed in a near whisper. "He used a master to go in on a dog barking. Finds these two guys screwing. One of them works in the governor's office. They fired him."

One floor above, Luke Mitchel backed away from the balcony into this room. His heart now pounded in his ears. He swore quietly. He knew the woman was going to jump. He took a deep breath, wiped his face, and bolted barefoot and shirtless for the open balcony door.

A collective hush fell over the crowd gathered at the main entrance. Faces and cell phones watched as a bare-chested man leaped over the railing of the balcony directly above the naked woman. The man grabbed the metal railing, swinging his weight up and over.

It took only seconds as Luke swung in a downward arc, glancing at the crowd, and the cement far below. Luke released his grip. Momentum carried his one hundred and seventy-seven pounds down, slamming into the woman. He held her as they crashed onto the balcony floor. Luke's foot slammed the sliding glass door, shattering the glass as they rolled to a halt.

The two security officers heard the thud, the breaking glass.

"Get in there," Gayle Turner's voice barked on the radio.

Luke was on top of the nude. He gasped for breath, lifting his weight off her. Shattered shards of glass fell from his back. Blood ran from the woman's nose. She moaned. Luke did not see the two security officers charging in from behind him.

"Get off her," an officer yelled, grabbing Luke's wrist and twisting his arm high into the middle of his back.

"Cuff him," the other officer barked.

TWO
SHOW AND TELL

MORE SECURITY OFFICERS were quickly on the scene. They carried the nude to the king-size bed. Her moaning continued. An officer brought a towel to wipe blood from her face. "Call an ambulance."

Luke lay on the carpet just inside the open slider, handcuffed, face down. The security watch commander, a gray-haired lieutenant, looked to the officers. "Who's he?"

One of the men glanced at the handcuffed Luke. "We found him on top the girl."

"I'm not a rapist. I'm from room—"

"Shut up," the lieutenant growled.

"Get a wheelchair up here," the watch commander added. "Get him out of here. Use a back-of-the-house elevator. Put him in the interview room. Mancini's on his way."

Luke heard the orders. His police experience taught him not to fight handcuffs or uniforms. He decided to keep his mouth shut.

After the wheelchair arrived, he was gathered from

the floor, covered with a sheet, and wheeled to an employee elevator. Handcuffed beneath the sheet, Luke's mind wasn't on his situation. He was thinking about the nude woman. Who the hell was she? Did he save her life, or did he puncture her lungs when he crashed onto her. He could hardly believe what he had done.

What drove her to the edge? Couldn't she run from life like he did? What the hell was she thinking? Time to think, reason, decide. Now, sitting in a wheelchair in handcuffs, he didn't feel like he had saved anyone. Jumping over a railing on the balcony. Remembering it scared the hell out of him. He wished he hadn't gone onto the balcony. *If* it hadn't been for the drone. He knew interfering in someone else's problems seldom solved your own.

Luke deliberately turned his thoughts from the woman. The moments ahead were more important. The wheelchair he sat in was pushed to a door stenciled *private*. An officer pushed a button beside the door. A buzzer sounded, the door opened, and they rolled Luke inside. There was another door directly in front of them. The metal door behind them closed and locked with a metallic thud.

Man trap, Luke concluded. He knew someone was watching on camera. In a man trap, the individuals entering or departing were trapped until they were iden-tified and allowed in or out. The Silver Palace may have been bigger and busier than the Wild River, but it didn't seem that much different. The conclusion brought him little comfort.

A buzzer sounded, a lock clicked, and the door in front of them opened. Luke was wheeled in. He spotted a camera high in a corner. The sheet was pulled off him. It was damp with perspiration. The handcuff on Luke's right wrist was unlocked. He was helped onto his unsteady bare feet. One of the officers gestured to a chair behind a desk. Luke sat down. His free wrist was locked to the frame of the metal chair. An empty chair across the table told him he wouldn't be alone long. He began piecing together images that would make sense to Barb. How could he explain this? He hoped she was still shopping.

––––––

BARBARA WAS DONE with her shopping. She returned to the suite she shared with Luke one floor above the *would-be* nude jumper. Her shopping trip had proven successful. She was carrying two bags. One held a new pantsuit. She knew Luke would like it.

She was surprised Luke wasn't in the front room. She looked in the bedroom. "Luke," she called, puzzled by his absence. Returning to the main room, she saw the open slider and froze. Fear rushed in.

"Luke," she called, louder now as she rushed onto the balcony to look over the rail. Below, the noisy crowd stood staring up, many with cell phones still in the air. "No!" Barbara screamed.

––––––

GAYLE TURNER quickly connected the dots. She checked electronic registration records at the front desk and found the would-be jumper's room was occupied by Dr. Martin Rogers and his wife, Jill. They had checked in at 3:10 p.m. on Friday. She found the related videos and froze photos of both. Photos of the doctor were provided to security working the casino floor. She wanted him found.

In the surveillance suite, fifty-six cameras were combing the card room, table by table, as others searched row after row of slot machines, trying to find a match for the photo.

Gayle was pulling up guest room records on the computer when a surveillance officer came rushing into her cubicle." Security says we've got another jumper."

"What!" Gayle said in disbelief.

"We're looking right now. Security said a woman came back to her room to find her roommate had jumped. That's all we've got."

"Well, it's not enough," Gayle said in frustration. "Get more details. Is security up there?"

The officer disappeared.

"Is there a full moon tonight?" Gayle muttered. Returning her attention to the computer, she hammered the keyboard. She found the guest room records from one floor above Dr. Rogers and his wife, revealing the registered occupant was Luther Mitchel. He had also checked in Friday afternoon.

Gayle had a team find the video. They watched on a monitor as Luke used a credit card at the front desk. He provided an address of 166 Cold Creek Drive, Verde Park, Rio Vista, Arizona. Gayle quickly Googled the name and found nothing. The next step was a frame-by-frame review of the video from the security drone hovering near where Jill Rogers stood nude and awkward on the rail of her balcony. Gayle watched as the blur of a man swung into the picture from above, slamming into the nude woman, sending them both crashing from the rail onto the floor to shatter the glass door. Seconds later, two security officers appeared, grabbed the man, and handcuffed him. The drone pilot had tightened on the images. Gayle saw the handcuffed, shirtless man was the same man identified as Luther Mitchel. There was no hint of sexual assault. Clearly, the man waiting in the interview room had risked his life to save the woman. Gayle put the video on hold as another officer approached. "Gayle, line four. It's Jack, down in the card room."

Gayle grabbed the receiver and punched the blinking line. "Jack, it's Gayle. Talk to me."

"We found Doc Rogers at a twenty-one table," the man answered. "We told him his wife was on her way to the hospital. He seemed unhappy about leaving the game."

"Get a limo from guest services. Drive him to the hospital."

———

LUKE WISHED he had his watch. The thought made him smile. He'd come to Vegas to forget time, forget who he was. Then the door opened. A woman in casual dress stepped in and closed the door. Handcuff key in hand she went directly to Luke's wrist shackled to the chair. She removed the handcuff. "Your name is Luther Mitchel. You're from Rio Vista, Arizona."

Luke massaged his freed wrist as the woman sat down across the desk from him.

"Luke instead of Luther," Luke said.

I watched the video," she explained. "We're sorry for the mix-up. I don't think I've witnessed such a heroic act. You could have fallen to your death."

"You're from surveillance?" Luke straightened in his chair. He suddenly had more respect for her comment.

"Yes, my name's Gayle Turner. I'm the director of surveillance. I hope you understand the situation looked much different to the officers coming into that room."

Luke straightened in his chair. He wanted to be taller than the woman across from him. "I'm the acting director of security at Wild River Casino," he told her, establishing common ground.

"You're a director?" Gayle was caught off guard. "Wild River. That's run by?"

"The Mojaves," Luke said, filling in the blank. "How is the woman?"

"One of my men is driving her husband to the hospital. He'll call after they get word on her condition. Your roommate was upset," Gayle said. "She came back and found you missing. She thought you jumped, but she now knows you're okay. She's still in your room."

Gayle lifted a cell phone from a pocket, dialed a number and reached across the desk, offering the phone to Luke. "I dialed your room."

Luke took the cell phone and put it to his ear. He waited only seconds before Barb answered.

"Hey, it's Luke."

Gayle could hear Barbara's loud voice.

"No, no," Luke said to the phone. "I'm fine. I'm downstairs. Yes, everything is okay. Calm down. Yes, me too. Same to you. See you in a couple. Bye." He smiled and handed the cell phone back to Gayle.

"When things like this happen, as you know, they get passed up the line. I called our director of security. I told him we had a jumper. Big crowd watching, taking pictures. That was before you put on your cape."

"My cape." Luke forced a smile. "I'd settled for a shirt."

"My boss told me to call the GM," Gayle continued.

"So, I did. GM's name is Greg Larson. I told him about the probable jumper, the big crowd, how you saved the woman's life. He's on his way in." Gayle glanced at her watch. "Security will give me a head's up when he's on property. He wants to meet you."

"I'm not exactly dressed for a meeting," Luke said, massaging a wrist again, trying to get rid of the imprint from the handcuffs.

"I'm getting Greg a CD of the drone shots. After seeing it, we knew the handcuffs were a mistake."

"So, it's all over. I can go?" Luke asked cautiously.

"I would appreciate you waiting to meet the GM."

"Okay," Luke agreed. "But first, can I go up to my room, assure Barbara all's well, and get a shirt and some shoes. I'm half naked?"

Gayle glanced at Luke's naked chest and shoulders. "I hadn't noticed," she said with a smile.

———

TikTok was to be the first to air an iPhone video of the nude woman on the balcony at The Silver Palace. The crowd was loud with cheers, shouts, and profanities. Far above the nude, who was swaying her arms to maintain balance, was a large bright sign announcing to the world, *The Silver Palace*. The crowd roared when the figure of a man bounded over the railing above the woman, swinging down to knock them both from sight. In minutes, the video amassed nearly two hundred thousand views, and the numbers were growing.

Greg Larson may have been the general manager of The Silver Palace, but the Saturday night traffic on the Las Vegas Strip didn't care. Larson's highly polished Maserati became the twelfth car in line at the valet when he reached the casino. There was an endless string of headlights and noisy horns behind him when his cell phone chimed. It was synced with the telephone in the Maserati. A panel on the dash told him it was his wife calling. He squeezed a button on the steering wheel. "I'm stuck in traffic. What's up?"

"Our daughter was on her iPhone watching TikTok."

"Isn't she always."

"True, but she doesn't always watch a naked jumper at The Silver Palace."

"TikTok," Larson complained, tightening his grip on the steering wheel. "Damn it. We can never catch a break. TikTok apparently has a hell of a lot more surveillance than we do."

"Thought you'd want to know," his wife said.

"Thanks," Larson said, and hung up. He gritted his teeth in frustration and pushed the Maserati into park. He climbed out and marched away. A protest of horns and curses filled the night behind him.

There were four valet attendants on duty at the main entrance to The Silver Palace. All were busy with arriving guests. Larson marched up to one of the valets and took the young man by the shoulder. Slamming his car keys into the man's hand, Larson said, "It's the red Maserati."

"What? Who are you?" the surprised valet asked.

"You only get to ask me that once," Larson warned as he continued his march toward the crowded front entrance.

The savvy female front desk manager recognized Larson as he approached. "Good evening, sir."

Larson acknowledged her with a nod. "I need a presidential suite. What have we got?"

"I'll have a look." The woman stared into her computer screen and began tapping keys.

Larson's attention turned to his cell. He logged into TikTok. His expression showed displeasure when he found the video.

The front desk clerk saw the GM's look and knew she needed to be quick and efficient. "The Starlight Presidential on the seventy-second is available, sir. Would you like a key?"

"I've got a key," Larson answered. "Call Blake Mancini. Have him meet me up there."

"Mr. Mancini isn't on the property yet, sir. I just spoke with Gayle Turner. She called us to say whatever Mr. Mitchel wanted was to be charged to the house."

"Mitchel...who's he?" Larson questioned.

"He's the guest that saved the woman."

Larson was annoyed—he felt ignorant and ill-informed. His fingers danced on the marble countertop. "And everybody knows about this?"

"Most in-house know." The woman's answer was a near apology.

Larson pushed his cell phone into his jacket. His displeasure was obvious. "Call Gayle Turner. Tell her to meet me on the seventy-second, and tell her to bring me some answers."

————

CNN WAS NOT FAR behind TikTok. They had new cell phone videos of the naked would-be jumper, which they labeled *Breaking News* at the top of the hour.

"Some viewers may find the following video disturbing," the anchor warned before announcing. "A naked woman intent on jumping to her death found the odds were not in her favor at The Silver Palace in Las Vegas tonight."

Seventeen million people watched CNN's video. Not only in the United States, but in countries around the world. "The man saving the woman's life has yet to be identified," the anchor concluded. "Perhaps it's a case of *what happens in Vegas, stays in Vegas*."

Proving an attractive naked woman standing on a balcony rail intent on jumping to her death in Las Vegas on a Saturday night was news, it went viral. Social media, streaming, and broadcast services across the country all presented the story and all had the same question. "Who was the hero? Who was this man?"

Nic Goss, a news producer at KTVK in Phoenix, Arizona, saw CNN's broadcast and thought he had the answer. His brother-in-law worked in surveillance at The Silver Palace in Las Vegas. Nic called him as soon as the thought entered his mind.

"I can't tell you crap," Howard Collins immediately said. He was on duty when Nic called. "Okay," Nic said. "Next time you want the condo in New Port Beach, you can kiss my ass."

"You're a real prick," Howard whispered into his phone. "The guy's name is Luke Mitchel. He's the director of security at Wild River Casino in Rio Vista, Arizona."

"Rio Vista? No way…"

———

BARBARA TRIED to calm herself after Luke's call, but all she could do was pace. Where the hell was he? His call helped, but that now seemed hours ago. She tried sitting in a chair, she tried drinking, combing her hair, but all she could do was pace and bite her nails. She put on the new jumpsuit, but Lady Gaga's show was now just an hour away. Barbara knew getting there was highly unlikely.

Lovers for some time now, Barbara and Luke were comfortable with each other. Neither felt a need to rush, although Barbara was close to inviting Luke to move in with her since he spent most of his nights with her. He had clothes in her closet, and a razor in her bathroom.

She found the idea comforting, especially after he invited her here to Las Vegas. Their suite was terrific. He was taking her to see Lady Gaga. Well, maybe. Now, from what the woman from security told her, Luke had saved some woman's life. Whoever she was, she had really screwed up their night.

Again, Barbara tried calming herself. Obviously, someone's life was more important than a Las Vegas show. Luke was an obvious hero. She smiled. She already knew he was. Determined to be rational, she sat down on a couch in the room and turned on the big-screen TV.

As the TV lit up, an attractive news anchor announced, "This just in. Luke Mitchel, director of security at the Wild River Casino in Rio Vista, Arizona, saved a nude woman from jumping to her death at The Silver Palace in Las Vegas."

Barbara's hands started to shake. She no longer heard the words. Her heart raced. "Oh, my god," she said.

CALVIN MANY-COATS and three other officers crowded around a TV monitor in the surveillance suite at the Wild River Casino.

"Holy crap."

Many-Coats gasped as a reporter said, "We've learned

Luke Mitchel is employed as head of security for a tribe of Indians in the Southwest where Indian gambling is legal."

"Oh, great," Greg Many-Coats said, throwing his arms in the air. "I'm so glad to hear we Indians are legal."

Horace Thunderhawk was Tribal Chief of the Mojaves. He was the force behind the dream that became the Wild River Casino. The task took twelve years. It added many more years to Horace's age. At eighty-one, he was an old man, but wise. He was often told he resembled the Indian on the silver nickel. Horace considered the comparison a compliment.

A chime from a bedside cell phone had awakened both he and his wife. A worried tribal member called to say he had just seen Luke Mitchel on TV. Horace and his wife moved to the living room and turned on the TV. They watched until, finally, a video of the nude jumper at The Silver Palace was played on the late news. At first, Horace was proud of what Luke Mitchel had done, but his pride turned to a smoldering anger when the two anchors wrapped up the story.

The male anchor looked to his female co-host. "So this pale face, who works for the Indians at the Wild River resort in Rio Vista, goes to Vegas where he saves a woman from jumping off the top of a casino. Sounds like we might be talking about the Lone Ranger."

"Let's call the Wild River in Rio Vista," the female co-anchor suggested. "Maybe Tonto will answer."

The two anchors laughed at their cleverness. Horace Thunderhawk was not amused. As a young man carrying a rifle in the Marine Corps during the Korean War, Horace had been nicknamed *Tonto* by his platoon sergeant. The name became a daily insult that haunted Horace until his honorable discharge three years later. He wasn't Tonto, he was a Mojave and proud of it. Horace threw his remote at the television set.

————

IN LAS VEGAS, the front desk manager proved to be savvy. She called the housekeeping manager as soon as the general manager walked away. When Greg Larson reached the presidential suite, the lighting had been turned on, and bottled water sat with a bucket of ice near a bar stocked with an impressive array of liquors. The suite's curtains were open to present an unequaled panorama of nighttime Las Vegas.

The fifty-six-year-old Larson had been in Vegas for thirty-two years, but the city's allure still held him captive and he knew it well. All of it. He could see light from the Luxor and from the Ferris wheel near distant Mandalay Bay. Larson had started as a bellman at Mandalay Bay, living on minimum wage and tips. He forced himself to turn away. Who the hell would want to die in a city like this?

"Get me surveillance," Larson said, picking up a telephone near the suite's bar.

"I'm sorry, sir. That number is restricted."

"I'm the damn general manager," he growled at the receiver. "Get them on the line."

The hotel operator did not argue.

"Surveillance, Turner."

"Turner, this is Greg Larson. I'm in the presidential suite. Find Blake Mancini. I want him, the guest that saved the jumper, whatever the hell his name is, and a CD of everything you've got, and I don't like waiting."

There was a pause before Gale Turner answered. "Sir,

I spoke with Blake. He's on his way in, but he has yet to arrive."

"You've got to be kidding me. We've got a full house. We're all over the damn news and he's not here. Where is he?"

"I can't answer that, sir."

"Okay, okay. Who's in charge if he's not here?"

"I am."

"Okay, Turner, you know what I need. So, get our hero guest, and get your ass up here. Understood?"

Larson slammed the telephone down and looked for the bar. "Not here," he yelled to no one in particular. "I'll crucify the son-of-a-bitch."

He selected a vintage Suntory Royal and poured himself a heavy glass. He turned back to the window. This time, his thoughts were no longer on the distant Mandalay Bay. He was worried about what to tell the press. Who did what, where, and when. He saw reporters earlier. They were gathering in the valet area, waiting and looking. He knew there was no playing catch-up with the press. Demanding bastards. Where the hell was Mancini? He was supposed to be the one with the answers. The prick. Larson gulped down the remainder of his drink.

———

Sunrise Hospital was less than two miles from The Silver Palace. Dr. Rogers was surprised when he and the driver from The Silver Palace reached the ER.

"That's him," a reporter shouted. Four other reporters, three cameramen, and everyone in the ER waiting area reacted.

"Doctor, why did your wife want to jump from a

balcony at The Silver Palace?" A microphone was pushed in front of his face. Camera lights and flashes followed.

"Get back," the driver from The Silver Palace ordered, pushing mics, cameras, and reporters away from Rogers.

The newly married Jill Rogers lay covered with a sheet in treatment room B, staring at the ceiling, planning her divorce. She was separated by curtains from a moaning senior who had been hit by a cab on the Strip, and a woman who swallowed a hundred-dollar chip at the Luxor.

"Jill," Dr. Rogers said, jerking the curtains aside. "What the hell were you doing? Are you nuts?"

Jill Rogers chose not to answer.

————

BLAKE MANCINI SAW the GM's Maserati when he wheeled his SUV into a spot in The Silver Palace's employee parking garage. He scrambled out, wondering how long the GM had been on the property. He was ready with a lie. He walked from the garage to an employee elevator. He rode with two housekeepers and an engineer with a toolbox. Mancini got off on the surveillance level. After being buzzed in, he found Gayle Turner at her desk. He was quick with his question, "Where's the GM?"

Gayle Turner was ready with an answer. "The GM wants you to wait in your office. I'll tell him you're here."

"Wait in my office? What the hell does that mean?"

BARBARA HAD TURNED off the TV. She was back to pacing, worrying. After a glance at her watch, she decided after another five minutes she was going to call hotel management and demand to know where the hell Luke was. Luke solved the problem by opening the door.

"Luke." Barbara gasped, bolting to him, ignoring Gayle Turner, who stood at his side. Luke took Barb in his arms. They kissed, hugged, and laughed. "Look at you," Barb said, wiping away tears. "You're dressed like Tarzan."

"Thank you, Jane." Luke smiled. Gayle closed the door behind them. "Barb, this is Gayle. She works surveillance. She's taking me upstairs to meet the GM."

Gayle offered a hand to Barbara who wiped her palm dry before they shook hands.

"Nice to meet you, Barb," Gayle said with a smile. "Would you like to come meet the GM? He wants to thank Luke for what he's done."

"What he did scared the hell out of me," Barb confessed, taking Luke's hand in hers to squeeze it.

"Think about it while I get some clothes on," Luke said. He kissed Barbara's hand, touched her face, and headed for the bedroom.

Barb took a deep breath, more a sigh of relief before she looked to Gayle. "I'm sorry. Could we start all over with your name?"

The two women sat and talked. Gayle explained her position in surveillance at The Silver Palace, and Barbara confessed she tended bar at Wild River. In a sense, they had a common denominator. It helped. Gayle took Barb candidly through the drama of the events. She was detailed and specific. Barb sat rigid, almost holding her breath.

"Bottom line," Gayle said in conclusion, "the man in your life is a hero. Spotlight is going to be on him for a while."

Barb nodded agreement and sniffed. "I thought for sure he jumped."

"He did…" Gayle smiled. "To save someone else's life."

Barbara passed on the invitation to meet the GM. "This is Luke's thing. Not mine. I think I'll stay here and get drunk."

————

THE DOOR CHIME sounded inside the presidential suite. Greg Lawson hurried to the door where he cleared his throat, straightened his jacket, readied a smile, and opened the door. An attractive middle-aged woman and a well-built, smartly dressed man in casual wear stood waiting. Greg Larson did not know he was looking at a man who was wearing clothes from a retail outlet on the first floor

"Gayle," Greg Larson said, offering the surprised Gayle Turner a hand. "Thanks for coming up." He turned his attention and hand to Luke. "And you must be Luke Mitchel. Congratulations, young man." He opened the door wide. "Come on in."

They sat on facing couches. Larson offered drinks as Gayle pushed a CD into the wide-screen TV's DVR. The TV lit up, and Gayle worked the remote.

"They say a picture is worth a thousand words," Larson said with a smile.

They watched in silence. Larson sat with his elbows on his knees, leaning toward the TV. Luke watched the GM as much as he watched the images on the screen.

"Play it again," Larson said when the action ended.

They watched the video again. The GM nodded, and Gayle turned the TV off.

Larson looked to Luke. "I don't know what to say."

His tone was sincere. "I've never seen anyone do anything like what we just saw—and in Vegas, that says a lot."

Luke wasn't sure how to reply. He looked to Gayle, then back to Larson as he wiped a sweaty palm on a knee, "First time I've seen it too," Luke said.

"I watched a video of it on TikTok," Larson said. "It was so dark and grainy it had to be homemade." He looked at the TV. "But this was stunningly real. What can we do for you? This place is yours." Larson gestured at the suite with a wave of his hand. "Anything you want. No charge. Everybody in Vegas is gonna want to give you something. You want money, a job, the best show. I'm not trying to buy you, I'm trying to say thanks."

"Thank you, but you don't owe me anything," Luke said.

"There's a lot of press downstairs," Larson said. "A woman jumping off of anything in Las Vegas isn't a first. A man risking his own life to save that woman is news. Big news. The press is going to find you. They're already here. They want to know who you are. See your face."

"I'm not sure," Luke said, hesitating.

Larson pushed to his feet. "The press are not going to go away. At some point, you're going to be forced to face them. How about we do it now…together."

THREE
RUNNING TO...OR FROM

THE PAPARAZZI, reporters, and cameraman, loitering around The Silver Palace's valet, front desk, and guest elevators, already knew what Luke Mitchel looked like. A reporter from the *Las Vegas Sun* had found a picture of him on the Internet from an article that had been posted online after his partner was shot and killed in Los Angeles.

The reporter had shared his find with all his cohorts. It was a professional dictate. Not only did the press know what Luke looked like, they had also discovered—via a housekeeping informant—that he was on the property. Collectively, they were wary when security officers offered them an escort to one of The Silver Palace's dark showrooms. There, they were told that Luke Mitchel would shortly make an appearance. It appeared Lady Gaga was to have competition.

After filtering into the idle showroom, the collective press was surprised when uniformed waiters joined them to take drink orders. They were even more surprised when told the drinks were on the house.

Orders were quickly changed from coffee or bottled water to vodka and orange juice, margaritas, and Tom Collins's. A reporter from the *Nye County Express* added a bacon and cheese on toast to go with his Bud Light.

Greg Larson was doing all he could to make the press comfortable. He wanted the story at The Silver Palace changed from focusing on a naked woman intent on jumping to her death, to a story about the guest at The Silver Palace, who became a hero when he risked his own life to save the life of another.

The difference was subtle, but so was the difference between being a winner or a loser. Larson, used to being a winner, was confident he could pull strings and get the pendulum to swing in his direction. He had already put out a text alerting in-house managers there was to be no mention of the would-be jumper's room number. Nor was there to be any name identity provided for the woman. Managers and staff were encouraged, at every opportunity, to mention The Silver Palace had an excellent record of guest safety.

As The Silver Palace's director of security, Blake Mancini knew he was in trouble when his text to the GM went unanswered. *Wait in his office*. What the hell was that supposed to mean? Mancini knew it had to be linked to his absence from the casino when the bitch decided to jump off the balcony. Had his wife, a former pool attendant, given him the release he wanted, he wouldn't have been at the massage parlor. Didn't she know he was in his prime? He had needs, desires, but no, he had to wait because his in-laws were visiting. Screw them. He was betting the naked jumper was linked to sex. Screw her too.

———

LUKE FELT COMPELLED to follow the GM's lead. The entire night had become a blur. He remembered jumping over the balcony rail to save the nude as a frightening experience that resulted in being handcuffed and pushed around in a wheelchair. Now everyone was calling him a hero. The title was uncomfortable. He was reluctant, but he was being carried by a tide of events bigger than himself. He made an excuse and took a moment to call Barbara on his cell from the bedroom of the penthouse. "Hi, honey…"

"Luke, are you okay?

"I'm fine…really. The GM is insisting I go downstairs with him to talk to the press about the lady who was going to jump. Would you like to come down?"

"Luke, this had nothing to do with me. I'll wait here. I'll be fine. I'll order something from room service."

"Okay," Luke said. "See you in a bit."

"Don't tell them you've seen me naked."

"What!"

Barb's tinkling laugh came down the line and touched his heart.

———

"LADIES AND GENTLEMEN," a male voice announced on the amplified sound system in the showroom where drinks were still being served.

A hush fell over the waiting reporters. Cameramen switched on equipment, soundmen aimed disks. "We are proud to present the general manager of The Silver Palace, Mr. Greg Larson."

The tall red curtains on the stage parted in the center to sweep silently aside, revealing the spotlighted, smiling and confident Greg Larson.

"What…no music?" a reporter from *TMZ* whispered sarcastically.

Larson captured the Vegas persona he was reaching for. He was wearing a hand-tailored fifty-four-hundred-dollar Aragona suit. Cameras were rolling, notes were being taken. He had them. The event was news, and he was driving.

Standing strategically behind Larson was a nervous Luke Mitchel. He stood exactly where Larson had positioned him. On Larson's left, in a similar position to Luke, was Gayle Turner. She wasn't nervous, not because she was the director of surveillance, but more because she had been a chorus line dancer at the Grand for six years. She was wearing her Vegas smile and style like a well-fitting persona.

"Thank you for coming," Larson said to the lights with practiced charm. "Welcome to The Silver Palace. We are here tonight to celebrate life. And nothing speaks louder in life than what we see with our own eyes. So, sit back, take a deep breath, and fasten your seat belts."

A large video screen scrolled down behind the trio on the stage. As the screen lit up, the stage lights dimmed. Larson led Gayle and Luke aside.

The press, drinks in hand, sat fixed, watching the compelling silent images recorded by The Silver Palace's drone. The shapely Jill Rogers balanced herself on the balcony railing. Her arms flailed as she looked down. The anxiety and fear on her face was amplified by the fact there was no audio. The silence in the sprawling room was deafening. Suddenly, Luke, dressed only in a pair of sweatpants, swung into the picture from above.

"Holy Shit," someone in the audience said aloud.

The video continued with the bare-chested Luke slamming himself into the woman. The two tumbled off the railing with Luke holding the woman in a tight bearhug. They crashed onto the balcony floor.

The silence in the room was broken by a single clapping hand. In the video, the bare-chested Luke, in sweatpants, was pushing himself up off the nude when two uniformed security officers burst into view. One of them grabbed Luke by the wrist, pushing his arm up into the middle of his back. A video edit cut the image of Luke being handcuffed. The screen images showed the arrival of an ambulance, followed by two paramedics and two security officers wheeling a stretcher out of the guest room and down the carpeted hallway to an elevator. More scenes followed, showing wide shots from a variety of fixed CCTV cameras showing the nude appearing on the balcony and then climbing awkwardly to the top of the railing.

When the videos ended, the screen retracted. Greg Larson, Gayle Turner, and Luke Mitchel returned to the stage, taking their previous positions. Each of their spots was marked with a taped X.

"Ladies and gentlemen," Larson smiled into the stage lights. "The word hero defines those demonstrating courage, outstanding achievement, and noble qualities. I think you would agree, the man in this video, saving this woman from what was certain to be a deadly fall, has them all." He gestured to Luke. "Allow me to introduce that man—Luke Mitchel."

Larson and Gayle started the applause, which was quickly picked up by a robust audience reaction. They joined in the clapping, many pushed to their feet.

Greg Larson motioned Luke to join him center stage. Luke was wishing he had never come to Las Vegas.

"Thank you," Luke said into the lights, adjusting the

microphone pinned to his shirt. "This really wasn't what I had in mind when I came to Vegas."

A splattering of laughter rippled across the audience. They were reading the honesty in his words. They weren't laughing at him. It was more a joining in with him. Luke smiled in appreciation. "I did what I think most would do. I didn't think about it before doing it. It was impulse. I saw the woman. I jumped."

A rush of questions came from the audience. It surprised Luke. He was careful with his answers. "How old are you? Were you in Vegas by yourself? Are you married? Did you know this woman? Where do you live? Have you seen her since then?"

Greg Larson was enjoying the moment even if Luke wasn't. Attention had shifted from a naked woman about to jump from one of The Silver Palace's balconies to the hero who saved her. Larson had realized long ago that the press was superficial. Tomorrow, they would be chasing after someone else, somewhere else.

Tomorrow, The Silver Palace would be back in the headlines, but it wouldn't be because of a naked woman on a balcony. It would be because Lady Gaga was becoming their headliner. The questions faded. Reporters were leaving. Deadlines had to be met. Breaking news was on its way to becoming something else—filler chat on the morning broadcasts.

After shaking hands again with Luke, Greg asked Gayle to escort Luke to his room and then excused himself.

Gayle led Luke through the busy back of the house with its rush of waiters carrying platters, uniformed dealers, and housekeepers pushing carts to an employee elevator.

"Are you and Barb married?" Gayle asked as they

walked. "I heard one of the reporters asking." They were waiting at the closed doors of an elevator.

"Married once, but not to Barbara." Luke smiled. "We're just friends. She also works at Wild River. And you?"

"Once for me, too." The elevator arrived. They stepped in. Gayle punched a floor number. "I'm sure you've heard, what happens in Vegas, stays in Vegas."

The elevator stopped. The doors opened, and three uniformed Latino housekeepers stepped in. They ignored Gayle and Luke as their Spanish chatter continued.

"Regarding the *what happens in Vegas* thing," Luke said over the talk between the housekeepers. "The GM said he's moving me up to the penthouse. If he was trying to impress me, it worked."

Gayle smiled. "Seventy-sixth floor. You are moving up."

————

Sixteen floors below, Blake Mancini was in the kitchen eating a fresh shrimp when his cell phone lit up with a text from the GM. *My office in fifteen.* Mancini was ready with his lie. His in-laws were in town. Making them part of the lie reinforced it. *Sorry boss, I was late, but I had to take my mother-in-law to urgent care in Henderson.* Who wouldn't accept that? It was family first. Everyone knew that. He found the GM's office door closed. Mancini checked his watch before knocking lightly.

"It's open," Greg Larson's voice boomed from inside.

Mancini opened the door carefully. Larson was behind his desk, looking out a floor-to- ceiling window. The nighttime glow and color from the Strip erased the night. iPhone in hand, Larson motioned Mancini to a chair in front of his desk. Mancini sat down carefully as if his movement may interrupt Larson's thoughts.

Larson went on with his call. "Wolf, I'll express the CD to you. You'll have it in the morning, and when are you coming out here? We got this great new German beer, Gaffel Kölsch something. You'll love it." He sat down in the high-backed chair behind his desk. "Okay, see you then. Good night." Larson looked to Mancini. "Where the hell were you?"

"Sorry, boss," Mancini said, straightening in the chair. "My wife's parents are in town. I had to take my mother-in-law to urgent care. Chest pains. She's gonna be okay, but traffic was a bitch."

Larson studied Mancini. Clasping his hands together on the desk, he interlocked his fingers. "You're a lying prick. You're fired. Get your ass off the property."

"Fired! For what?" Mancini was shocked. "Taking my mother-in-law to a doctor."

Two plain-clothed security officers stepped into the room. Mancini looked at them and recognized both. Their arrival shook him. "What the hell are they doing here?"

Larson unlocked his fingers. "I called your house. Your wife told me she thought you were here."

Mancini pushed onto the edge of his chair. He looked at the two security officers and then Larson. "I…I drove my mother-in-law there myself."

"You are even dumber than I thought," Larson said. "Your mother-in-law told your wife to tell me hello while we talked. I put them in a king a couple months ago. Now, these two are going to escort you down to your car. You don't stop anywhere, you don't talk to anyone, you just get the hell out."

Mancini pushed onto his feet. He felt ill. "Boss, let's talk. We can—"

"Get him outta here," Larson said, looking at the two officers. Mancini knew it was over. He turned and took wooden-legged steps to the door.

"Blake," Larson called.

Mancini paused, turned—maybe there was a chance.

"I lied. I didn't really call your wife." Larson smiled.

———

IT WAS dark when Luke and Barbara drove away from The Silver Palace. At least dark by Vegas standards. They found their suite and room service was all comped, but after the telephone in the room never quit ringing, followed by knocks on the door, they both knew it was time to leave.

Saying the day had been long was an understatement. Luke wrote the GM and Gayle Turner a thank you note on a Silver Palace letterhead he'd found on the room's desk. He sealed it in an envelope, along with the room key, and left it on a table beside the undisturbed king-size bed. Hand in hand, they took a final look at the panoramic view of Las Vegas and walked out.

Their drive to Rio Vista from Vegas was one hundred and seventy-seven miles. Some of it was wide interstate, but most of it was down narrow, twisting lanes through the middle of nowhere. They were eager to get home. Luke answered Barb's questions about the press conference, but talk had somehow become a challenge. After the first hour, Barb fell asleep.

Luke wondered what it was he was driving toward. He had been so eager to get away. The plan hadn't gone very well. *Was Rio Vista home*, he asked himself during the drive. Was he driving home or running away again? The question left him cold. He adjusted the car's heat. He had to admit he'd been running from things most of his life.

The Marine Corps had offered refuge. Luke welcomed the opportunity to shoot someone. At least until death got in the way. He ran from that, too. He wore his military uniform and ribbons to his LAPD oral interview. They hired him, and he took refuge on the streets of LA until death took his partner. Then he ran again, finding a hiding place with a tribe of Indians.

He found the Mojaves gave much more than they took. Although, death once more had come hauntingly close when he found Jim Todd deceased in the parking lot. Was Vegas another runaway? He had to admit it was. But it seemed fate had a much different plan. This time, instead of death chasing him, he chased it.

Somewhere, a woman he had never met, whose name he didn't even know, was alive because he came between her and death. The realization was comforting. He wasn't driving away—he was actually driving home. Maybe it was because the woman sleeping beside him had made it home for him. He reached out to lay a hand on her jean-covered leg.

Dawn came in the last hour of their drive. Bright, sunny, sprawling desert. It felt like home. Barb's SUV was parked beside her trailer. Luke parked in front. He turned off the car. He was surprised at Barb's sober glance as she gathered her jacket and purse. "Luke, maybe it would be better if you played *meet the press without me*." She opened her car door while he hesitated with surprise. "You know they're going to find you." She climbed out of the car, opened the rear door, and gathered her travel bag. "I'll call you later. Thanks."

Luke watched as she walked to her door. Never looking back as she unlocked it to disappear inside.

Luke reasoned the hero who drove from Las Vegas to Rio Vista had just got run over by a disappointed woman. He started his car and drove away. Luke's grand plan to share his heart, mind, and soul with Barbara was gone, and so was she. It was sobering and painful.

He drove out of the trailer park, uncertain what to do or where to go. The thought of driving to his own trailer was less than exciting. It was a comfortable double-wide three miles away, ironically decorated by Barbara. The dismal thought of going there made the choice easy. He turned onto US 95 and headed for the Wild River Casino. There, he would find refuge, familiar faces, rules, and routine. Barbara might be pissed at him, but at Wild River, he was in charge. There he was *the man*.

———————

THE SPRAWLING PARKING lot at the Wild River Resort was dotted with a mix of cars, pickups, and SUVs. Several of them had ski boats on trailers behind them. *Not a bad morning crowd,* Luke thought as he wheeled into the parking lot. He hoped he would find Many-Coats in the security office.

Many-Coats was bright and ready to take over someday. Luke found satisfaction in the knowledge. He had taught the kid well. Luke parked, locked his car, and headed for the front door. The morning sun felt good as he walked. It was going to be hot. There was a uniformed security officer with a valet attendant standing at the casino's front door. Luke recognized the man. Dan Williams. He was a big man. High side of forty. A drinker. Been fired from Fresno PD. Luke had hired him. Casinos, it seemed, were refuge for many ex-cops.

"Morning, gentlemen." Luke nodded as he reached the two men. Carson reached out an arm to block his path while he keyed his radio, "Blue six to Desert eye. Luke Mitchel has arrived. Sorry, sir, you're gonna have to wait here."

Luke was shocked. "What!" He gave Carson a hard look.

"Blue six, I'm on my way," a filtered voice announced on Williams's radio. Luke recognized Many-Coats's voice.

Luke's shock quickly turned into anger. Barbara's chill, mixed with Williams's Marlboro breath, pushed him to the edge. "Get out of my way." He pushed Williams's arm aside and opened the door.

Many-Coats, once a smiling, respectful subordinate, intercepted Luke near the front desk. Many-Coats's expression wasn't its usual user-friendly self.

Many-Coats raised a hand, motioning Luke away from the front desk.

"What the hell is going on?" Luke demanded.

"Sorry, Luke. The Tribe met last night," Many-Coats explained. "GM called me this morning and said you've been banned."

Two uniformed security officers arrived. They assumed positions behind Many-Coats. Luke knew they were reinforcements. He had seen this before. Hell, it had been his job to announce the same to others. Two women behind the front desk were watching. Luke clenched his fists.

Many-Coats saw it. "Luke," he cautioned, "don't make this ugly."

Luke was confused. Was he the same man who left

Las Vegas being called a hero? Luke's mouth was dry, his words strained. "I've got things in there. Lot of it personal."

Many-Coats nodded. "I know. We'll have someone bring it over to you."

"How thoughtful," Luke said.

Guests at a nearby table stopped eating to stare at the two men. The words and the body language told them it wasn't going well.

Many-Coats stood silent. Luke's eyes went from Many-Coats to the two officers, then around the room. He knew it was a last look. He inhaled a deep breath and unclenched his fists. There were no words left. Luke nodded soberly, turned, and walked away.

FOUR
DREAMS DO COME...

LUKE'S STOMACH was in a knot. His ears pounded with the beat of his racing heart. He was overwhelmed. It was a bright, sunny warm day, but his life was once again plunged into darkness.

First Barbara and now his safe place to fall had stabbed him. Why? What had he done? How could this be? He was supposedly a hero. He'd saved a life only to find it was costing him his own.

He'd had it all under control. Success, promotion, excitement, reward. It was all in his hands. It was safe, secure. Barbara said she loved him, but suddenly, unexplainably, and painfully, it had all slipped through his fingers. The men and women who were once those closest to him, those who knew his heart, were now betraying him. The reality of it blinded logic. When he reached his car, he kicked the door, leaving a dent.

A mile from his trailer park, Luke stopped at a liquor store to buy a bottle of Jack Daniels. He wanted something to make the day go away. The Cactus liquor store was familiar and comfortable. He'd shopped at it often.

They had fresh hoagies and about anything else a man could want.

There was a Native American wearing coveralls and a ponytail ahead of him with a case of beer. The man was older with skin darkened by the sun and age. Luke watched as bony fingers counted out payment with bills and coins dug deep from a pocket. The Tribe owned a multi-million-dollar casino, but few of the nearby residents wanted or had credit cards.

The kinship he'd found with the Tribe was gone. It was likely everyone within fifty miles would know of his firing by sunset. Well, they could kiss his ass.

He stepped aside as they slid his case of beer off the counter and moved for the door. They never looked back.

"How are you today, Chief?" the unshaved clerk asked as Luke shoved his bottle of liquor onto the counter along with a credit card.

"How's things at Wild River?" the clerk added, processing the card.

Luke was going to lie, but the clerk saved him by continuing, "I was over there last night. Won sixty-eight bucks outta a slot." His smile widened. "You want a bag?"

————

LUKE'S double-wide trailer was hot. He turned on the AC, filled a glass with ice, then Jack and Coke. Heavy on the Jack. He left the curtains closed and sat in the living room. "Damn Indians," he said aloud, and then emptied his glass.

People, he told himself, slouching on the coach, could only hurt you if you allowed them to. An idea promoted by a shrink the LAPD insisted he talk to. Screw them too, and screw Barbara, and the whole tribe.

It was dark and almost ten o'clock when he heard the noise in his carport. He switched on an outdoor light and opened the door as an SUV, lights on, drove away into the night. There were five cardboard boxes sitting on the cement behind his car.

In the first box, Luke found his framed honorable discharge from the Marine Corps, a gold embossed LAPD appointment certificate, several pictures of combat in Afghanistan, and a color photo of his then six-year-old daughter. The collection was from a wall in his office. He wondered how the office looked. Was it empty?

In the other boxes, he found a checkbook, six silver dollars, and a paper Bible with a faded black cover given to him by a Chaplin whose name he couldn't remember.

For a moment, he thought about the war. He could hear the thump of mortars, the snap of rifle fire, flashes in the darkness. Seemed the war wasn't really over. Just far away.

————

TWO HUNDRED MILES AWAY, it wasn't dark. The lights of the Las Vegas Strip were on. There were no signs, inside or out, announcing time or temperature, just the glut of colorful digital lighting inviting all in. On the third floor of The Silver Palace, the general manager, Greg Larson, was at his desk. There had been no announcement that Blake Mancini had been fired, but in Vegas, official word wasn't necessary. In Vegas, word of mouth was faster than social media. As a result, many were already applying. Three resumes for director of security lay on the desk in front of Larson.

After studying them carefully, page by page, he pushed back in his chair and looked to Charlotte Johnson, his director of human resources, who sat waiting in front of his desk.

Charlotte Johnson was a Black woman, five-ten, forty-two years old, and even by Vegas standards, beautiful. She had become The Silver Palace's HR director five months after becoming the GM's lover. Sometimes, during their lovemaking, they joked about who seduced who. Charlotte had once been the head of housekeeping at The Silver Palace. Housekeeping in Las Vegas ranked right up there with nudity. If guests didn't like what they saw, be it a topless chorus line or their suite, they weren't coming back.

That reality, coupled with Charlotte's bilingual abilities—she spoke fluent Spanish thanks to her Latino ex-husband—made her a natural. Nearly fifty percent of the city's labor force was Hispanic. She not only spoke Spanish, but she also understood the character and lifestyle of Latinos.

Charlotte had spent her day preparing applicant resumes for The Silver Palace's next director of security. It was a critical position. Critical because of the millions in cash and property the resort offered by opening its doors to the world, day and night, three hundred and sixty-five days a year.

Although The Silver Palace had yet to announce they were accepting candidates for the position, HR had received thirteen applications. Charlotte wasn't sure if it was the Vegas small-town persona or Greg Larson's big mouth. Likely, he had bragged about his tumultuous firing of Blake Mancini.

Charlotte spent the afternoon reducing the number of applicants to three. She knew Greg Larson would rate repartee with a new director as critical. Above all else, Larson wanted someone who would tell him when they might be heading toward an iceberg.

Larson studied Charlotte for a moment before he spoke. She knew he had an ability to separate their private relationship from business. For the moment, it was business.

"I know two of these men," Larson said with a sober look at Charlotte. "They both have good jobs. One at Caesars. The other at the Luxor. They're chasing money. I don't want somebody who's wants this job just for more money. I want somebody who wants the job, more than the money."

"Okay, let me make sure I understand," Charlotte said. "You want someone who doesn't care about money, doesn't have a job, and who you know really well."

"Don't be a smart-ass," Larson said. "These guys applied because they've heard we're without a director. We gotta find someone else."

Charlotte pushed out of her chair and gathered the three resumes from the desk. "I'll find him," she said.

"Stay in touch." Larson gave her a smile. "If you know what I mean."

———

FIVE BLOCKS FROM THE STRIP, on East Sierra Boulevard, Blake Mancini sat at a bar in the *Flesh & Fashion Gentleman's Lounge*. The music was loud, and the three shapely scantily clad waitresses, as well as the barkeep, were busy. Mancini was glad as it provided him a lost-in-the-crowd refuge.

For once, he wasn't interested in bare asses. They surrounded him, but he was lost in alcohol and anxiety. He'd left home at his usual hour and said goodbye with a smile to his in-laws and wife. His wife would now think he was at work. Why would she think otherwise? He cringed and drank the remainder of his third drink.

He was old and overweight. Being fired didn't mean the end of a career in Las Vegas. There were over one hundred and fifty casinos and hotels. They all needed security. The problem was there were more than one hundred and fifty men, all younger, all better looking, with just as much experience, chasing the same jobs— and most wouldn't have to explain why they were fired from one of the big dogs on the Strip.

Along with Blake Mancini's position as director of security at The Silver Palace came a mandated vetting by the state gaming commission. When he passed the commission's background check, he was issued an ID card and a CCW permit. Blake Mancini, sitting at the bar, drinking while surrounded by tourists, locals and near-naked Vegas wanna-be-beauties, was wearing a fully loaded Glock 43X.

He knew he would receive prompt notice from the gaming commission that all of his rights were suspended with his termination, including his right to carry a concealed weapon. It was only a matter of time. The clock was ticking. Either he told his wife, or her deep Vegas roots would deliver the news.

Gigi Mancini was once a beauty. She still turned an occasional head, but like her husband, she was, by the Vegas standard, old. Old in Vegas was tough to market. His Vegas *juice* as a director, provided access to headline shows, the best tables in the best restaurants, and rooms for friends and family. Telling his wife he had lost it all was going to be a challenge. Money could make a loss of perks less painful, but he'd lost that, too. Who wouldn't miss a couple hundred thousand a year? Mancini knew he was at the top of the shit list.

Revenge emerged from his frustration, and Mancini welcomed it. Pouring alcohol on it was like pouring gasoline on a fire. Through the flames haunting him, Mancini could see the prick who caused it all, Greg Larson. Mancini wanted him dead.

The idea made him think of the loaded Glock under his jacket. He pictured himself kicking Larson's office door open and firing a hail of shots into the bastard's chest. Mancini tapped his empty glass on the counter, signaling the set of tits behind the bar that he wanted another.

————

THE HR DEPARTMENT at The Silver Palace was busy. They were down forty-nine employees. The Palace employed 10,206 employees. Profit disclosures were not available to the public. Profits were only disclosed to the invisible coalition of Chinese investors who remained out of sight. Just send the money.

In addition to The Silver Palace's sixty-two floors, its two wings housed 6,908 guestrooms, three indoor pools, a waterfall with a river, a spa, seventeen restaurants, nine bars, and a shopping arcade. Allow me to suggest you look for the meaning of the word! There was only one resort casino larger. Three blocks away stood the mother of them all, the MGM Grand. However, Larson often argued, "The Grand might be bigger, but the Palace is better."

As the director of human resources at The Silver

Palace, Charlotte Johnson knew the GM held the power. In addition to being the GM, Larson was also her lover. Discretion was their watchword. One of them was married, and it wasn't Charlotte, which gave her the ability to bring him down with a simple sexual harassment complaint and a multimillion-dollar settlement. The reason she hadn't done it was simple—Greg Larson trusted her. Few men had.

Charlotte wanted to ask Larson if he loved her, but she hadn't. His marriage seemed stable, so was it just sex, or was it the fabled curiosity about sex with a Black woman? There were many unknowns in their relationship, but trust outweighed them all. It was Larson's trust that kept her at her desk looking for a relevant candidate for the resort's director of security.

"Think beyond the traditional," Larson had told her after passing on the candidates she'd presented earlier. She didn't tell him the three he'd rejected had already been filtered out of seventeen.

She tried to understand why he didn't like them. What was it he was looking for? Uncertain, tired, and frustrated, she turned her attention to the *Desert Sun*, the big dog of the daily newspapers in Vegas. A copy was always waiting on her desk. Certain she would find an article on the nude, intent on jumping from one of their balconies to a near-certain death, she unfolded the paper.

Larson's attempt to keep it off the front page had obviously worked. She finally found the story on page six. It was titled—*Heroic Guest Saves Woman From Deadly Fall*. Charlotte read on, the hero, thirty-eight-year-old Luke Mitchel, from Rio Vista, Arizona, ironically serves as director of security at the Mojave Wild River Resort and Casino.

An idea took root in Charlotte's brain. Did Greg Larson know this man was an experienced security director? Had he, in his rush to manipulate the press, overlooked who and what Luke Mitchel was? If Greg wanted an out-of-the-mainstream idea, she had it. "Jim," Charlotte yelled to her assistant in the outer office, "get in here."

————

LUKE MITCHEL CHECKED his cell phone to make sure it wasn't dead. It wasn't. The phone simply hadn't rang. He'd hoped Barb would call. She hadn't. Maybe someone from the casino. They didn't call either.

How the hell could they get everything done without him. Luke didn't like the answer that came to mind. He got along fine after Jim Todd's death, and they were obviously doing fine without him now.

Alcohol hadn't solved Luke's problems. It only brought him new ones. He had a headache and an upset stomach. He had finally quit drinking. Now, he wished he could quit thinking—especially of Barbara. Okay, the Tribe was done with him, but why her. When he needed her most.

His double-wide trailer was no longer a refuge. Now, it was just a haunted place, a place he didn't want to be. Luke wanted to despise the tribe for what they had done but couldn't. People, even the Mojaves, did things with a reason. They just chose not to tell him what the reason was. It had simply been, *get out, you're banned*.

Maybe they were in a conspiracy with Barbara. When he wrapped it all together with their Vegas getaway, it became even more baffling. In Vegas, he was a hero, but here, he was an asshole. He decided to have another drink. Screw another headache. They could all go to hell. Maybe he would go back to the Marine Corps. At least there, he knew who the enemy was. He also knew the Corps didn't want old men. And then he realized who his enemy was—himself.

He was pouring a glass of Jack when his cell phone finally rang. It was on an end table in the living room. He bolted to it. Maybe it was Barbara. They could talk. She would understand. "This is Luke," he said into his cell, hoping he didn't sound out of breath.

"Hello, Luke, my name is Charlotte Johnson. I'm the director of human resources at The Silver Palace in Las Vegas. How are you this afternoon?"

Luke considered telling the woman the truth. He lied instead." Fine. How can I help you?" He set his glass of Jack aside.

"I called the Wild River Casino," Charlotte explained. "The gentleman I spoke with gave me this number."

Luke did his best to think of a reason for the woman's call. Had he left something in the room? Did they now want money for their suite?

"Uh-huh," he said, waiting for what he knew was going to be a more painful truth.

"First, allow me to compliment you on your heroism here at The Silver Palace," Charlotte continued. "Your courageous act was certainly appreciated. I hope in spite of what had to be challenging circumstances, that you enjoyed your stay."

"I was treated well," Luke granted.

———

CHARLOTTE GLANCED at the notes on her desk. She had a printout from his registration form. She had Googled

Luke Mitchel to find the online history of his employment with the LAPD as well the press when his partner was shot to death.

She'd also run a property and title check on his double-wide trailer, checked his credit scores, and his three credit cards, all current. She ran a DMV history on his Arizona license plate as well as his driver's license, which was due to expire in June.

She looked for Luke Mitchel on Facebook, chat rooms, and in email services. She'd found none and considered that a good thing. A search of service records resulted in finding Luke's voluntary enlistment in the Marine Corps as well as his honorable discharge.

She had made a call to the LAPD's HR department to verify the terms of his employment. Their only comment was his resignation was voluntary. A similar call to the Mojave Tribe's HR resulted in a *no comment*.

An online query for criminal arrests and civil lawsuits produced a record of a VA home loan, a divorce, and information identifying him as the father of a female child. She also searched medical histories but found no red flags.

Before making her call to Luke, she spoke with the front desk, housekeeping, and room service. She called surveillance and asked for a CD of every CCTV image with Luke in it.

Gayle Turner delivered the CD. Charlotte knew Gayle had played a key role in identifying Luke as a hero as well as the security director at Wild River Resort. Her impression was important.

"This man was more than just a hero," Gayle said as they watched the CD in Charlotte's office. "He had character."

When Charlotte finally made the call to Luke, she knew with whom she was dealing.

"Before I continue," Charlotte said, "you know the importance of confidentiality?"

Luke was puzzled. What the hell was this woman talking about. He gave the answer he knew she wanted. "Yes, I do."

"Thank you." Charlotte was relieved. "I'm calling to see if you might be interested in becoming part of The Silver Palace family."

"Part of the family?" Luke was puzzled.

Charlotte understood the anxiety she heard. She knew she had to be cautious. "I'd like an opportunity to talk with you in person."

Luke's apprehension yielded to suspicion. He was wary. "Listen, lady, I don't know who you are or what you want. Nor am I buying what you're selling. I finished with all my talk about Vegas before I dove away. Have a good day." He clicked his cell phone and ended the call.

Charlotte was shocked. She listened to the dial tone in her ear for a moment and then hung up. "Damn," she said aloud.

Luke went back to his drink. He wondered what the call was about. What did they want? An opportunity for more publicity, hype for the casino, photos? Whatever it was, he didn't want to be part of it. Screw them. They were worried about their freaking image, while he was worried about his life.

His cell rang again. Luke looked at it and drew in a breath when he saw the area code was 702. He was irritated. What part of my hang-up didn't she understand? He answered in the middle of a ring.

"Allow me to be direct and brief, Mr. Mitchel," Charlotte said, pressing the telephone close to her mouth.

"We have a position open for director of security. If you're interested, call me." Now, it was Charlotte's turn. She hung up.

Luke stared at his cell phone in surprise.

————

CHARLOTTE TRIED TURNING her attention to other business—there was lots of it, but her thoughts kept returning to Luke Mitchel. Her call didn't go exactly as planned. So much for her novel idea. Seemed the carrot she dangled wasn't all that appetizing in Arizona. It was hard for her to imagine someone not being interested in working at The Silver Palace, especially if they were already in the business. Anyone working for Indians had to be an eccentric.

Luke Mitchel seemed to prove the point. She tried picturing what the Mojave's Wild River Resort might look like. An abandoned, remodeled K-Mart with a new sign in front came to mind. Good place for an ex-cop from LA. The telephone on her desk rang. She picked it up. "Charlotte Johnson."

"Miss Johnson," Luke's voice said in her ear. "I'm sorry I hung up earlier."

Charlotte read Luke's tone as sincere.

"Can we set our telephone practices aside? I'm interested in an interview," Luke said, "but there's a problem."

"A problem?" Charlotte said.

"My Indian friends aren't friendly anymore. I was locked out when I got back from Vegas. Banned. I don't know why, but you don't have to be a genius to think there's a link to what happened."

Charlotte was surprised. "But what you did was a

good thing. I spoke with the Mojaves earlier. They made no mention of this."

"How very Indian of them," Luke said. "You're the director of human resources. If someone called you to ask about an employee's history what would your answer be?"

Charlotte knew he was right. Her mind raced. Ironic —a hero with problems, but his candor impressed her. There was nothing for him to gain with a confession. Her gut provided the answer. "I think we should proceed, Mr. Mitchel."

Luke quit holding his breath. "Thanks, and it's not Mr. Mitchel. It's Luke."

Charlotte's eyes and fingers went to her computer as she cradled the telephone to her neck. "I can set something with our GM for the day after tomorrow. Does one in the afternoon work? If you need a room, I'll be glad to make a reservation. No pun intended."

"I'd like that."

"Check in with me after your arrival. The interview should last no longer than…well, we'll allow the GM to decide."

"Got it," Luke said.

"Thank you for calling back, Luke. I look forward to meeting you."

Luke tossed his cell phone on the couch. "Hot damn!" he shouted.

After the call from Charlotte Johnson, all Luke could think of was how fortunate could one man be? Could it be true? Was it real? He tempered his excitement with the thought that maybe the interview was just another gift from the GM. Another thank you. He didn't want to believe that. He knew he made a good impression on the GM, but a chance to become a director of anything in

Vegas had never entered his mind. Even if it was all air kisses, he was excited. His thoughts turned to Barbara. He doubted she would share his excitement, let alone even answer her phone. He decided it best to wait before trying to make contact.

Luke rummaged through his clothes. He paused when he found a pair of Barbara's jeans. He really wanted to tell her, to share the news with someone. He pushed the jeans aside and selected a suit jacket. He put it on and looked in the mirror. It looked formal, dark. He put it back. Blue, brown, light green, none seemed right and then he remembered why The Silver Palace had called. If it was real, a true chance, then the call was because he was Luke Mitchel. They wanted something different. They wanted to take a chance.

Las Vegas was the kingdom of chance, the city of hope, a place where a dollar slot could send you away with more money than you ever dared dream. It was also a place where you might lose your ass. The Grand, the Luxor, Caesars, none of them were built with winners' money. Losers built them. The only thing the winners and the losers had in common was *chance*…now Luke had one, and it was a big one.

He selected a tan sports jacket. He'd wear it over a black tee shirt with black jeans. Hell, it was what he wore every day at Wild River. If Las Vegas was interested in Luke Mitchel, he was going to dress like Luke Mitchel. The odds were in his favor. He realized he was beginning to think like a gambler.

Luke brushed the wrinkles out of the sports jacket he'd chosen, then pulled out a black tee shirt, black jeans, black belt, black underwear, and black socks. He wondered if anyone would care if his underwear was color-coordinated. The thought made him smile.

After his wardrobe selection, he went into the bathroom to pack his shaving gear. There, he found more of Barbara—lipstick, Chanel perfume, Dove deodorant, and a toothbrush. Luke forced thoughts of her away.

He had a day to get there. Packing made it real—but was it? He needed to learn who he would be meeting with. He went to his laptop and Googled The Silver Palace. Eleven ads and promos appeared, presenting an array of photos depicting suites, crowded pools, and headline shows. All encouraged him to make reservations. They weren't cheap.

He searched through the hype only to be presented with options to The Silver Palace's rates at lesser resorts in Henderson and Boulder. He found an article posted by the Nevada Hotel & Casino Gaming Association announcing the grand opening of The Silver Palace. The article was four years old. Another compared the bottom line earnings of the top five resorts in Las Vegas. The Silver Palace was number three. Their earnings were in the billions. There was little doubt they could afford him.

Luke turned his Googling on the GM, Greg Larson. Nine Greg Larsons appeared. The first was a dentist in San Diego, the second, an attorney specializing in motorcycle accidents, and the third, a life coach in Beverly Hills. Greg Larson, the GM of the Silver Palace, remained hidden somewhere in the shadows of the Internet. Luke was not sure how to dig out more information. Maybe it was best if he went in cold.

Now he'd settled on what to wear, and a car wash and gas was next on the list. Dirty cars seemed the exception in Vegas, at least it appeared that way, and Luke wanted to blend in. He gathered his car keys and tried to remember the location of the car wash. He asked his iPhone, and *Siri* was quick with an answer as well as directions and drive time. It was two point eight miles. He was headed for his car when the haunting reality came back—was he running *to* something or *from* something?

Luke was almost to the car wash when he saw an orange traffic cone in the middle of the street. A uniformed Border Patrol agent stood beside it. The agent's patrol car sat at the curb with its emergency lights flashing. Luke slowed to a near stop as did the car in front of him. He watched as the agent looked at the drivers ahead of him before waving them on.

Illegal aliens in Arizona were not unusual, nor was the search for them. All routine, Luke thought, running his window down as he reached the officer.

The uniformed agent looked at Luke from beneath his wide-brimmed *Smokey Bear* hat. He was a young man, midtwenties, dark eyes, and a uniform tailored to show off his fitness.

"Hey, are you Luke Michel?" the agent asked, laying a hand on the roof of the car to look down at Luke. The brown eyes studied him. Luke was surprised by the question. Why the hell was the Border Patrol asking him who he was?

Luke gave the only answer he could. "Yes."

The agent gestured to the shoulder of the street in front of his patrol car. "Pull over to the curb."

Luke was puzzled. "What's this about?"

The agent cut him short. "Pull over to the curb." There was no room for negotiations. Luke pulled to the curb in front of the patrol car and stopped. The agent followed him. When he reached Luke's open window, he spoke. "You know Calvin Many-Coats?"

Luke was even more surprised. "Yeah, I know him. What does he have to do with this?"

The agent looked down at Luke behind the wheel. "Calvin's my brother-in-law. He asked me to do him a favor."

Luke looked up at the agent's face. It was shadowed by the wide brim of his hat. He didn't know what to say. He was worried. Was the Tribe going to get in the way of his interview in Vegas? What role was the Border Patrol playing in all this?

"Listen," Luke said, it was nearly a plea. "I don't know what you want? But—"

"I don't want anything," the agent said, cutting Luke off again. The agent then reached beneath his protective vest. He pulled something out and dropped it in Luke's lap. "That's called a dream catcher. Calvin wanted you to have it." The agent turned and walked away. A moment later, the patrol car sped by Luke and disappeared into the distance.

Luke looked at what had been dropped in his lap.

His three years with the Mojaves had taught him much about Indian lore. The dream catcher was big medicine. Made by hand, a dream catcher was believed to do exactly what its name implied—catch dreams.

Luke cradled the item in his hands. His heart was racing. A dried, dark three-inch piece of snakeskin had been molded into the shape of a heart. Shoestring stripes of hide were laced around the snakeskin and pushed through small colorful beads. Another longer strand of leather hung from the bottom of the heart and sported a dozen dangling multicolored beads. The craftsmanship was obvious. Luke closed his hand carefully over the dream catcher. Tears welled in his eyes. Had the gift from his Indian friend given birth to the dream he was living? Luke knew the answer.

FIVE

PICTURE THIS

IT WAS like Andy was leaving Mayberry. Luke had never dreamed of leaving Wild River. Hell, he never dreamed of finding it, but now he was torn between his love for the Indians—no matter how badly they had treated him —and the excitement waiting in Vegas. That was if it wasn't all a pipe dream.

It had been another day with a silent phone. He fought an urge to call Many-Coats and thank him, but he had learned Indians never did anything expecting thanks. Luke stopped for gas at the AM/PM mini-mart on 95 next to a KFC and a Walmart. After filling his tank, he drove north on 95. The last monument in his changing world, the Wild River Resort, slid by on the left. It was tall and glistening in the sun, but he could see much more than the glass façade. He could see Barbara, her naked beauty, her voice. He could see Many-Coats and Jim Todd. He could hear the clatter of the slots and the shouts from winners. It was all his, once. Now, it was fading behind him.

Luke drove toward the Nevada state line. He thought

about life in Las Vegas. Where did people live there? He had seen little of a city whose population was now near a million. Where were they? Where were their homes?

He remembered a TV show about the rich and famous in Vegas. Payne Newton was featured as the Godfather of Las Vegas, but he was hardly typical of those calling Vegas home. Where were those living on tips? Was there a minimum wage in Vegas? An electronic chime from his cell phone ended his thoughts. He picked up his iPhone and answered. "This is Luke."

"Luke, it's Barbara," the familiar voice said.

Luke wasn't sure what to say, but the fact she called, excited him. He was trying to think of something when Barbara solved the challenge.

"I miss talking to you," she said. "I was worried. Calvin told me what happened. Are you okay?"

"Yeah," Luke said. "I'm good."

"I owe you an apology. I was a bitch. I'm sorry. Can we get together? You know, just hang out and talk?"

Luke's heart raced. It was obvious Barbara had no idea where he was or what he was doing. "Barb, I was going to call you. I'm going to Vegas. They called and—"

Barbara cut him short. He could hear the displeasure in her voice. "Back to Vegas?"

"They called and…"

"Then why didn't you call me?"

"I was going to call, but—"

"Goodbye, Luke."

"Barb, listen…" Dead air sang in his ear. Luke looked at the cell phone and then tossed it. "Shit," he growled.

Where was his head? Why was he in such a fog? Why hadn't he called her? That's all she wanted. Why didn't he invite her?

She knew him as if she were his wife. Was that it?

Was he afraid she was just another woman who would leave him? Was that the real reason he couldn't draw her closer? Did he love her, or was he just in love with her flesh? Could you share physical love and not emotional love? The answer was simple. He had screwed it up.

In an effort to escape the painful thoughts, Luke turned on the car radio. Creedence Clearwater Revival filled the quiet rush of his speeding car with the sounds of *Bad Moon Rising.*

I see the bad moon a-risin' I see trouble on the way I see earthquakes and lightnin' I see bad times today

Don't go around tonight Well it's bound to take your life There's a bad moon on the rise

Hope you got your things together Hope you are quite prepared to die

Looks like we're in for nasty weather One eye is taken for an eye.

Luke turned the radio off and tramped on the accelerator.

———

"I'm GOING FOR A HAIRCUT," Greg Larson announced to his executive assistant as he marched out of his office, pushing an arm into his suit jacket.

Jackie Fallon, the attractive thirty-year-old brunette, glanced up from her computer. "And you'll be back when?"

"Depends on my barber, doesn't it." Larson pushed another arm into his jacket. "Anyone calls, tell them to go to hell."

"Tell them *go to hell.* Got it," Jackie said in a businesslike tone.

Larson shared the back-of-the-house elevator with a

bellman, a waiter, and two engineers. They recognized Larson, but none spoke. They knew his disdain for small talk, or was it just small talk with the *invisibles*.

Leaving The Silver Palace, Larson drove his Maserati to the Meadows Mall. The shopping precinct was popular with both locals and tourists. It housed big-name anchors and a mix of Vegas specialties. Combined, there were one hundred and twenty-two businesses. It was a busy place, which was why Larson picked it.

He parked at the rear of the mall in the midst of other cars. Walking to the front of the mall, Larson waved at a passing cab.

————

LARSON HADN'T NOTICED the Ford SUV following his Maserati from The Silver Palace to the mall. Nor did he notice the driver of the SUV had stopped and was taking pictures with a telescopic lens when Larson hailed the cab.

Blake Mancini was excited. He knew he was finally onto something. He put the SUV into gear and fell in line two cars behind the Larson's cab.

————

CHARLOTTE JOHNSON HAD ARRIVED at the condo fifteen minutes earlier. She turned and kicked off her heels, put on some music, and poured drinks. Charlotte looked at the condo's furnishings. She guessed it was costing Larson four or five grand a month. He told her he'd leased the condo after they became lovers, but Charlotte suspected she wasn't the first woman to have a key. However, she was determined to be the last.

She heard a key in the lock. Larson opened the door. Charlotte smiled and moved to him. They kissed passionately.

When their lips parted, Charlotte purred, "Welcome, said the spider to the fly."

"Thank you, ma'am." Larson accepted the drink she offered.

Charlotte sank into a cushioned chair as Larson tossed his jacket aside, loosened his tie, and sat down across from Charlotte.

"I have a surprise for you." She smiled seductively.

"I like surprises," Larson said, pushing one shoe off and then the other.

"I've found you exactly who you want for your new director of security."

"Tell me about him." Larson rattled the ice in his glass. "And don't tell me he's a know-it-all from another casino where his friends just gave him a farewell party he'll never forget. That would not be a good surprise."

Charlotte pushed out of her chair to kneel on the carpet in front of Larson. She put her hands on his knees. "Remember Luke Mitchel?"

"The boy scout who saved the jumper?" Larson answered. "Yeah, I remember him."

"What if I told you he's coming in for an interview?" Charlotte moved her hands to Larson's feet. She rolled a sock down and pulled it away. "You want someone you can trust. Someone not owned by another casino. Someone this town will know is exclusively yours. Try Luke Michell"

"I'll be damned," Larson said with a smile.

Charlotte tossed a sock aside and pulled the other away before reaching for Larson's belt. Polished nails loosened the buckle, then found the zipper which she pulled down slowly. "Speaking of betting my ass."

————

BLAKE MANCINI PARKED beside a Walgreens drugstore across the street from where Larson had climbed from the cab to walk into the Desert Flower Condominiums. He missed a picture of Larson going in, but he was betting whoever went in would eventually come out. Maybe Larson would come out with some bitch he might recognize.

Mancini assured himself this was about sex. Expensive sex. It was often said a picture was worth a thousand words, but this picture was going to be worth a freaking million, maybe two million—right out of Larson's fat, hand-tooled leather wallet. Mancini settled in his seat. Excitement was finding its way to a growing erection as he imagined Larson inside screwing some young shapely staffer with big tits.

Mancini quickly found, however, that two hours of waiting in his SUV had its challenges. He let the car idle in the heat to run the AC, but now he worried the engine would overheat. After he got the money from Larson, he was going to move the hell to Alaska.

He watched two couples, one pushing a shaded baby cart, and two men enter the condo complex. An overweight woman, not worthy of a picture, came out. Mancini struggled with the growing discomfort in his bladder. He thought about going into Walgreens. *No, I'm not buying anything, I just have to piss.* But the fear he might miss Larson coming out, or a skirt he might recognize, stopped him.

Finally, in desperation, he decided he'd open the

driver's door just a crack and piss. Damn, he had to go. He unzipped, opened the door of the SUV and was hit by a blast of heat. He saw a Styrofoam cup in the gutter and reached down to grab it.

Hurry, he pleaded silently with himself. If he didn't hurry, he was going to piss his pants. He unfolded the gritty cup and shoved his penis in it and let loose. He sighed with relief, tilting his head against the headrest, and then he felt it. Warm urine was soaking the inside of both of his legs. The cup was leaking. He pushed the door open, tossed the cup and pissed all over the floor mat.

"Shit," he growled. In the center console, he found a napkin from *In-N-Out*. He cursed, mopping his pant leg. He looked up and was shocked to see a cab pulling to the curb in front of the condos. Greg Larson emerged from the entrance. Mancini grabbed his camera, but Larson climbed into the cab, and it pulled away.

"Son-of-a-bitch." Mancini was still cursing when the woman came out. Mancini recognized Charlotte Johnson immediately. The bitch had sent a formal termination letter to his house. He raised his camera and shot frame after frame as a second cab arrived.

———

LUKE MITCHEL'S Las Vegas suite was more than comfortable. He tried watching TV in both the living room and the master bedroom. A drink from the well-stocked bar helped him decide on the living room. He called Charlotte Johnson's number shortly after arriving. Her voice invited him to leave a message.

"Miss Johnson, it's Luke Mitchel. I'm here. Thank you for the room. It's more than nice." Luke wasn't prepared for her voicemail. He paused awkwardly, trying to think of words. "I'll probably be here when you call. If not, I'll be close and you can call my…" An electronic beep told him time had run out. Luke looked at the house phone in his hand, damned it, and hung up.

The windows in Luke's suite provided him with a panorama of Las Vegas, but the traffic and the crowded sidewalks were all distant, and like the suite, quiet on the other side of the glass. Perhaps it was the quietness of the suite that annoyed him. This wasn't the Las Vegas seen in commercials with smiling, attractive couples laughing, drinking, and gambling, and then he realized what it was. He was alone, lonely in the haunting quiet.

Memories of sitting alone in the dead silence of a police interrogation room after his partner was shot, coming home to a house filled with nothing but silence and a note from a wife who wasn't there. Add the silence from his cell phone after Barb's hang-up, and the sting became real.

He could still hear Barb's words. *"Can we get together? You know, just hang out and talk?"*

Remembering his answer made it even more painful. *No, I'm on my way to Vegas.* No wonder she terminated the call. Why didn't he say, *come with me? I'll come get you.*

He was where most people in the world wanted to be, Las Vegas, but he was lonely. Beneath him, a casino was full of smiling faces, dinner was being served in the restaurants, and the showroom was filling with those waiting on Miranda Lambert's performance.

Luke finally realized what it was he had to do. He didn't give it much thought. He just knew he had to do it. He found his cell phone and dialed Barbara's number. He knew she'd be at work. He pictured her behind the bar in the lounge at Wild River. She answered calls at work.

He'd be quick, *Barb, I'm sorry. I miss you. I love and I wish you were here.*

He was still working on the words when he heard her cell ring. He waited for her voice. After the fourth ring, he got his answer. "You've reached Barbara Nichols. I can't take your call right now, but if you'll leave a message, I'll return your call soon."

Luke hung up. She knew who the call was from and chose not to answer. "Damn it," he muttered.

———

BLAKE MANCINI WAS in no hurry to go home. Things hadn't been good there in a long time, but they were significantly worse after Charlotte Johnson's letter confirming his termination arrived. His wife was the one to open it.

"You sonofabitch!" she screamed. "Why didn't you tell me? What did you do?"

It wasn't what he had done. If she had been a wife instead of just some aging sex symbol, who ironically never wanted sex, he'd still have his job. Would she have reacted differently if he told her? He knew the answer.

Mancini's first stop was at a hands-on car wash on West Sahara. He wanted the urine off the mat and the stench out of the warm SUV. He tipped the attendant an extra twenty-dollar bill.

It was cooler now. The afternoon heat was surrendering to nightfall. In Las Vegas, the dinner hour came late, but so did the guests. He missed dinner with his wife, although dinner with her was much like sex. Rare.

As the SUV went through the carwash, Mancini's attention turned to the camera hanging around his neck. He pushed the *menu* button and then *images*. Charlotte

Johnson appeared. He clicked again and again, eleven times. She was tall, smartly dressed, with perfect hair. The bitch was not only Black, she was beautiful. He could only imagine how she looked naked. That prick Larson knew. The thought made Mancini smile. He may not have naked pictures of Charlotte, but the ones he had were worth a million. Looking at the images a second time he found three of them had the address of the Desert Flower Condos in the background. He was pleased. He had no pictures of Larson coming out of the condo, but Larson didn't know that. In Vegas, it was what you didn't know that cost the most.

───────

LUKE WAS HUNGRY FOR A DRINK, but a clear head for his interview was far more important, so his drink became a Diet Coke, straight up. He wondered if Barbara would return his call. Not likely. He tried to remember the last time they made love. It was easier to remember when they didn't. Could it really be called making love? If that was true, where had the love gone? Apparently, love was no longer in Rio Vista. It was now in Las Vegas.

Where he was, and what he was there for, considering he was banned by the Mojaves after the fiasco with the would-be naked jumper, staggered his mind. How could it all be *chance*? Was it all part of the Vegas persona, or was God at the wheel? He hoped it was God. Did the would-be jumper realize what she had done? Did she care? What drove her onto the balcony naked? Why did she want to die? Luke wondered if he really had the right to interfere in the woman's decision.

Was Luke a hero or just someone taking a chance? Then again, he was in the city of chance. There was a fine line between chance and dreams. Many-Coats's dream catcher came to mind. Did it really have relevance, or was it just another example of Indian smoke and mirrors? He decided it had no power, but this didn't interfere with the gratitude he felt for Calvin Many-Coats.

He thought the Indians were bastards for how they'd handled things, but oddly, he missed them. Maybe he'd call Many-Coats later. Maybe it was best he didn't. He didn't want another hang-up.

Luke fell asleep with the Diet Coke in hand. When he finally woke up, he drank the now warm soda, put in a wake-up call for seven a.m., and climbed into the king-size bed. The bed seemed big. The last time he was in bed in Vegas, it was with Barbara. Luke finally fell asleep, wondering how his now eight-year-old daughter would feel about visiting him in Vegas.

———

IT WAS LATE, even by Vegas standards, but Greg Larson was still in the GM's office. He returned from his "haircut" to learn the Chinese investors for The Silver Palace had sent an email saying they were going to call at five p.m. Hong Kong time. They were a pain in his ass, but there was no choice. Money made the rules. The Chinese investors made the rules.

Larson called his wife. "The Chinese are playing who's got the money," he told her. "Conference call, five p.m., Hong Kong time. That's three a.m. our time."

"Don't get so upset, Greg," Neomia Larson cautioned.

"Why? Because I mentioned the Chinese. You wanna drive in and help me calm down? I'll kick Bill Marr outta the penthouse and we'll blow the Chinese off."

"No, thanks," Neomia said. "I prefer sex at home."

"Okay, but wait till I get there," Larson said. However, he was grateful she'd declined his invitation. He wondered if two Viagra in twenty-four hours created a health risk. He'd taken one before his afternoon meeting with Charlotte Johnson. He had three more tablets hidden in his desk.

"Get some rest, Greg," Neomia urged.

"I've already got a room waiting. I'll take the call there."

After calling Neomia, Larson did the math. He hadn't become the GM by watching the clock. The Chinese investors had the money, but he was the captain of the ship. He decided it was time to make a walkabout to ensure there were no icebergs in sight.

He liked property walkabouts. As the GM, he received daily reports from every one of the many departments. They appeared on his computer. Occupancy, both present and ten-day projections. *The drop*, bottom line money, collected by security from slots, table games, and other revenue sources. Engineering, status of the infrastructure. Operational revenues, house monies on hand for cash payouts, and material supplies. Food and beverage, meals served, restaurants, bars, and staff cafeteria. Security, incident reports, internal and guest related. Human resources, current vacancies, staff, apps. There was a dozen more. Larson reviewed them daily, but there was no substitute for a hands-on see-and-tell. He put on his tie and jacket, checked his appearance in an office mirror, and headed downstairs.

The casino was busy. Larson remembered someone had done a study about why serious gamblers liked the night. Maybe because human nature felt the darkness of night made it easier to hide—to bet without being seen, maybe bet the kids' college fund and not feel guilty about it.

Larson walked through the card room. He was glad to see they were busy. Especially the *twenty-one* tables. The dealers were smiling, chatting with players. The players usually tipped when they left a game. Feeling their dealer was part of the gamble made even losing somehow fun.

He noted most of the players had drinks. Players usually didn't leave a game until their drink was empty. So, House Rule Number One—keep the drinks full. Slots, table games, or roulette. Larson eyed them all. The drink glasses looked good. Ordering from, or having a drink delivered by one of the many scantily clad waitresses helped the flow of alcohol. The waitresses made good money. Most came from tips. Come on, this was Vegas.

Carpet was in good shape, lighting okay, floor polished. The lounge was busy with serious drinkers and two attractive women he was certain were prostitutes. Illegal in Vegas and Clark county, but...

A siren went off in the middle of the slots. Cheers followed. Larson, like others, went to see. A gray-haired senior stood pointing at his machine. He had won a thousand-dollar jackpot. Those crowding around patted him on the back.

Larson made a mental note of the machine number. He would look at the ratio between money played and money paid out later. He knew odds were the house had already collected a serious amount from the so-called winner. He was pleased to see the old man's reaction had encouraged those playing nearby. Money was finding its way home.

The kitchen, like the card room, was busy, noisy, and

filled with an aromatic mix of cooking as an army of servers prepared plates. Larson spotted the executive chef near a wide grill at the back of the room. The kitchen was coping with orders for a dinner for eleven hundred members of the American Association of Real-tors. Each had the option to order chicken or steak. The hot, expansive gas range was crowned with both. The executive chef, Klaus Bayer, was a German that Larson had found while on a retreat in the North Limestone Alps. He was a big, noisy man dressed in a white uniform stained with spots and remnants of splattering. He wore the traditional Toque Blanche—the chef's white bonnet —set low on his eyebrows. He was barking orders to his minions on either side of him tending the meats.

"What's cooking, Chef?" Larson asked, patting Bayer on the shoulder.

The chef burned a look at Larson. He hated cooking jokes. "I'm busy," he said with a thick German accent. "You want small talk, go to McDonald's."

"Good talk," Larson said and moved on.

His next stop was employee dining. The steak smelled good and whatever was served to guests was also served to employees, free. The employees in line ahead of Larson were all being asked for ID cards by a young F&B attendant sitting on a stool at a gate to employee dining.

"ID," the attendant ordered when Larson reached him.

"My name's Greg Larson," he said to the twenty-five-year-old wearing an earring. "That mean anything to you?"

The young man made no move to open the gate. "Maybe if you were Kit Carson?" He smiled at his clever-ness. "But you're not. No ID. No food. That's the rule."

Behind Larson, the line grew as more employees joined in.

The complaints started from those in the line.

"What's the problem?"

"Come on. Move it."

"Listen, kid," Larson said, leaning into the young attendant. "Showing ID to get in the dining room may be the rule, but I made the damn rules. You're a nobody, and I'm the GM. Now open the damned gate or you're going back to Pizza Hut."

Suddenly, the line was quiet. The attendant opened the gate.

"Thanks," Larson said.

He selected a tray and followed others down the buffet line. He chose a well-done steak, a baked potato, and lima beans. The room was crowded. Most were eating or relaxing. Some were asleep.

Larson wondered how many employees were there—several hundred, he guessed. Lot of free chicken and steak, but then reminded himself he was among them. He regretted getting in the kid's face. Soon the story would be told throughout the Palace, but there was nothing to be done now.

Where to sit became another challenge. Most of the tables had three or four employees. Tray in hand, Larson searched and then he saw Gale Turner, the director of surveillance. She was sitting alone, reading something. Her empty plate announced her meal was over. Larson moved to her table and paused. "May I join you?"

Gayle looked up from her reading. She was surprised. "Of course." She gestured to an empty chair.

Larson sat down. He was relieved. He didn't know Gayle well, but he felt she had proven herself during the incident with the jumper.

"It seems I'm not the only one working tonight," Larson said, salting his steak.

"You may have forgotten, Mister GM," Gayle said, "bad guys and cheats are like bats. They come out at night."

Gayle's tone was friendly. Larson decided he liked her. She wasn't beautiful, but she filled the Vegas requisite for *attractive*.

Nice hair. Good color. Makeup balanced. Breasts the right size. Her blouse revealed just a hint of separation. She was dressed casually, but nothing identified her as an employee. Surveillance persona, Larson decided. It explained why she was sitting alone.

No one was sure what Gayle was—and in Vegas, what you were was a lot more important than who you were.

Larson knew he had news Gayle would be interested in. Surveillance was a subdivision of security, and the new director of security would be Gayle's boss.

"Glad I found you," Larson said, cutting his steak. "I have news you may find interesting." He raised his fork with a cut of meat.

"I had the chicken," Gayle smiled. "One of those who didn't make it across the road."

Larson smiled as he tasted his steak. "You remember Luke Mitchel?"

Gayle nodded. "I do. A man and a night that will be hard to forget."

Larson looked directly at Gayle. "He's scheduled for an interview tomorrow. Director of security. What's your gut tell you?"

Larson noticed his words impacted Gayle. He was skilled at reading expressions and hers had surprise written on them. He could see she was working on an answer. He cut at his steak again as her fingers toyed with a paper lying face down between them. Gayle surprised him by picking up the papers to push them in front of Larson.

"I remember Luke Mitchel," Gayle said.

Larson's eyes scanned the paper. Luke Michel's name was printed on it. Along with his address, occupation, employment history, skill set, credit rating, character queries, divorce circumstances, child support, and relationships. Larson laid his fork aside. "Good answer," he said.

SIX

ONE FOR THE MONEY

LARSON HAD a standard room on the thirty-sixth floor of The Silver Palace. The room was good news. It meant the penthouse and the luxury suites were sold. Some big rodeo thing was going on. Everyone in Vegas seemed to be talking like wannabe cowboys. Shoes off, Larson laid on one of the double beds to watch *Batman* on a movie channel. From what he saw of the film, he decided Batman would make a piss-poor GM.

The telephone rang. It was precisely three a.m. It was the Chinese. If nothing else, they were punctual. Larson turned off the TV and had the receiver in hand before the third ring. "This is Greg Larson."

"Mr. Larson," a young Chinese female with an accent said in his ear. "I am calling on behalf of Starman Wind."

"Yes, I've been expecting your call."

"My name is Mia Kum. I am secretary for the group. I'm here with Mr. Chang and Mr. Yang. I speak on their behalf this afternoon. Both gentlemen, as you know, rely on, what is the term, interpretation?"

"Yes, I understand. Please give both gentlemen my

regards." Larson could hear male Chinese voices in the background.

"Thank you," the young voice continued. "Both Mr. Chang and Mr. Wang want to compliment you on your quarterly report. They are pleased with your management."

Larson knew the Chinese wanted something. His management style was confrontational. He knew the Chinese were more diplomatic. First, they would kiss his ass. He was hoping they weren't going to kick it. "I'm happy they are pleased. How may I be of service today?"

"One moment please," the young voice said. She spoke in Chinese with the male voices in the background.

There was quick chatter and then the girl spoke into the telephone again. "Mr. Chang and Mr. Wang are planning a business trip to your country. They will be arriving..." She paused and spoke again in Chinese to the two men. Then again to Larson. "Plans are still being formulated. They estimate about three weeks. Will a telephone call in advance suffice?"

"Of course, anytime," Larson said. "I welcome their call as well as an opportunity to make them comfortable."

"They will be spending two nights in your city. We hope you will be able to offer accommodations."

"They will be comfortable here at The Silver Palace."

One of the Chinese men spoke in the background. The girl answered him and then spoke again to Larson. "The two gentlemen will be visiting your city after business in New York. Although they have been to Las Vegas before, they are not familiar with all of your customs."

"I will be their personal host."

"Thank you, but I am told they will be tired and do

not wish to impose. There will be no need for formal meetings. Just casual inquiries."

"What can I do to make their visit more comfortable?" Larson asked. He swung his feet to the floor.

"Associates have told them about what is called, the *Hard Rock Hotel*, saying it has an interesting atmosphere. They would like to visit it but understand most visit the Hard Rock with companions."

Larson now understood where the conversation was going. "I'll be glad to arrange for female companions to accompany them. Would they prefer Chinese?"

"No, the preference is Caucasian. They have learned attractive female Caucasians are preferred at the Hard Rock."

Attractive white whores…Larson shook his head. Las Vegas had the best money could buy. No chopsticks for these two. "The gentlemen will not be disappointed," he told the interpreter. "I will have companions waiting."

"We must ask," the young voice continued. "The visit be keep private, so competitors do not gain, what is the word…an advantage."

"Privacy is assured," Larson said.

The girl again spoke in Chinese to two men. Larson waited. "Thank you, Mr. Larson. That is all."

"My pleasure," Larson said. "Thank you. I look forward to their visit." He hung up the receiver, smiling. Not only was he the general manager of The Silver Palace, he was apparently also a pimp.

————

LUKE WAS UP EARLY. Thoughts of his interview with GM, now just hours away, were filling him with anxiety. They had to know he had been banned at Wild River. Banned was Mojave for *get the hell out*. Now, the challenge was to explain it.

And what was with the woman from HR? *Call me when you arrive*. Obviously, she belonged to the club chaired by Barbara Nichols.

He tried to remember the last time he had an interview. Wild River, obviously. Before that, it had been the LAPD. His work history consisted of the Corps where he was discharged, the LAPD where he quit, and Wild River where he had just been fired. This interview probably wouldn't last long.

The thought this was just another thank you from the GM kept creeping in. If it was, what would he do next? Did he really believe he had a chance to become director of anything in Vegas?

Maybe he'd go online and look for work. Vegas was full of guys carrying guns. He'd become a guard. The thought was a painful one—a director down to a guard. Luke had no answers.

He walked to his window and watched traffic on the Strip. Cabs, buses, and limos crowded the street. Luke decided it looked like the city was yawning, waking to a new day. If ever there was a new day, ready or not, this was it.

Wild River, Barb, Calvin Many-Coats, Rio Vista—all of them gone. The silence of his once-busy cell phone was all the proof needed. The hope one of them, any of them, would call, was now unrealistic—their involvement in his life, reduced to memories.

———

JACKIE FALLON WAS NOT surprised when she arrived at her desk in the general manager's executive office. The door to the GM's inner office was open. The lights were off. Greg Larson had yet to arrive. No surprise. Jackie knew of his scheduled three a.m. call from the Chinese.

Larson often bragged of his nighttime endurance, during his early day adventures as a bellman, valet, front desk manager, yada, yada, yada, but it was Vegas bullshit. Everyone needed sleep. Even in a town with no clocks.

Jackie ordered coffee and a Danish from room service—a privilege of the GM's executive assistant. She looked at the day's schedule on her computer. The director of rooms was demanding a meeting ASAP.

Jackie knew what it was about. The grapevine had its reliable sources. The rooms director had a near knock-down-drag-out with engineering over the paint color for the executive suite bathrooms. She knew what color the GM would pick. She knew Greg Larson well. It was her job to make his job as smooth as possible, and Jackie was good at it.

After a review of the day's schedule, she checked her voicemails. As usual, there were quite a few. House-keeping was having issues with supplies. They were critically low on shampoo. Valet had another stolen car. That one would go to guest services. Security was reporting a guest slip and fall. Bathtub. Injury alleged, but nonapparent. Employee dining needed additional staff. Asley Collins from guest services wanted the pent-house reserved for a Turkish prince. Verified high roller. The chef wanted to comp two rooms for friends visiting from Germany. Jackie made notes as needed. None of it would be shared with the GM. As the GM's executive assistant, Jackie had *juice*, and *juice* was the oil that kept Las Vegas running.

After checking her own voicemails, Jackie dialed in the pin number for the GM's private voicemail messages.

She'd been given the pin by IT. They didn't ask why she wanted it. It was good to have *juice*.

Greg Larson didn't know Jackie regularly listened to his private messages, but then he had no need to know. In Jackie's mind, anything the GM did was her business, and usually listening to his messages gave her a head start without him knowing.

"You have three new messages," a recorded female voice announced in Jackie's ear. The first caller was Larson's wife. Jackie recognized her voice. "Greg, time and circumstance permitting, would you please bring home dinner from your Japanese restaurant, whose name I can never remember. Pick whatever you want. I like it all. No later than eight. Bye"

The second message was from the GM of Hard Rock. "Greg, it's Dennis at Hard Rock. Got your message. Glad to help. Give me a call."

Jackie was betting the call from the Hard Rock related to the Chinese. She made a mental note to ask Larson about their late-night call. A female voice on the third message sounded familiar. Jackie put a face on it. It was Charlotte Johnson.

"Greg, it's almost midnight," Charlotte's recorded voice said. "Just wondering if you were still *up*." The woman's tone, as well as her phrasing, was suggestive. Jackie stiffened in her chair and pressed the receiver tighter to her ear. "Is your zipper up?" Charlotte's voice questioned. "When I saw it at the condo, it wasn't. Be my pleasure to check it. Call my cell when you can. You have my number…I've got yours."

The telephone went to a dial tone after Charlotte hung up. A shocked Jackie looked at the receiver in her hand as if it were on fire, and in a sense, it was. She hung it up slowly, carefully.

———

"Good morning, sunshine," Larson boomed as he marched into the office.

Jackie, still dealing with shock, looked at him quizzically. Larson, dressed in suit and tie looked rested, eager.

He continued to his open office. "Great looking blouse," he said. "Did I buy that for you? Makes you look good."

Larson paused in the doorway of his office. He was puzzled by Jackie's sober look. He studied her. "This is the part where you say, *good morning, boss. Hope you had a great night.* And yes, I'd like a coffee. Thank you."

Jackie forced a smile. "Good morning, boss. One coffee, on the way, And I hope you had a great night."

"That's my girl," Larson said.

———

Gayle Turner was in The Silver Palace's surveillance suite. The room was blue-gray with light patterns from the banks of CCTV monitors capturing in-house activity. A tip from the DOS at the Wynn brought Gayle in early. An attractive, well-dressed couple in their early thirties had manipulated a roulette wheel and walked away with nearly fifty thousand dollars. The crew at the Wynn forwarded a video.

The couple claimed they were staying at The Silver Palace. After watching the video with her crew, Gayle programmed the images into the facial recognition system. She set an alarm so that when either of them found their way into The Silver Palace's sea of cameras, they would be watched. In addition to watching them, surveillance needed to know what they did, and how they did it.

Gayle turned her attention to reviewing the in-house guest list. Most cheats were good, and Vegas attracted the best of them. But they were crooks, and even the best crooks sometimes made mistakes. Names were among them.

She was scanning the names of in-house guests when she spotted the name, Luke's name—room 1832. Gayle knew he was here for an interview with the GM. If you had a meeting with the GM for anything, you needed an edge. She hoped she'd given him one when she recommended him to the GM.

Gayle gave in to the impulse. She picked up the telephone and dialed Luke's room. All she had in mind to do was welcome him and wish him good luck with his interview.

When the call went unanswered, a digitally recorded female voice spoke, "The guest you are trying to reach is not available at the moment. At the tone, please leave a message."

Gayle wanted to speak with Luke. She wasn't ready for an electronic beep urging her to speak.

"Luke, it's Gayle, Gayle Turner. I wanted to wish you luck…I don't mean luck, I mean…" Her words were awkward. "The reason I'm calling…"

Beep. The second beep told her it was over. She hung up, equally awkward. This was the man who could become her boss. Was she kissing ass? What would he think?

JACKIE FALLON THOUGHT her day couldn't get any worse, but it did. She was still thinking about Charlotte Johnson's implied sexual voicemail when the woman walked into her office. She was Black, tall, attractive, and dressed for success.

"Hello, Jackie," Charlotte said. "Is Greg in?"

Jackie's voice got stuck somewhere in her throat. She turned her difficulty into a cough. "Sorry. Yes, he's here."

"Charlotte," Larson shouted from his office. "Get in here."

Charlotte offered Jackie a smile and moved toward Larson's office.

"Jackie," Larson said to his assistant. "There's a guy named Luke Mitchel. Let us know when he gets here."

"Yes, sir."

"Charlotte, close the door."

Jackie watched as Charlotte stepped into Larson's office and closed the door.

"Holy shit," she mumbled.

———

LUKE THOUGHT ABOUT LUNCH. That's as far as it went. He walked by Palace Burgers, Fish & Fries, Myra's Taco's, plus several formal-looking indoor restaurants. None of it worked. No appetite. That was a shocker.

He was convinced he was living the longest day of his life. He had spent the last hour and a half walking everywhere he could. He lost twelve dollars in a slot machine, another twenty at roulette, and he was now toying with the idea of playing *twenty-one*. A glance at his watch changed the idea. It was time. He headed for the elevators, checking his cell as he walked. There were no messages.

He spotted a restroom in the long hallway leading to the GM's office. It would be his last chance for a look in a mirror before the interview. Inside, he stood in front of a full-length mirror. He'd considered wearing a tie. Las Vegas appeared to be the last place on earth where men still wore jackets and ties, but he couldn't bring himself to do it.

He'd opted for a khaki sports jacket over a black tee shirt. They needed to know who he really was. He took a deep breath and headed for the hallway.

It was exactly one o'clock when Luke opened the door to find Jackie Fallon at her desk. "Hello. My name is Luke Mitchel. I have an appointment with the general manager."

Jackie nodded and pressed a key on an intercom. "Sir, Luke Mitchel has arrived."

"Send him in."

Luke recognized Greg Larson's voice.

Jackie pushed up from her chair and walked to the GM's door. Luke followed her lead.

Both the GM and Charlotte stood as he entered. Larson walked around his desk to offer Luke a hand. They shook. "Good to see you again, Luke. This is Charlotte Johnson, our HR director."

Charlotte offered a hand to Luke as Jackie stepped out and closed the door. "We spoke on the telephone. A pleasure to meet you in person."

Larson returned to the chair behind his desk. "Sit down, Luke. Would you like coffee, water?"

"No, thank you," Luke said. He followed Charlotte's lead and sat in one of the chairs facing Larson's desk.

It was quiet for a moment as Larson studied Luke.

"So, you're looking for a job and we've got an opening. You know what you want. I know what we need. How can we put this together?"

Luke sat with his elbows on the arms of the chair. "Before I came here, I looked at The Silver Palace online. I also Googled you. I know who you are and where you've been. I know you've done the same with me or I wouldn't be here." He exchanged a look with Charlotte.

"Okay, so let's get to it," Larson said, pushing back in his chair. "You got fired. The Indians threw you out. What happened down there?"

"I don't know," Luke said. "I wish I did, but the Mojaves make the rules."

"When did they fire you?" Larson pressed.

"I found out I'd been banned—locked out—when I got back after the jumper."

"We know you've got guts, we've seen that, but we need someone with more than guts. I want someone I can trust," Larson said. "I fired the last guy because I could no longer trust him."

"Which tells me if I violate your trust, I'll be fired."

"You think you can do this job?"

"I carried a gun in Afghanistan, I wore a badge in Los Angeles, and I worked for the Mojaves at Wild River. Yeah, I can do the job," Luke said. "Money didn't bring me here. A woman on a balcony did. What followed hasn't felt very good, but this fits. I know crooks, and I know cards. I can read both. I'm an experienced supervisor. Until recently, I ran a casino. I programmed slots, supervised drops, set camera positions, dealt with dishonest guests, theft by employees, and interacted with the state gaming commission."

"You may have been a director of security for a bunch of Indians, but being a director of security in Vegas is far tougher," Larson said. "Here, we have no disturbances, no scenes, no sirens. You can't call for back-up. We have ten thousand two hundred and six employees, and at times, more than twenty thousand guests. They all want to be winners. Employees steal our blankets, pillows, toilet paper, tools, and everything else that's not nailed down. They use drugs, they get drunk, and they get ugly. And that's not counting our millions in cash. A lot of it in the open, waiting on thieves, card sharks, cheats, and skimmers. We invite them in, and we give them a chance. An honest chance. If we cheat them, our casino is going to be empty in a month. Then there's the state gaming commission. They're going to surprise you with audits and inspections every month. The Silver Palace is like a beautiful woman. She's nice to look at, but she's high maintenance."

"I'm not looking for easy," Luke said. "It wasn't easy jumping off a balcony, but I did. It wasn't easy being handcuffed and called a rapist, but I was. I didn't complain, I didn't sue, I didn't hide. All it got me was one night here and fired. Yeah, I want this job."

Larson found Luke a tough read. He looked to Charlotte. She had been quiet, hands folded in her lap. "Charlotte, what are your thoughts?"

Charlotte straightened a wrinkle in the hem of her skirt before exchanging a look with both men. "Clearly, Luke knows the qualifying factors for the position as well as understanding who we are." She looked to Larson. "You've made it clear what the position requires as well as what you expect of a candidate. I think what we need to do is go to our neutral corners and think about what's been said and decide."

"Agreed," Luke said, standing up. He extended a hand to the GM.

Larson stood. They shook hands.

"I would be privileged to be part of The Silver Palace," Luke said. "I'm confident in my ability to do the job. As for the importance of trust—you already have mine. Thank you for your consideration."

Luke thought it best not to go on at length. Keep it basic. He was anxious, but not about to show it. He turned his attention to Charlotte, offering her his hand. She stood and shook it.

"A pleasure meeting you, ma'am."

"Likewise, Luke. Thank you for coming in."

Luke left the room, closing the door behind him. He knew they would talk. He offered Jackie a nod. "Thank you."

Luke disappeared into the hallway, the door closing behind him.

"Nice meeting you, too," Jackie said to the empty office.

———

IN THE GM'S OFFICE, Larson drummed his fingers on his desktop. He appeared deep in thought.

Charlotte sat down and crossed her legs. "Well?"

"Hire him. A hundred and five," Larson said.

"Why so much?"

"I want him to owe me."

"I thought trust was the issue?"

"Money buys trust," Larson said.

———

LUKE WENT to his room and took off his jacket. He was pouring a drink when he saw the flashing light on the bedside telephone. He picked it up and dialed. An operator answered, "Good afternoon, Mr. Mitchel, how may I assist you?"

"My message light was blinking."

"I'll be glad to play your message for you. Please stay on the line."

"Thank you."

There was a voice and then a female voice came down the line. "Luke, it's Gayle. Gayle Turner. I wanted to call and wish you luck. I don't mean luck, I mean…" Her words were awkward. "The reason I'm calling… *Beep…*"

Luke sat his drink aside and dialed the operator a second time. "Gayle Turner in surveillance, please."

"I'm sorry, sir. That number is for employees only. I could have surveillance call you?"

"That would be fine."

Luke waited. The telephone remained silent. He walked to the sliding glass door and pushed it open. Hot air swarmed in around him. The noise from traffic reached up from the Strip. He looked at the patio, then the railing. The idea of jumping over it seemed unimaginable. He pulled the slider closed.

The telephone rang. He reached it on the third ring. "Hello."

"Luke, it's Gayle Turner."

Luke could hear the faint sound of a car horn. He guessed she was on her cell, driving.

"Gayle, thanks for calling."

"I heard you're scheduled for an interview with the GM," Gayle said. "I wanted to wish you luck."

"Let's see," Luke said. "The director of surveillance calls to wish me luck getting a job as her boss. That's almost as crazy as me jumping off a balcony."

"Not quite, but hopefully it means your interview should go smoothly," Gale said.

"My interview with the GM is over."

"Over?" Gayle was surprised. "How did it go?"

"I'm in hover mode," Luke said.

"Call when you hear something."

"Will do. Thanks, Gayle."

Luke felt good about her call. Her words seemed sincere. He knew the decision belonged exclusively to the GM, but it was reassuring to have Gayle and the HR director on his side.

Luke picked up his drink, downed it, and poured another. Waiting. He been waiting for Barbara to call, waiting for Calvin Many-Coats, and now waiting on a call from the GM. Here he was, in the heart of Las Vegas, among millions, waiting for anybody to call. Did the GM of the Silver Palace ever call anybody? Not likely. Maybe they would send him a postcard.

————

BLAKE MANCINI DECIDED he'd waited long enough. While his wife was out spending money they no longer had, he was looking at the photos of Charlotte Johnson coming out of the condo complex. She had been meeting Larson, who fired him for getting a massage. Larson fired him when he was doing far worse—a real prick move.

What would the investors of The Silver Palace think about their married GM secretly screwing a subordinate female employee. The thought made Mancini smile. Either Larson was going to come up with a couple million, or the photos were going to the investors and the public.

Mancini was ready. His plan was damned near

perfect. He took a deep breath, picked up the telephone, and punched in a series of numbers. The phone at the other end rang twice before Jackie Fallon's familiar voice answered, "Good afternoon, executive office, how may I assist you?"

"Jackie, it's Blake Mancini. I need to speak with the GM. It's important."

"Hello, Mr. Mancini, let me check, please."

Mancini knew what Jackie was saying. *Let me see if Larson is willing to take your call.* He waited. Worrying, wondering. His heart raced. He hoped his voice wouldn't reflect his anxiety. What if Larson didn't answer? He had no plan B. It all depended on the prick he was waiting on.

"Hello, Blake." Larson's gruff voice in his ear surprised him.

Mancini bolted straight in his chair.

"I'll get right to it," Mancini said. "You're gonna meet me at the Meadows Mall tonight. I want you to park right where you did the other day. You know, when you walked off to take a cab to your meeting with Charlotte Johnson at the Desert Flower Condos."

The silence that followed was deafening. Mancini took another breath before he continued. His fear was easing, yielding to Larson's silence. "Tell you what, Greg, if you're not…"

Larson cut Mancini short with an angry challenge, "Listen, you piece of shit, I'm not meeting you anywhere."

"Okay," Mancini said. "Did I mention I've got photos, asshole. You wanna see them or should I just forward them to your rice-eating investors?"

Silence answered him. Mancini chewed on his lip as the seconds passed.

"I'll be there," Larson said in a near whisper. His tone was softer, less angry. It was almost a plea.

"Eight o'clock, straight up. Come alone. I'll flash my headlights when I see you."

"What is it you want, Blake?"

"We'll talk when you get there." With a finger stab, Mancini terminated the call. He smiled and slammed a fist onto his desk, causing his wife's dog to start barking in another room.

SEVEN
ALL THE KING'S MEN

Luke sat slumped in a chair in his room at The Silver Palace with the TV on. Drink in hand, he stared at the TV. An episode of *Friends* was playing. Ross was fighting a losing battle with a vacuum cleaner. Luke watched, but his mind wasn't on Ross's problem. He had his own.

Here he was in the midst of a city of millions, not counting those who came to Vegas for fun, waiting on an answer from a man he hardly knew, for a job in a place where he couldn't find all the doors. Most people had a plan for their lives. Most knew what they would be doing tomorrow. Luke wasn't sure what he'd be doing in the next hour.

He decided his problem was he had put his fate, his future, in the hands of others. Someone else was deciding if he'd have a good day or a bad one. He knew he had to change the situation, going to change, but he had no idea how. A solid knock on the hall door put his thoughts on hold.

It was probably housekeeping for an early turndown, maybe fresh towels, or another gratuity from management. *We're sorry you didn't get the job, but please enjoy this nice basket of fresh fruit that came by truck three days ago.*

"Coming," he called, sitting his drink aside. The impatient knocker hammered again on the door.

Opening the door, Luke's cynical attitude yielded to shock. Standing in the hallway was a stoic-looking Greg Larson.

"We need to talk," Larson announced. He marched by Luke into the room. He looked around the room. "Anybody else here?"

"No, sir," Luke said, closing the door. He was both worried and puzzled.

Larson saw Luke's drink glass beside the chair aimed at the TV. Larson pulled a chair, positioning it so he faced Luke. "Sit down," he said with a look at Luke. "And let's lose the TV."

Luke turned the TV off and sat down. He expected he was about to be told it was a pass. They had picked someone else for the job. He'd be driving back to Rio Vista in the morning. Luke drew in a breath to steady himself. They could all go to hell. He wasn't about to grant anyone, especially this man, a look at his disappointment.

"I need your help," the sober Larson confessed with awkward effort.

"What can I do?" Luke asked.

"I need your trust. Man to man."

Luke read Larson's expression. He could see the desperation. "Anything you say stays between us."

Larson reached to pick up Luke's glass. He smelled it, and then downed the remainder of it.

"You're hired," he said. "A hundred and five a year. ID, drug test, Nevada gaming, we'll catch up with all that shit. First, I've got a big fucking problem."

Luke masked his surprise. He poured two new drinks. "I'm listening."

Larson tasted his liquor. "Blake Mancini. He was the previous security director. He lied to me. I fired him."

"Got it," Luke said.

Larson gave Luke a hard look. "The sonofabitch called me tonight. He says he's got photos."

"Photos of what?"

Larson paused and stared into his drink glass. "Photos of me and a woman who isn't my wife."

Luke's features remained neutral. "What did he say he is going to do with these photos?"

Larson downed his drink. "He didn't say. He didn't have to. He told me to meet him tonight. But whatever he does, I'm screwed. *GM seduces the HR director*—It'll be headlines here in Vegas. The investors will fire me as soon as they hear about it. My wife and seventeen-year-old daughter will be history."

Luke agreed. The GM was screwed. He tried not to show his own response to the GM's admission he was having an affair with the HR director.

"Using the threat of these photos to make you come to a meeting is blackmail—a felony. Call the police."

"He'd make bail in ten minutes. Then the photos will be on TV, the Internet, and everywhere else ten minutes after later."

Luke knew Larson was right. His mind raced. "Tell me about this guy. What's he like—clever, smart, ballsy? What about his nerve?"

Larson thought about Mancini before answering. "He's an admin. He loves paper. He knows the business. Came to us from the Luxor. Good recommendations. I obviously underestimated him."

"Sometimes you have to fight fire with fire," Luke said.

"I'm listening," Larson said.

"Someone's trying to blackmail you. What if you turn it around? Blackmail them?"

"Go on."

"This guy's demanding a meeting. What if you went to the meeting wearing a wire? We could use his own words against him."

Larson thought about it. "How can we do this?"

"You'll have to wear a mic."

"I can do that," Larson said.

"Can you get the equipment?"

"Small mic and a recorder? We must have that somewhere with every other security gadget in this place."

"Surveillance," Luke suggested.

"Give me the phone," Larson said.

Eight minutes later, a surveillance supervisor knocked on the door. When Luke answered it, he was met by an attractive thirty-year-old blonde carrying a cloth Silver Palace shopping bag.

She gave Luke a suspicious look. "Is the GM here?"

Luke reached for the bag. The woman stepped back. "Sorry, I don't know you."

"You will," Larson told her, pushing by Luke to grab the bag from the woman.

————

BLAKE MANCINI SAT behind the wheel of his SUV in the parking lot at the Meadows Mall. Darkness didn't seem to have an impact on would-be shoppers and tourists. The sprawling lot was a sea of headlamps. Every time a set pulled into the parking lot, Mancini tensed, hoping it would be Larson's red Maserati. He counted eleven cars before vowing not to count anymore, but he did.

Finally, car number sixteen proved the counting was worth it. The set of headlights became Larson's red Maserati. The car slowed and pulled into a space two rows away. There was an open parking space next to the Maserati. Mancini started his SUV and pulled into it. He stopped with his driver's window facing Larson's.

He rolled his window down. "You're late," Mancini said, sarcastically with an over-exaggerated glance at his watch. He was enjoying his moment of feeling in charge.

"I'm here."

Mancini was about to speak when a young couple walked between their two cars.

Mancini waited until they were out of earshot, but the couple was followed by a gray-haired woman with a shopping bag walking in the opposite direction. He waited as a car pulled in on the other side of Larson's Maserati. A couple climbed out, locked their car with an electronic chirp, joined hands, and walked away.

Larson was annoyed by it all. He climbed out of the Maserati and looked to Mancini. "This is nuts. I'm going inside." He walked toward the mall entrance.

"Prick," Mancini grumbled, but he pulled the keys from the ignition, grabbed a canvas shopping bag from the passenger's seat, scrambled out, and followed Larson.

Larson walked to an empty table in the food court and sat down. The dining area was busy, but no one seemed interested. Mancini approached and looked around, as if expecting to be followed. He burned a look at Larson and sat down across from him, holding the canvas shopping bag in his lap.

"You always have to be in charge, don't you, Greg?"

"Cut to the chase, Blake," Larson said.

Mancini dug in his canvas bag, lifting out a digital camera. He sat the camera carefully on the table between them. "What's the cliché? A picture is worth a thousand words."

"Pictures of what?" Larson asked cautiously.

"Pictures of who," Mancini corrected, tapping the camera with a finger. "How about Charlotte Johnson, maybe the Desert Flower Condos. You remember being there?"

"You sonofabitch," Larson said with restrained anger. "You're blackmailing me?"

"No," Mancini said. He leaned into the table. His feeling of power returning. "It's not blackmail. Think of it as my separation bonus."

"How much?" Larson was blunt.

"Two million," Mancini said. "Two fifty now and two fifty every two months for the next eight months. Cash. I'll give you a bank account number."

"Two Million, eight months. All of a sudden, you're an accountant?" Larson could barely keep his rage under control.

"Not an accountant," Mancini said, pushing back in his chair. "Just a millionaire." Power was now on his side of the table.

"The camera goes with me?" Larson suggested.

Mancini raised a hand to lay it atop the camera, "You get the camera when I get my final payment."

"How do I know you won't screw me?"

"You'll just have to trust me."

Mancini could see Larson's anger but knew the man across from him was powerless.

"As I told you, Blake." Larson's confident tone and character were suddenly back. "You're fucking fired. You're getting nothing. Not a fucking penny. I'm leaving now." He pushed to his feet.

Mancini was stunned. He stared after Larson as the GM walked away, hardly noticing Luke's approach. Luke pushed Mancini's hand off the camera and sat down in Larson's empty chair. He reached into his jacket and lifted out a small tape recorder. Pushing the camera aside, he sat the recorder directly in front of Mancini.

"Who the hell are you?" Mancini asked.

"Your worst fucking nightmare," Luke answered. His tone and body language were not to be ignored. "If your ass moves off that chair, I call the police. Blackmail is a felony. You want a ride in a police car, try getting up and walking away."

"Blackmail! I don't know what the hell you're talking about."

"Every word you said to Greg Larson is on tape. Look around. See all the cameras. They'll prove you were here, and the tape will prove why."

Mancini was in shock. He took a deep breath, "Blackmail! This is blackmail…"

"More like karma than blackmail," Luke said. "You set this in motion and now it's going to stop."

Mancini wiped a damp palm on his trouser legs. "I have a right to know who you are?"

"Nope… You gave up your rights when you started this shit," Luke said.

Reaching out, Luke pulled the camera to his side of the table. He was using a tactic the LAPD taught him— *command presence*. Never give a suspect an opportunity to object, keep the threat level high, and make the contact harsh, brief, and creditable. Mancini made no move to object. Luke sensed he had him. Shock and awe was working.

"And as of this moment it's over," Luke said. "You're

leaving with nothing. No camera, no pictures, no money. If you ever talk to anyone about this, your ass is going to jail. Now get up and get the fuck outta here."

"Listen," Mancini pleaded, raising his hands as if in surrender. "I don't…"

"Shut up," Luke ordered. "I said get up and get out. We're finished. Now do it."

Mancini pushed to his feet using his hands on the table to control the sudden weakness in his knees.

Luke moved a hand to the camera. The message was clear. Mancini no longer owned it. He understood. He wanted out, away. His mind was wrapped in anxiety. His plan had collapsed on him like a wet roof. He took a final look at the tape recorder, turned, and walked away, hoping somehow to leave his fear behind.

Luke watched until Mancini's form merged into the stream of customers in the food court. When Mancini was gone, Luke reached for the camera bag. His own hand was shaking.

EIGHT
PICKING UP THE PIECES

LUKE WASN'T surprised when he opened the door to his guest room to find Larson waiting for him. Larson, drink in hand, bolted to his feet. He noticed Luke was carrying the camera bag. Luke offered the bag. Larson set aside his drink and dug in the bag.

"Do I have to ask?"

"We got him," Luke said.

Larson dug the camera from the bag and hefted it. "The photos, they're in here?"

"I didn't look," Luke said. He took off his jacket and sunk into the closest chair. "I feel like I should wash my hands."

"Pardon me all to hell," Larson said, as he searched the controls on the camera. "Like you never screwed an employee."

"I never got caught," Luke said.

Larson found the review button on the camera. He stared at the viewer as he punched the button time and time again. Images of Charlotte at the condo appeared.

"That sonofabitch." Carson thumbed through the pictures. "You think he'll cooperate?"

"He doesn't have a choice."

Larson finished looking at the images. He pushed the camera back in the bag. "I can breathe again," he said. He took a glance at his watch. "It's late. let's call it a night." He had the pictures and wanted out of the room.

"Agreed," Luke said.

Larson extended an open palm to Luke. Luke pushed out of his chair. They shook hands. The firm grip and Larson's expression told Luke it was sincere.

"Thanks, Luke. I'll put out a blast email in the morning telling the world you're now the man."

"Thanks."

Larson moved for the door. "Get some rest, you're going to need it."

"Yes, sir."

Larson was no sooner gone than the telephone rang. Luke gave up on looking for a soda in the refrigerator and answered the call. "Hello."

"Luke," the familiar voice of Gayle Turner said in his ear. "I got a call from my night supervisor. She said the GM called and asked for a wireless mic and a tape."

"True," Luke confirmed, not knowing what else to say.

"And it was delivered to your room?" Luke could hear suspicion in her tone. She wanted answers.

"Yes."

"She said the GM was with you."

"Yes."

"What's going on?"

"I understand your curiosity, Gayle, but this can't go any further," Luke said in a respectful tone.

The line was silent for a moment before Gayle said, "I get the feeling this means your interview went well?"

"Yes. I got the job. I was going to call, but it got busy."

"Congratulations," Gayle said. "I'm glad. "

"Thank you," Luke said. "Maybe tomorrow you could help me learn where all the doors are."

"Glad to. Good night, Luke."

Luke went back to his search for a Coke. He found one and drank it down in three gulps. He turned the TV on. Anderson Cooper was mumbling something sincerely on CNN. It didn't matter. Luke wasn't watching. He was thinking about Gayle's call and the congratulations she offered.

He was now the director of security at The Silver Palace in Vegas. Who knew? Gayle, Larson, maybe Charlotte Johnson...and Blake Mancini, if he was smart enough to connect the dots.

He wanted to tell the world, but Barb and Calvin Many-Coats weren't taking his calls. He'd made love to Barb and promoted Calvin Many-Coats. Calvin was now most likely the security director at Wild River. What a difference a night in Vegas could make.

You may think you were following a plan, but then there was reality. What was it the chaplain said in Afghanistan—*If you wanna make God laugh, tell him your plans.*

Luke's plan had been to get away from it all and spend a couple nights in Vegas with Barbara. Turned out there were no quiet nights in Vegas. The woman he saved from jumping didn't come to Las Vegas to jump off a balcony, and he didn't go there to save her. But the paths of two strangers crossed, and like a bolt of lightning, their lives changed.

Luke felt as if he was now part of a bigger plan. He

didn't know what was around the corner, but he liked the feeling. Fasten your seat belts and put your tray in an upright position. Luther Michell was piloting the plane. The Coke can slipped from his hand to the carpeted floor. It was empty and Luke was asleep.

————

SIX MILES away on the third floor at the Macoon Inn on West Sahara, Lawrence Jenkins, a twenty-one-table floor manager from The Silver Palace was meeting with two card room dealers from Atlantic City.

Jenkins had just finished his PM shift at The Silver Palace. The three men sat around a table as one of them skillfully dealt individual cards from a deck. The cards were face down on the table. The back of each bore the colorful logo and design of The Silver Palace. All three men studied the cards.

"Ace," Goss said confidently, baring a gold-capped tooth. He adjusted his glasses and stabbed a finger at one of five cards lying face down on the table. Jenkins reached and turned the card over, revealing an ace of spades.

Parsons dealt another card.

Goss looked at the card carefully before he spoke. "Ten of hearts."

He smiled, glancing over his glasses at Parsons and Jenkins. Jenkins reached and turned the card over revealing a ten of hearts.

"Where's the mark?" Jenkins asked with a look at the two men.

"You can't give up what you don't know," the unshaven Parsons said as he gathered the cards. His easy manipulation of the cards reflected his skill set.

"Okay…" Jenkins raised his open hands as a dealer would. "I don't want to know. Give me my money and I'm out of here."

"This deck is going with you," Parsons said, exchanging a quick look with Goss.

Jenkins shook his head in disagreement. "Our deal was three nights. We're done."

Goss laid his glasses aside to dig in an inside jacket pocket and pulled out a wad of folded bills. He peeled away individual bills, stacking them in front of Jenkins.

"Nineteen thousand, three hundred and thirty-three. All the president's men."

Parsons deliberately pushed the deck of cards and the cash to Jenkins. "Our deal was three nights, but there's three of us, right? That makes the two of us a majority, and two of us want three more nights."

"Screw you," Jenkins said, gathering the money.

Goss reached and tapped the deck with a finger. "Don't ruin a good thing. You know the money's good. How about two nights?"

Jenkins shoved the folded bills into a jacket pocket. "Okay, two nights," he agreed. "Then we're done."

"Deal," Parsons said, getting to his feet. Goss followed. Jenkins picked up the deck of cards, pushed them into a box and then into a jacket pocket. "Where are you getting these Silver Palace cards?"

"Internet. Your place is so ignorant they sell fucking cards," Goss said.

"Tomorrow night," Parsons said, as Jenkins moved for the door. "I'll be in at eight. Frank in on the half. He'll lose a couple hands, bitch, and then ask for a new deck. That's when you put our deck in. We milk the cow and then we celebrate. Maybe get laid." Parsons and Goss laughed.

Jenkins opened the door and was gone.

Goss gathered two bottles of beer from a small refrigerator. He twisted the caps off and offered one to Parsons. "I don't trust that prick."

"Let's see," Parsons said. He drank from his bottle. "We're stealing their money, but you don't trust them. Pretty ironic."

———

BLAKE MANCINI WASN'T sure where to go or what to do. Getting fired after failing to get a hand job was depressing enough, but his attempt at extortion and blackmail had not only failed but completely backfired.

He had surrendered to fear. It cost him his camera and his pride. He couldn't go home. His wife would read him. She would know something had happened and then the questions would start. Not only the questions, but the accusations. About what? About how he treated her, how he lied to her, how he cheated on her.

Plus, there was her dumb ass dog. It pissed on the leg of their coffee table every night. It barked at him every time he raised his voice. If his wife didn't have such great tits, he'd leave her.

He sat at the bar in the Bare Minimum Gentlemen's Lounge while near-naked, bare-breasted young beauties danced on the bar above him. The music was so loud he could feel it on his chest.

Three vodkas and an erection put an end to his immediate concerns. He knew he could have any of these girls, but he also knew they weren't cheap. Tourists pushed the cost up for everyone. Blake knew where the cheaper slags hung out—on The Strip near New York New York. They were not only cheaper, but quicker.

After two hours of watching dancing young tits with pierced nipples, he headed for his SUV.

Mancini knew he had to be careful driving. He'd done it before. Drinking and driving wasn't that difficult. Especially in Vegas. Shit, all you had to do was get in between cars in the traffic and go with the flow.

For most of the world it was late, but Vegas wasn't like most of the world. It was more like the center of the world. When the evening shows emptied out across the city, it was time for late-night drinking, dancing, and getting laid. Blake Mancini belonged to the *get laid* crowd.

He followed traffic on the crowded Strip to New York New York. Plan A was pick a good-looking bitch, negotiate a price, and get a head job. When the deed was done, he'd go home. His wife would be in bed. Bitching and complaining would wait until morning. The dog would bark when he got there but he'd kick its ass.

Mancini saw the street sign for Frank Sinatra Drive next to the New York New York. He wheeled his SUV onto the side street and began looking for whores. He'd gone only half a block when he spotted her. A tall, busty, shapely Black beauty in heels and a short leather skirt. He looked at her. She looked at him. Damn, he thought, this would be like having Charlotte Johnson.

Running a window down on the passenger's side, he pulled to the curb between two parked cars just ahead of the woman. He could hear her heels clicking on the cement sidewalk.

"Hey," he called as she came into sight. "What's a good-looking woman like you doing out here all by yourself?"

The Black woman paused, looked at him, and placed

a hand on her hip. Damn, she was fine. Gold dangling earrings and long hair twisted up into smooth folds.

She answered him with a white smile. "You wanna change that?"

Mancini pushed open the passenger door. "Come on in, said the spider to the fly."

The woman accepted his invitation. Her fragrance climbed into the passenger seat with her.

"Before we drive off into the night, let's get a piece of business out of the way," Mancini said, deliberately adjusting his erection as he spoke.

"We talking price or preference?" White even teeth asked.

Mancini was eager. He wanted her head between his legs.

"Sixty bucks. Three twenties," he said. "I know a spot a block away. Heads it is."

"I don't mean to be rude, but show me the money?"

Mancini fumbled awkwardly in his jacket for a money clip. Pulling three twenties from the clip, he offered them to the woman. She took the bills, folded them, and slipped them into her bra.

"You didn't ask my name," she said, lifting a badge case from her purse. The star-shaped silver and gold badge of the Las Vegas Metropolitan Police stared at Mancini. "You can call me *Officer Clark*. You're under arrest for soliciting prostitution." The mouth full of white, even teeth smiled.

A marked police car, lights flashing, braked to a hard stop beside the SUV. Two uniformed officers scrambled out. Mancini's erection faded.

———

AWAKENING in his chair to voices on the TV and windows filled with sunlight surprised Luke. He bolted out of his chair. He was late, needed to catch up, get with the program, and wake up. The good news was he got the job. The bad news was he got the job. So much for relaxing in Vegas. Luke's mind filled with the challenges ahead. He had a lot to do, and sleeping late wasn't part of it.

A rushed shower and shave followed as Luke planned priorities. The *daily drop.* How much revenue did The Silver Palace's gaming tables bring in every day? He had counted slots and tables. His guess was sixteen million a day. Figure another nineteen million from rooms, food services and entertainment. Thirty-five million a day. He would have to learn the time security collected the drop from the card rooms and slots.

Traditionally, the drop team would collect during the early morning hours—three a.m., four a.m.—when crowds were their thinnest. The actual count itself took place in the count room, which was protected by sound-proof walls, man trap doors, and heavily armed security officers both inside and out. Some you would see, some you wouldn't.

Revenue pick up by armored car was another critical procedure Luke would be responsible for. He knew the daily pick-up times needed to be random, quick, and out of public view. Once the metal door swung shut on the armored car, responsibility for safe-keeping belonged to someone else. He knew he'd be able to find times, proce-dures, and related security deployments on the computer in his office. Wherever the hell that was.

Another pressing issue was Luke identifying himself. He was now director of security at one of the big dogs on the Vegas Strip, but he'd met very few of the management team and even fewer in what would be his two-hundred-plus security team. He needed to meet them all.

He guessed security at The Silver Palace would be divided into three shifts. Each would have a daily formal briefing as the new crew came on duty. It might only be two briefings if they were working twelve-hour shifts. Luke preferred eight-hour shifts. He believed it provided better performance.

As soon as possible, he needed to start attending every security team briefing to introduce himself and meet the men and women who would be working for him. That needed to be done promptly. And then there was an array of managers he needed to get to know—rooms, food & beverage, cash ops, engineering, slots, card room, and more.

He had two-hundred-plus on staff, but to ensure the safety and welfare of nearly twenty thousand guests and visitors, he needed even more help. Housekeepers and bellmen were key. They saw and heard nearly everything and usually they'd talk. Drugs, guns, money, missing guest room furniture, and more. When you saw where people slept you got to know them well. Luke knew he would soon be visiting the daily briefings for every department. He needed them, and hopefully, they knew they needed him.

The only manager he had met was Gayle Turner, which gave him a place to start. As the director of surveillance, Gayle would know where all the doors and windows were, and Luke needed to learn all he could about the towering sixty-four floors of The Silver Palace. He needed to know who did what, where and how, in every one of the many departments—there weren't going to be enough hours in the day.

After dressing, Luke called room service. He ordered

eggs over medium, fried potatoes, bacon, sausage, sour-dough toast, oatmeal, orange juice, a sweet roll, and coffee. After placing the order, he turned on the TV to catch up on the latest Las Vegas news. The ring of the telephone changed all that. He had it in hand by the third ring.

"Luke Mitchel."

"Good morning, Mr. Michel," Jackie Fallon's voice said in his ear. Apparently, her day was starting much earlier than it did for most executive assistants.

"Good morning," Luke said, wishing he could remember her name from the meeting in the GM's office.

"I'm calling at the request of the GM. How soon can you be available?"

Luke felt a stirring of alarm. "Give me five minutes."

"Thank you. I'll tell the GM you're on your way."

Luke slipped on his shoes, grabbed his jacket and was moving out the door just as his room service order arrived. Luke parked the cart in his room, thanked the attendant, took a piece of bacon, and sniffed the rest.

He remembered how to find the back-of-the-house elevator from the night of his arrest. Most remembered it as the night he saved the nude jumper. He remembered it as the night security handcuffed him. He shared the elevator with three Hispanic housekeepers, an engineer in coveralls, and an attractive female admin from somewhere.

The GM's *get your ass down here* call had Luke worried. Lots could go wrong with what they had done the night before. If it had, his advice to the GM would be blunt—call the police.

Blackmail was a threshold for violence. It was his job to keep violence out of the house, and he was determined to do that. The GM, Charlotte Johnson, and Blake Mancini were targets. You could argue whose targets they were, but the past twenty-four hours proved they were all at risk.

Luke wished he had a gun. He'd carried one at Wild River. The real world dictated someone in his position carry a firearm. The threat of armed robbery, terrorists, drunken or drugged armed guests or employees, could not be ignored. The Silver Palace had over ten thousand employees. Most knew where the money was, and there was a lot of it. Luke was determined to make prevention the watchword.

He felt an acute sense of urgency when the elevator came to a halt on the fourth floor. His anxiety grew even more as the elevator doors opened to reveal Gayle Turner walking by.

"Gayle," Luke called.

She looked Vegas fresh. Her hair was pulled up into a soft bun. Her makeup made her look like she was ready to be a guest on *Good Morning America*. A form-fitting blouse and pants added to her success in business look.

"Good morning, Chief. Jackie said she called you."

They began walking together toward the GM's office.

"What's going on?" Luke asked.

Gayle held up a printout she carried. "If Jackie hadn't called you, I would have. Something's wrong in twenty-one. They're down one hundred and sixty-two thousand. A little over fifty per night for the past three nights."

Jackie Fallon was behind her desk when Luke and Gayle entered. She offered an acknowledging smile, pressing a button on an intercom. "Sir, Luke Michell and Gayle Turner are here."

"Send them in," Larson's filtered voice said.

"Congratulations, Mr. Mitchel," Jackie said.

"Thank you," he said, following as Gayle led the way into the GM's office.

Tom Roberts, the card room manager, was sitting in a chair facing Greg Larson's desk. Larson, jacket off, was behind his desk in his high-backed chair. Luke could see from the GM's face that the mood in the room was serious. Two chairs waited beside the card room manager.

"I'd say good morning, but it isn't," Larson said. "Luke, this is Tom Roberts, our card room manager. Tom, this is Luke Mitchel, our new director of security."

Tom Roberts stood to shake hands with Luke.

Luke thought the man looked more like a college freshman than a card room manager. He was young, clean-shaven and dressed like a male model. Luke was aware his sports jacket and black tee shirt made a totally different fashion statement.

"Tom, you already know Gayle," Larson said as Luke and Tom finished evaluating each other and sat down.

Gayle offered Roberts a look of acknowledgment.

"We're here," Larson said, rocking forward in his chair to rest his elbows on his desk, "because we've got a fucking thief downstairs."

Luke loosened his grip on the arms of his chair. He kept his face blank, deciding to follow Gayle's lead.

"As you are well aware, we count every penny of our money every day." Larson scanned the faces in front of him. "And after it's counted, they tell me how much money we've made. They never tell me how much we've lost, because we shouldn't be losing money."

The trio in front of his desk remained silent.

"That was until the last three nights," Larson said. "Tom, you claim this morning we're short over one hundred and fifty thousand from twenty-one."

If Tom Roberts was alarmed, he didn't show it. It was his poker face learned in the card room, Luke decided.

"I'm sorry I had to report this," Tom Roberts said without emotion. "But the odds of it being just chance are six hundred and fifty-eight million to one."

"And I'm the one who has to explain this to our investors," Larson said. "But you three are the ones who are going to find the weasels who are taking our money. As slick as this is, I'm betting employee involvement."

Larson looked at Gayle. "Surveillance missed something. I want a review. Minute by minute, hour by hour, until there's nowhere else to look. Tom, you got a dealer or a pit boss with shit on their shoes. Turn them inside out. Find me this sonofabitch. Now, go get it done."

The three facing the general manager, pushed to their feet.

"Luke, you stay," Larson said.

Luke stood while Gayle and Tom Roberts left the room.

Larson waited until the door closed. "I put out a blast memo announcing you this morning. Now the whole world knows you're the man. As we speak, housekeeping is putting together your office. You've got a room here in the Palace for as long as you need but find a place to live off-site. We've talked salary. We pay a signing bonus of five grand. That will buy you drinks until your first paycheck so get an account opened somewhere and get the number to Charlotte. Human resources will get you an ID and a company iPhone. They'll cover your moving expenses from wherever you lived down there with all those Mojave who loved you so much. You have any questions, Charlotte's got the answers."

Luke nodded his agreement, but there was still a six-hundred-pound gorilla in the room and both men knew it.

"So, say it," Larson urged.

Luke took a breath. "My job is to protect the house. You're head of the house."

"You're talking about my relationship with Charlotte," Larson said bluntly.

"That's exactly what I mean," Luke said.

"Allow me to remind you I came to you seeking help," Larson said. "I know I created a shit storm, but the storm has passed."

"Until very recently, you and Charlotte were the only ones who knew about your affair. Then Blake Mancini discovered you and the number changed from two to three."

"Get to your point," Larson urged. He didn't like what he was hearing.

"When you came to me, the number changed from three to four."

Larson knew Luke was right. He ran both of his hands over his face. He felt his stress level rising.

Luke waited. He had said enough.

Larson took in a breath and let it out slowly. His usual broad shoulders slumped. "So I have to do something about it?"

"Your words. Not mine."

Larson nodded agreement. "Okay, now get the hell outta here."

Luke turned and quietly left the room.

NINE

LOOKING IN ALL THE CORNERS

LUKE FOUND Gayle Turner in surveillance. She already had a team reviewing the *twenty-one* tables. It was a big task. They started with the tables for the past ninety-six hours. There were forty-six *twenty-one* tables. Gayle had also requested the dealer sign-in sheets. Surveillance was hoping to find wrongdoing on a CD recording before interrogating a suspect. This would be critical to not only resolving the current problem but also provided a proactive path to preventing a possible reoccurrence.

Luke was pleased with Gayle's initiative. Being the new guy, he knew he would be playing catch up. He appreciated Gayle's experience since, on this caper, he would be riding on her back.

"Help me get a handle on this place," Luke asked as he stood with Gayle in the shaded surveillance unit.

Most of the blue-white light came from multiple CCTV screens filling the space. Gayle had five monitors on her desk. Three of them sequenced through a variety of images from the front of the house, the cash cage, slots, and the card room.

One of the others showed the count room—a bright, reinforced, windowless room with a mantrap entrance. Six women in blue, loose-fitting, sleeveless blouses counted bills, house tokens, and coins while a uniformed armed security officer and a manager watched, seeming to be bored. The fifth screen showed a wide shot of the front entrance where a stream of guests moved in and out.

A tall, thick glass wall separated Gayle's desk from the main surveillance deck where sixteen wide CCTV monitors filled the walls with live colored video images from the back of the house to the front. Most were sequenced, running through a program, switching from one fixed camera to another. Joysticks for the PTZ—pan, tilt, and zoom—controls, stood on two desks along with an illuminated computer screen, keyboard, mouse, radio, earphones, and multiple-line direct dial telephones.

The constant hum from the screens, computers, and radios filled the room with a low-frequency rumble. Two surveillance agents, one male and one female, dressed in casual streetwear, sat watching the screens. Both agents held remotes. A female supervisor sat at a desk on the far right of the surveillance deck.

"We have two-thousand-seven hundred and thirty-three cameras," Gayle told Luke. "The big dog is number three." She pointed at the number above the wide screens on the other side of the glass wall.

"That's our facial recognition system," Gayle said as they watched the CCTV image scan quickly from one face to another as people entered the casino through the wide six-door front entrance.

"Let's say Mandalay Bay identified a cheat. They send us a photo. We program the image into our system, and the next time that bad guy walks through our front door, we get a heads up."

Luke nodded as Gayle continued. "Another system that works great is Alf. Alf is an AI—artificial intelligence—algorithm linked to camera number five."

Luke looked for the number above the appropriate screen.

"Alf looks at everyone and anything that comes through our doors that could be a threat. The program reads body language, dress, tattoos, scars, hair, eye color, and more. When it sees something it doesn't like, we get an alarm."

"Impressive," Luke said.

"We record all twenty-seven hundred and thirty-three cameras onto CDs. The majority in gaming are PTZ. Every guest or employee is covered by a camera. Guest floors and elevators have fixed images from every angle. We never violate guest privacy. No cameras in any guest room. The back of the house, including all corridors, hallways, kitchen, and parking decks are covered. We also look at all exterior doors, the river, our waterfall, and the pool as well as every cash point in the house. If it happens in-house or outside, we're going to see it and record it."

"This loss in twenty-one should have been covered by surveillance," Luke said.

"Absolutely," Gayle said.

"That makes you vital, Gayle," Luke said. "It also makes you my number two."

"I'm all in," Gayle said. "And there is more. In addition to our primary cameras, we have a variety of special ops hardware. We do regular electronic sweeps of the GM's office and yours looking for listening devices or cameras."

"Have you found any?"

"Not yet," Gayle said. "We also sweep the jet before each flight."

"Jet?" Luke asked.

"Bombardier Global 7500. It's hot. We can do a pick-up in the mideast and be home for dinner. She's in a private hangar out at Harry Reid International."

"Who decides who qualifies for our jet?"

"GM, guest relations, or us," Gayle said. "Every time they get an order to fly, Jackie calls us."

"What about covert. Let's say an employee is dealing dope in the stairwell on the thirty-eighth floor?" Luke said.

"There's a fire extinguisher there," Gayle said. "We turn it into a camera. We can put a concealable on a button on your jacket, or in a clock on the wall. In short, just about anywhere. They provide video and audio. Then there're our drones. We have eight of them."

"Seen them," Luke said, remembering the drone from the night of the jumper.

"They can stay in the air for about seventy minutes," Gayle said. "We've all been to drone piloting school. They're pretty user-friendly."

"I'm impressed," Luke said.

"And last but not least, the team reviewing CDs for twenty-one is working in the briefing room next door. We've got a couple laptops in there."

"How many troops do you have?"

"Four each shift," Gayle said. "Three worker ants and one supervisor. Factor in days off, investigations, two IT guys, one deputy, two card room plain clothes guys, and total hands-on, and we're talking eighteen on the team."

"Got it."

"Let me introduce you to my day-watch supervisor,

my number two," Gayle said, reaching to key an inter-com. "Candice, can you come in here please."

Candice Harmon, an attractive, shapely thirty-year-old blonde dressed in a short-sleeved form-fitting blouse and Levi's with exposed knees, walked through the open door to Gayle's office a few moments later.

"Candice, this is our new director of security, Luke Mitchel. Luke, this is Candice Harmon."

Luke and Candice Harmon shook hands.

"I believe we met last night," Candice said.

"I remember," Luke said, returning her smile.

The woman's hand was warm and gentle, but her grip said *don't screw with me.* Luke hoped his palm didn't feel sweaty.

"Pleasure to meet you again, Candice. I understand you have a team looking at CDs from twenty-one," Luke said.

Candice nodded. "It's got to be somebody with hands-on. We're looking at dealers, pit bosses, and who's at the table."

"Keep me in the loop, please," Luke said.

"Yes, sir…"

"Luke, please," he said.

"Candice is also a licensed realtor here in Vegas," Gayle said. "So, when you're ready to buy that six hundred-thousand-dollar property up at *The Lakes*, give her a call."

Luke granted the two a smile. "I better keep moving."

"Good idea," Gayle said. "We'll obviously stay on this from our end."

———

LUKE FOUND a female dealer waiting at one of the *back-of-house* elevators. "Can you tell me what floor human resources is on?"

"The ninth," the dealer answered. "Turn left when you get off. Can't miss it. You a new hire?"

"Yeah," Luke said, offering a hand. "Luke Mitchel. I'm the new security director."

The woman took Luke's hand and smiled. "You're the guy who saved the jumper."

———

LUKE FOUND the HR office humming with activity. Five admins were busy either at their desks or walking in and out of offices. An inner door in the busy complex was posted with the nameplate *Director*.

Luke wondered if Charlotte would be around. He hadn't seen her since his interview with the GM, at which time he had no idea the two were involved. He speculated if Greg Larson had spoken with Charlotte after last night's meeting with Blake Mancini.

He knew he was in a challenging position as the new head of security, but his problems paled in comparison to theirs. He hoped the blackmail threat was over, but that was only part of the issue. Their path out of the swamp was filled with threats. He hoped they could find their way through.

Eleven new hires sat in the HR waiting room. Luke among them. There were five housekeepers, two engineers, a front desk agent, a chef, a cashier, and Luke. He learned who and what the others were by listening. Listening was part of his skill set. Anxiety led to talk. Especially talk among strangers. They were called in the order they had arrived. Luke was sixth.

They took Luke's picture for an ID card, advised him that the Nevada Gaming Commission prohibited gambling by management, provided him a debit card for salary deposits, explained health care benefits, issued him an iPhone which required a signature, took a sample of his hair for drug testing, issued him a black master key card, and three silver keys that opened every door in The Silver Palace. Luke's signature was required again. He was cautioned that duplicating the card or keys was prohibited.

He completed a lengthy mandated Nevada Gaming Commission background application, silently wondering what they would think of his termination by the Mojaves. His signature was required on a limited liability form restricting his carry of a concealable firearm—CCW—was limited to a forty caliber Glock with a fifteen-round magazine. Carrying a firearm in The Silver Palace was restricted to security department personnel. CCW on the property and off was governed by Nevada State law and the policies of the state gaming commission.

"Do you understand and agree to each of these terms?" the young HR clerk asked, pointing a finger at yet another required signature blank on the form. The girl was at least ten years younger than Luke. He signed without comment. He was too early to apply for a Nevada CCW permit.

"When you obtain a permit for a CCW from the state, we require a copy to put in your file."

Luke chose not to comment. The girl leafed through the voluminous file she carried. "Do you have any questions?"

Luke gave a curt, "No," and moved away, glad it was over. He wasn't sure why the girl's age was an issue for him, but he knew it was. He needed to work on his ego.

He stopped at the front desk in the HR waiting room. More new hires had arrived. They looked as anxious as the ones with whom he had sat. "Could you direct me to the security director's office," he asked the desk clerk quietly.

————

PAUSING when he reached the door of his office, which had a plaque on the door which read *Director of Security*, he found his pulse racing. He smiled when he realized he felt good. He used his black master key to open the door. The lights were on, which surprised him. So did the size and furnishings in the room. It smelled fresh and clean.

Set in front of Luke's executive desk between two padded chairs were several stacks of cardboard boxes. Atop the desk sat two computer screens, a keyboard, a multi-line telephone, a police scanner, and a flat, clear calendar. A printer sat atop a wide credenza behind the desk.

The wall adjacent to the desk housed rows of wide-screened videos depicting a variety of live CCTV shots from the casino floor, the kitchen, the cash cage, count room, the parking garage, the front entrance, and the hallway approach to his office. As Luke took it all in, his emotions swung between excitement and anxiety.

The fact the office had once belonged to Blake Mancini, a man he threatened, gave Luke an odd feeling. Was he dancing on a grave? He hoped the world wouldn't see it that way.

"Sorry, sir," a female voice said behind him.

He turned to find a young, uniformed housekeeper with a baggage cart.

"There were many. I got the boxes. So, I come back."

"You cleaned my office?" Luke questioned, knowing the answer.

"Si." The housekeeper smiled. "HR, they called and say get it done."

Luke returned the woman's smile. "You've done a nice job."

He welcomed HR's thoughtfulness, but wondered how Charlotte Johnson would feel if she knew he was aware of her relationship with the GM. She was a victim. The GM made her that. Luke knew it was probably a story without a happy ending, a story still unfolding. Was Blake Mancini going to stay quiet? Would the GM end the affair? Would Charlotte Johnson buy it? Would the investors want the GM fired for creating a cover-up? *Welcome to the big bucks club,* Luke concluded, trying to bring himself back to the moment.

He helped the housekeeper load the remaining boxes onto her cart. "I appreciate what you've done," he said as the woman prepared to leave. He wanted the impression she carried away to be a good one. The woman smiled as if she understood.

———

GREG LARSON'S morning wasn't going any better. He ordered Jackie Fallon to call the head of HR and have her report to his office without delay and to advise the executive committee their scheduled ten o'clock meeting was being pushed to one o'clock.

Jackie assured the GM she would make the calls. She

did not tell him she knew about his affair with Charlotte, but she knew something was wrong, very wrong.

Had word got out the GM and Charlotte were having an affair? Why didn't he call Charlotte himself? Obviously, they had communications. Why the official tone?

Jackie was worried. If the GM was fired, would she lose her job? A new GM would want a face he knew. All of a sudden her knowledge of the affair was hanging over her like a wet blanket. Jackie shoved her worries aside and started dialing Charlotte's extension.

————

Luke sat at his desk test-driving the high-backed cushioned chair. He went to work searching desk drawers. In a center drawer, he found a badge. It was star-shaped with Silver Palace imprinted above an image of the seal for the State of Nevada. *Director of Security* rimmed the bottom in bold gold letters beneath the state seal and four stars.

The badge was configured with a clip, which Luke used to attach it to his belt just forward of the Glock he'd brought with him from Wild River. The pistol was from his days with the LAPD. Together, they were much more than a badge and gun. Luke was beginning to feel like a director of security. A knock on his closed office door put an end to the thoughts.

"It's open," Luke called, expecting the housekeeper was returning for some forgotten item, but a housekeeper didn't open the door—a uniformed security officer did.

"Morning, Chief. Thought I'd come up to introduce myself and say welcome." The man smiled and extended a hand. "My name's Lopez. Mario Lopez. I'm the day-watch commander." He was a fit man in his thirties with short dark hair, wearing the silver bars of a lieutenant on his uniform collar and a holstered Glock on his service belt.

Luke stood and shook Lopez's hand.

A radio on Lopez's duty belt and the scanner on the desktop interrupted them.

"Gate Keeper Twenty. Housekeeping is reporting a DB in the shower, guest room two-twelve. DB is confirmed. Fox Six is on site requesting back-up."

Lopez nodded to Luke as he keyed a microphone clipped to his collar. "Roger, Control. Tell six I'm on my way."

"I know what a DB is," Luke said. "I'll go with you."

————

CHARLOTTE JOHNSON HURRIED the end of an interview with an accounting candidate after the alert appeared on her desktop computer screen: *The GM is requesting you in his office—ASAP.*

"Thank you for coming in," she told the middle-aged balding man. "We'll be making our decision in the next few days."

Were all bean counters balding? Charlotte was beginning to believe it was true. She walked out with the candidate, but her thoughts were with Greg Larson. What was going on, and who was in trouble? Was there an issue with the new security director? Why hadn't Greg called himself?

Jackie Fallon was at her desk in the GM's outer office when Charlotte arrived. Jackie paused from her work and offered a smile. "Good morning, Charlotte."

"Good morning, Jackie." Charlotte smiled back. It

was her practiced corporate smile. The GM's assistant was probably ten years younger, had the quintessential Vegas body, and probably knew Greg almost as well as she did. Charlotte had long ago decided the only reason Greg hadn't seduced the girl, or at least tried, was because of her age.

"He's expecting me?" Charlotte asked, pausing before approaching the GM's door.

"He is," Jackie said. "Please go in."

Charlotte rapped lightly on the door before opening it. Larson was behind his desk, telephone in hand. He nodded to Charlotte, gesturing to a chair in front of his desk. "As soon as you're done with the police get down here," Larson said into the phone. "We need to talk." He terminated the call.

"Police?" Charlotte asked, crossing her legs.

Larson did not look happy. She knew him well enough to know the difference between business and pleasure. This was business.

Larson tossed his cell phone onto the desktop and looked at Charlotte. "Guest suicide. Housekeeping found the woman hanging in a shower."

"I already heard," Charlotte said. "You know how housekeepers talk." She was trying to keep the conversation light. "Is today business or pleasure?"

"Today's different," Larson said, leaning his elbows on his desk. "I'm sorry to tell you we're no longer a secret."

Charlotte tensed. "What do you mean?"

"You and me. Our affair."

"What?"

"Blake Mancini followed us. He took pictures. He wants money. Lots of it." Larson wasn't about to tell Charlotte that Luke had already resolved the situation.

He needed her to think there was still a threat—and there was, if Mancini somehow came back at him again.

Charlotte uncrossed her legs and leaned toward the desk, "He can't do that. That's blackmail." She was shaken. "Mancini's a revenge-seeking prick. No one's going to believe him."

"Charlotte," Larson said bluntly. "He took pictures. At the condo."

"Pictures!" Charlotte blurted.

"Yeah, pictures. And anybody who sees them is going to say, the GM seduced a subordinate."

Lines were being drawn. Charlotte could feel it. "Don't compliment yourself on the seduction part, Greg."

"Okay," Larson agreed, raising his hands in surrender. "I count myself fortunate, but no one is going to give a shit how I feel."

"How long have you known this?" Charlotte questioned.

"Long enough to know we have to end it," Larson said candidly.

"End it! Is that what I am? A fucking end!" She was loud, angry.

"Charlotte," Larson pleaded. "Listen to me."

"I have, Greg, and look what the fuck it got me."

"Please, listen," Larson pleaded. "No one cares what Blake Mancini says. He's a liar, but we have to be careful and deny everything."

"Deny everything." Charlotte was spitting mad. "Sounds like an end to me?" Tears welled in her eyes. Her words were filled with emotion. "How comforting."

"You have options. I don't," Larson said.

Charlotte pushed to her feet. "Options? Try this one, Greg. Fuck you." She turned and bolted for the door.

Larson stood. "Charlotte, wait."

———

LUKE WAS SITTING with Jackie Fallon in the GM's outer office when Charlotte swung the inner office door wide. Luke and Jackie had both heard the tense exchange but neither acknowledged anything. Charlotte marched by them without a word and disappeared into the hallway. Jackie did her best to ignore it. She cleared her throat and then keyed her intercom. "Sir, Luke Mitchel is here."

"Send him in," Lawson's filtered voice answered. "And Jackie, get me a Starbucks," Lawson called from his office. "One for Mitchel, too."

Luke nodded and moved for the open door.

"Close the door and sit down," Lawson ordered.

Luke nodded and did as asked, sitting in the chair beside the one Charlotte pushed aside on her way out. The chair looked empty. He could almost feel the emotions.

"Not to negate the impact on a victim's family," Luke offered, trying to ease the tension. "The shower-hanging upstairs has been ruled a suicide by the county coroner. Boyfriend failed to show for their wedding."

Larson didn't seem interested. He studied his inter-twined fingers on his desktop. "I told Charlotte we had to end it."

"How'd she take it?" Luke asked.

"Hard, damned hard," Larson said softly.

Luke nodded but didn't say anything further.

Lawson straightened his posture. His elbows came back to the top of the desk. He studied Luke. "We've got another problem. A big one."

"If you're talking twenty-one, surveillance is reviewing recordings. We'll be on it tonight."

"I'm not talking twenty-one," Larson said. "I'm talking gold. Vegas gold."

"Gold?" Luke said. "I don't understand."

"This is going to be a lot for your first day," Larson said. "But I'm passing the buck to you."

Luke could see the anger and frustration on the GM's face. He straightened in his chair.

"We had forty-eight gold bricks. Now we've got forty-five. Cutting to the chase, someone got us for two hundred and sixteen thousand dollars worth of gold. Three gold bricks. Two pounds each. You have to find this sonofabitch."

Luke gritted his teeth. He was annoyed. Nobody had said anything about gold on the premises. "Where was this kept?"

"Count room. Stacked and hidden underneath the count table."

"There are cameras in there—PTZs and at least twelve fixed," Luke said.

"You think I don't know that?"

"Okay," Luke said, trying to understand. "Forty-eight bricks of gold. Three are missing. Who reported it?"

"The bricks belong to the Chinese. They don't trust American money. They like gold."

"One more time. Who reported it?"

A rap sounded on the door.

"Come in," Larson barked.

Jackie entered with a tray of coffee. She sat the tray on Larson's desk and retreated without a word.

Luke welcomed the chance to breathe. He was both angry and frustrated.

"Again," Luke pressed, "who reported the gold missing?"

"Our director of cash operations," Larson said, and then sipped his coffee. "Caroline Summers. We go back eighteen, maybe twenty years. I was valet, she was front desk at the Flamingo. We dated. That was before either of us were married. Caroline's no thief. If she was, why would she be telling me the gold was missing?"

Luke shook his head. "I can't protect what I don't know about. I thought we agreed trust was a must between us. Now I'm getting crapped on over something I knew nothing about."

"You're right, I'm sorry," Larson said, raising a hand as if in defense. "I didn't like it either, but the damned Chinese swore me to secrecy. Who the hell could have seen this coming?"

Luke knew he had no way out. Secrets aside, he knew he now owned this. He allowed his body to sink in the chair. "How many people know about the theft?" Luke asked. He knew a mountain had now been pushed across the desk to him.

"Me, Caroline, and now you," Larson said. "As I told you, the Chinese don't like banks. People lose their asses. Gold doesn't go broke. So, the Chinese ordered me to have a stash of gold. Last count we had twenty-five million nine hundred and twenty thousand downstairs in pure fucking gold."

"Do the Chinese know some of their gold is missing?" Luke asked, uncertain what was next.

"No—and they're not going to. This has to stay quiet. They come here every quarter and they always count the gold. That's why it's always lights out, cameras dark, when they're in the count room. They're going to be here in three weeks. You get what I'm saying?"

"You know that's a violation of the gaming commission policy. They'll slap us with a fine you won't forget."

"I work for the Chinese, not the gaming commission. They're your problem, not mine."

Luke's mind was racing.

"So the Chinese count this gold with the cameras off. Not likely they steal from themselves. So, it's someone else," Luke said, trying to gain his elusive confidence. "You can't walk out of the count room with a two-pound brick in your pants."

Larson leaned into his desk, aiming his words at Luke. "Here's a news flash—go over to Circus Circus and you can watch a six-ton elephant disappear in front of five hundred people. All on camera. This is Vegas. Shit happens here whether you got cameras or not."

"Got it," Luke said, trying to turn his mind to the task. "Three people know about this missing gold. You, the head of cash ops, and now me."

"Your point?"

"Until your coffee got here, I didn't know the gold was missing," Luke said. "Which means the circle is getting wider."

"Exactly," Larson agreed. "Do whatever you have to do, but do it quietly," Larson said. "And get it done. The clock has the Chinese climbing all over it."

"Who discovered the theft? Was it Caroline or another employee?" Luke asked.

"Caroline," Larson said. "As head of cash ops, she inspects the count room routinely. This morning, she lifted the cover over the bricks. Engineering built her the frame, but they didn't know what would go under it. Few people know the gold is there. Caroline found three missing."

Luke stood and shook his head as if to clear it. He

was a worried, disappointed man and he made no effort to hide it. "We talked about trust when you hired me. None of it was in Chinese. Or so I thought."

"Luke, I'm sorry," Larson offered with sincerity.

"Yeah, me too," Luke answered, moving for the door.

TEN

ALL THINGS BRIGHT AND SHINEY

LEAVING THE GM'S OFFICE, Luke found his self-confidence shaken. His new title had bigger challenges than he could have imagined. He needed help. If he had learned anything as a cop and in casinos, it was the reality you could do little without help. The GM had just proven that point.

Luke knew he would need the trust and help of others. There were two in particular he had to trust— surveillance director Gayle Turner and his day-watch commander Mario Lopez. His gut told him they were solid, but the reality was he didn't have a choice.

The first thing he did when he reached his room was call Gayle Turner's cell. "Gayle, it's Luke," he said when she answered on the second ring. "Please track down Mario Lopez. I need to see both of you in my room. ASAP. No word to anyone else."

"Will do," Gayle assured.

In lieu of lunch, Luke grabbed a drink from his well-stocked fridge along with a bag of peanuts. Looking around, he realized housekeeping had been through. The king-size bed was made, the floor vacuumed, and fresh towels supplied.

His cell phone gave its electronic chirp. He assumed it was Gayle calling back, but he was surprised when he saw the caller ID. He punched the answer button.

"Barb, hello."

"Thought I'd surprise you," Barb said, her tone light-hearted.

Luke's mind filled with a rush of thoughts.

"Thanks for calling," he said awkwardly.

"Wild River Casino isn't the same without you," Barb's friendly voice assured. "I miss you."

"The tribe didn't give me much choice."

"Everyone knows that. Where are you?"

"Vegas," Luke said. "I got a job."

"A job?"

"Director of security at The Silver Palace."

Now Barbara was surprised. "Wow. You're not coming back, are you?"

"I still have my double-wide," Luke said, avoiding a direct answer.

"And I'm still pouring drinks at Wild River. Director of security at The Silver Palace. Wait till Many-Coats hears this."

"I haven't forgotten you, Barb."

A knock sounded on Luke's door.

"Barb, I have to go."

"I like talking to you, Luke," Barb said.

"I like talking to you too," Luke said, but the phone had gone silent.

He realized he had saved one woman only to lose another. He didn't think he loved Barb, but the painful reality was there was no one else.

The knock sounded outside the door again. Gayle

Turner and a uniformed Mario Lopez were waiting when Luke opened the door.

The duo sat on a couch while Luke pulled a chair to sit facing them.

"I've got some information to share with you. It has to stay between us. Is that understood?" Luke paused and looked at their faces. He wanted agreement. He needed their help. The choices were few. Luke searched for a commitment.

"I'm in," Gayle said.

Lopez nodded and said, "Confidentiality is part of the job."

Luke took a deep breath and let it rush out of him. "Okay, here's the situation. The GM just told me we're short a quarter of a million in gold bullion."

"Gold bullion?" Gayle said.

"Three gold bricks. About two pounds each," Luke said. "There's a stash under the count room table belonging to the Chinese. There were forty-eight bricks. Caroline Summers, the head of cash ops, checked the stash this morning. Three were missing."

Gayle and Lopez exchanged glances, but neither spoke. Their attention returned to Luke.

Luke was puzzled. "You're not surprised?"

Lopez shrugged. "No disrespect, Chief, but we know about the gold bricks in the count room. It's our job to know."

"But we haven't heard anything about gold being missing?" Gayle added almost apologetically.

Lopez leaned forward, resting his elbows on his knees. "It's our job to know what's going on. People talk. We listen."

"Okay." Luke accepted the reality. He was annoyed. It seemed he was the only uninformed and misinformed individual at The Silver Palace. "But you haven't heard a whisper about the theft?"

"Nothing," Gayle said. "Mario and I talk every day. Exchange rumors, scams, events. We've heard nothing."

"Nothing," Lopez confirmed.

Luke made no effort to hide his frustration. "Someone stole three gold bricks. The circle of possibilities is small. When the count room is occupied, we've got uniforms and guns in there, right? More guns outside the man trap. All of which says our thief, or thieves, are going to be faces we know."

"I don't understand. This really isn't possible," Gayle said.

"Possible or not, it happened." Luke fixed Gayle with a hard stare. "You need to go over every inch of surveillance footage and find us someone with a gold brick in their pants. And you need to do it fast before someone asks why the hell we have surveillance?"

Luke turned his look to Lopez. "The Chinese are coming in three weeks. They're going to count their gold. That means we solve this as fast as possible, or we may end up missing like the gold."

"What can we do?" Lopez said, his expression serious.

"We've got to keep this quiet. People may know the gold is in there, but the only ones who know about the theft beside us are the GM, Caroline Summers, and whoever has the sticky fingers."

"We listen, but we don't talk," Lopez said.

"And we need The Silver Palace to appear to be operating as normal," Gayle added.

"Exactly," Luke said. "Let's start with the personnel assigned to the count team. Who are they?"

"David Williams and Grant Edwards," Mario

answered. "I rotate them. They've both been here since day one."

"We also still have to find the crook in twenty-one," Gayle reminded them.

"The crook in twenty-one is strictly your problem," Luke said. "Yes, it needs to be dealt with, but the theft of the gold takes precedence over everything else."

After the conversation with Gayle and Mario, Luke went to his office. He needed to get his first foothold into the investigation. His police experience, coupled with what he had learned in casino security, taught him the person reporting the fire was sometimes the one holding the match.

He sat at his computer and requested HR provide him with the files for Caroline Summers—the head of cash ops. In minutes, the digital info was delivered to his desktop computer.

Luke studied the file. There was a picture enclosed. Summers was sixty-one-years-old, a recent widow, but still Vegas attractive. Her husband had died of cancer three years earlier after thirty-one years of marriage. She had been with The Silver Palace since the grand opening.

Her prior employment included positions as cash ops for New York New York, Boulder Station, the Flamingo, and a Wells Fargo Bank. She had lived in Vegas for twenty-six years. She earned one hundred and eighty-six thousand dollars a year plus a bonus, and she resided in a mortgage-free million-dollar home in Shadow Mountain Estates.

She had no children or dependents, and a personal credit debt of sixty-seven hundred dollars. She had two traffic violations and no arrest record. She owned two cars, a boat anchored at Lake Mead, and two Yorkies. She had a total of seventeen paid vacation days pending.

Her most recent employment review showed her as a skilled and experienced department head with a high degree of trust.

Luke was still reviewing the file when a knock sounded on his office door. He clicked the computer to a screen saver.

"Come in."

A man in his early fifties with a uniform shirt that announced his issue with weight, stepped into the office.

"Hey, Chief," he said with a smile. "Daniel Payne. I'm your PM watch commander." Payne hesitated until Luke stood, then he stepped forward to offer a hand. The two men shook.

"Sit down," Luke directed. "I apologize for not getting down for your briefing, but being the new guy got in the way."

"I can imagine," Payne said. "Still, a lot of us remember you from the Saturday night jumper."

"A night to remember," Luke agreed.

Payne reached into a uniform pocket to pull out a folded envelope. He slid it onto the desk, pushing it toward Luke. "Count that as dues for your first month."

Luke gave Payne a puzzled look.

"My first month dues?" Luke picked up the envelope and opened it. Inside was a wad of one-hundred-dollar bills.

Luke pulled the bills from the envelope and counted aloud, laying them in a row. "One hundred, two hundred, three hundred." Luke continued counting until he reached eleven hundred dollars.

Payne smiled as he watched.

"What is this?" Luke asked, looking from the spread of bills to Payne.

"Your percentage. Monthly gratuities. For your services," Payne explained.

Luke studied the hundred-dollar bills for a moment then looked back to Payne. "Why are you collecting this?"

"I'm the senior lieutenant," Payne said. "I collect the dues and make sure they get divided properly."

Luke returned the bills to the envelope. "There's no easy way to say this, but this has to stop. Extorting money for our services is prohibited. This is going back to the general fund."

"Wait a minute," Payne said, straightening in his chair, forcing a less than convincing smile. "This is Las Vegas. You worked in Arizona, didn't you? With Indians, wasn't it?"

"Mojaves, to be exact," Luke said. "They didn't like extortion either. So, one more time, Lieutenant. No more collections. We don't sell our service, we provide it. Do you understand?"

"Yeah, I got it." Payne's displeasure was obvious. "I was following the policy Blake Mancini set in motion. Lot of people aren't going to like this. An extra buck means a lot to some."

"Gratuities are acceptable," Luke said, folding the envelope shut. "But soliciting is prohibited. Anybody in security who does this will join Mancini on the other side of the fence. Do we understand one another?"

Payne pushed awkwardly to his feet. His leather service belt with its holstered automatic groaned. He struggled to hide his anger. "Yeah, I got it. I'll pass the word." He turned to the door.

Luke shoved the currency into the center drawer of his desk. Payne pulled the office door closed with a solid thud as he exited.

———

IN SURVEILLANCE, Gayle Turner sat at her desk studying a deck of playing cards spread face up in an arch atop her desk. Candice Harmon and several other surveillance officers stood looking over her shoulders at the cards.

"Tom Roberts called," Candice said. "As soon as the player in the number three spot started winning, suddenly he's up twenty-eight thousand. Parsons, the dealer, then puts a new deck in play. There's no reaction from anyone at the table. You're looking at the cards he dealt."

"You see anything," Gayle asked, as she continued to study the spread of cards.

"Nothing," Candice confessed.

The telephone on Gayle's desk rang. She grabbed it. "Surveillance. Uh-huh. Okay, thanks. We're on it." She hung up. "That was Tom Roberts. Player three is now up thirty-one thousand, and we've still got nothing."

———

LUKE WAS STILL at his desk when the telephone rang. It was Gayle. She briefed him on the ongoing twenty-one situation. Somehow, they were being hustled in real time but had no idea how it was being done. Luke headed for the surveillance office.

There, he joined the others, watching the live video feed from the twenty-one game, the suspected cheat, and the spread of cards in front of Gayle. The group of five around Gayle watched in stone silence. Luke studied the cards spread in front of her.

"This is the deck pulled from the table?" Luke asked as his eyes roamed the cards.

"Yes," Candice said.

Luke had seen marked cards before. He'd even discovered them in play. Now, his eyes searched, looking for hidden marks or a slight difference in color or design. He found nothing.

"We can't just let this dick walk away," Candice said as their collective frustration grew.

"What if we banned him?" Gayle suggested. "We pull him out of the game. Take his picture, take our money, throw his ass out and tell the world he's a cheat."

"And a good one," one of the male surveillance officers said.

"Got it!" Luke said with excitement.

Attention turned to him as he watched the live surveillance images from the game. "He's in the number three seat, right?"

"Yes," several voices answered at once

"Look at him," Luke urged.

"So, we're looking," Candice said. "He's a male cock, midthirties, maybe five-ten."

In response, Gayle used a PTZ to tighten the image of the cheat.

"Wearing glasses and a light-blue shirt. Come on," Candice pleaded. "What do you see?"

Luke surveyed the faces around him. "Anyone here wear glasses?"

One of the male surveillance officers reached into a pocket and produced a set of prescription lenses. "Just for reading," he said, offering them to Luke. Luke grabbed the glasses enthusiastically and put them on. Glasses in place, he looked at the playing cards in front of Gayle.

"Got him," Luke said. Looking through the prescription lenses, he spotted a subtle single faint dot above the letter I in the ornate Silver Palace background print on the playing cards. He lifted the glasses away and looked again. The dot was gone. "Now you see it," Luke said with a satisfied tone. "Now you don't."

Candice grabbed the glasses. "Let me see..." She pushed them on and looked at the cards. "Wow! We do have the sonofabitch."

Gayle was next. After she looked at the marked cards, the glasses were quickly passed to the others.

"The good news is we know the cards are marked," Luke said. "The bad news is an employee put this deck in play."

Gayle quickly went to work with the PTZ on the twenty-one table where the cheat sat. She rewound the images until finding Larry Parsons, the twenty-one card room manager doing the routine task of rotating a fresh deck of cards. Tom Roberts, like others in the card room, paid little attention. All seemed routine.

"Shall we get him?" Gayle asked.

"Yeah, get him," Luke said.

They resumed their watch of the live video from the twenty-one table as two uniformed security officers approached the cheat. The officers surprised the man when they tapped him on the shoulder and gestured him out of his chair. The cheat acknowledged them and began gathering his winnings. The officers instructed him to leave the chips on the table. He was led away, wearing glasses.

Gayle made a call to Tom Roberts. "Tom, it's Larry Parsons."

The crowd of curious surveillance personnel watched in stone silence as Tom Roberts left his desk and walked to Larry Parsons, the twenty-one manager. He tapped

Parsons on the shoulder, spoke with him briefly, and then led him away.

"Send me an email on how you put this together," Luke said. They all knew it was his gift. "Copy the GM and the card room manager. They'll be happy with the results."

Luke patted Gayle on the shoulder and moved for the door. The silence behind him gave way to a mix of cheers and laughter.

———

CHARLOTTE JOHNSON HAD SPENT most of the day behind her closed office door. Anger had given way to pain and then desperate hope. A hope that Greg Larson would call. She laid her private cell phone on her desktop where she could reach it quickly.

It rang three times. Each time she prayed, *God, please let it be him*. It wasn't. It was her sister, then her housekeeper, and finally her vet. Her cat was due for a shot and a checkup.

Eventually, her watch, a wall clock, and the digital date and time at the bottom of her desktop computer told her the HR staff was gone for the day.

James Bergman, her competent gay assistant, had read the tea leaves. He knew there was trouble. He didn't know what, but he made certain her telephone and computer stayed quiet. Maybe, since she had made the inevitable decision to leave, she'd take him along to wherever in the hell she was going—all she knew is it would be somewhere other than The Silver Palace.

The thought of leaving the Palace was painful, but staying for what reality revealed was a one-sided love, would be even more painful. She mentally composed an email at least fifty times as well as a voicemail, but neither took form. The words had been said, the lines drawn, the curtain closed. Greg Larson was more than a GM. He was an open wound in her heart.

Charlotte was uncertain what to take when she left. She had already gone through her computer, deleting everything personal. Simply walking out seemed best. No notes, no goodbye, no farewell, just an empty office. She wondered how long they would wait for her to return before the empty office became an obvious vacancy. Let Greg Larson explain it to the executive committee.

Her emotions swung from memories of their love-making to a desire for revenge. Charlotte knew waiting any longer was futile. She took a last look around her office, put on her jacket, gathered her purse, and walked out. She hoped and prayed she would run into Larson as she walked to the back-of-the-house elevator. She didn't. She shook her head and thought, *fuck the prick*.

————

WHEN LUKE RETURNED to his office, he found a covered tray sitting on the floor outside his closed office door. He smiled, remembering he had ordered a sandwich just before he got the call from surveillance. He gave into curiosity and reached down to lift the lid. The sandwich looked dried out. However, he needed fuel. Knowing where employee dining was, he was headed for a back-of-the-house elevator when he saw Charlotte Johnson standing in front of the closed elevator doors.

He considered calling out to her. Then he remembered sitting in the GM's outer office with Jackie Fallon when an emotionally wrought Charlotte had charged by them. He didn't know what he could say to her, but ignoring her would make him a coward.

"Charlotte," he called.

When Charlotte turned and saw Luke, she had a moment of panic—*he must have heard the angry exchange between her and Greg.*

The elevator solved her problem. A chime sounded as the car arrived and the doors parted. Charlotte gave Luke a slight wave then stepped into the elevator and pushed the door closed button.

Luke could easily imagine why the woman didn't want to share the elevator, but he was worried about her. She had recruited him. He also understood how Greg Larson could fall in love or at least lust with her. However, the rule was *you could screw down but you couldn't screw up.* He didn't want to think about his similar situation with Barb. He hoped their relationship survived. He hoped Greg Lawson and Charlotte would survive. He wondered how love could get so screwed up.

He pushed the button for a down elevator.

———

THE TIMELINE for the GM's day was typical. Larson was nearing his eleventh hour at The Silver Palace. The timeline was the only thing typical. The three-hour meeting with Windstar Promotions, the company providing broadcast and social media marketing for The Silver Palace, had proven futile. He didn't know if it was the fact their proposals were crap, or if it was the fact his whole day had been total crap. Larson's personality usually enabled him to hide from crap days by ignoring them. He usually let them bounce off him then turned his back, forgot the details and names, and simply smiled at everything.

But this day had started when a pastry chef had lost a finger. Then there was the unexpected loss of eight hundred room nights when the Wynn's GM outbid him. Another blow came with the unexpected resignation of the head of engineering, who was in the middle of remolding the Palace River. Without giving notice, he was moving to Saigon for who knows why...

In reality, Greg knew these were the typical events of another day in big dog hospitality. The problem really was that his heart had been cut out of his chest and dropped in his lap. Charlotte Johnson was the one with the knife, and somehow he couldn't let it *bounce off*.

His life, his career, his family were all on the line, but he didn't care. He had only one care—Charlotte. He couldn't leave without seeing her again. He wanted to believe it was over. He wanted to believe he loved his wife and daughter more than getting laid by the beauty who ran HR, but then there was reality and reality's name was Charlotte Johnson.

Was it love? He didn't care what it was called? He regretted the coming storm of angry words, he regretted anyone who got hurt, but he knew his relationship with Charlotte wasn't over. The day couldn't end without truth, and truth was down in the HR office, and he was going after it.

Larson shared an elevator with a bellman and a cart loaded with luggage. The kid looked young. He didn't recognize Larson. "How's your day been?" Larson asked between floors.

"Good." The bellman smiled. "We've got a meat packers convention in-house. Nice people. Many of them never been to Vegas. Great tippers."

Tippers, Larson thought. The bellman was living on minimum wage and tips. Hell, maybe someday the kid would be a GM. Didn't seem so long ago that he was living on tips. The kid and his cart of luggage got off at the next stop.

Larson had to use his black master key to get into the HR office, but while the lights were on, nobody was home.

The reception area and the eight cubicles comprising the sprawling HR complex were quiet. The chairs and desks all sat empty. Light from unwatched computer screens gave the room a haunted feeling. Larson crossed to the door of the director's office. He hoped Charlotte would be inside. They seldom left the property without saying good night to one another.

He silently said a quick prayer, but realized God had better things to do than involve himself in what happened between the GM and the HR director. Apparently, neither God nor the Chinese were going to be of any help.

Larson thought about intimate relationships at The Silver Palace and knew he'd been hypocritical when dealing with them. The title of GM was proving to be a hot mess, but he wasn't ready to give up on Charlotte.

He knocked lightly on her office door. Silence answered. He tried the knob and found it locked. He called Charlotte's name, but there was no response. He used his black key again. The door buzzed, and the electronic lock clicked open.

Larson pushed the door wide and found the office empty. She was gone, but he could feel her spirit in the room. It looked like her, smelled like her. Then he realized she was really gone. He couldn't explain the feeling, but he knew it was true. She was no longer part of him. Like the empty office, she was just a memory.

He walked around her desk and ran an open hand over the back of her chair. It was smooth and warm. He moved to the chairs that sat facing her desk. The desk looked large and empty. He took a deep breath and sank into one of the chairs being careful not to make any noise, as if noise might somehow disturb the foreboding silence.

The telephone on Charlotte's desk rang. Its electronic ring was loud in the stillness. An orange light blinked on the instrument. It rang three times before a recorded voice spoke.

"You've reached Charlotte Johnson, director of human resources at The Silver Palace. I'm not at my desk right now, but at the tone, leave a brief message. I'll return your call as soon as possible."

Greg Lawson listened as an electronic beep sounded. The caller hung up without leaving a message. Larson decided Charlotte Johnson had done much the same.

ELEVEN
SEX AND THE CITY

LUKE FOUND the employee dining room. He also found a hamburger, french fries, a Starbucks iced coffee, a cup of rice pudding, a piece of pineapple upside-down cake, and a brownie. Employee dining was busy. He sat alone but didn't feel alone with the bustle going on all around him. Ten thousand employees, maybe a third of them on duty.

Above them, scattered across sixty-eight floors, were nearly thirty thousand guests. All excited, all hopeful. The card room, slots, restaurants, shops, showroom, and more were all busy and all trusting security to keep them safe and secure. Luke, more than anybody, knew they had no clue.

Not many came to Vegas thinking about their security or anybody else's. Security, they assumed, was a given. It wasn't. Luke finished his iced coffee and went looking for his security officers.

The PM watch was on duty. He figured there would be forty-plus on duty. He needed to introduce himself and ask if they'd heard about the twenty-one table arrest.

The thought of the arrest made Luke smile, especially as he'd been the one to spot the scam.

Luke decided to start in the card room. He'd seen three uniformed officers there, along with another two in slots. He was crossing through the smiling, noisy crowds around the roulette tables when he saw her sitting at the bar.

He wasn't sure what made him look at her. Long blonde hair pulled back, large breasts, tanned legs. A tattoo on her calf. A drink glass and purse sat on the bar at her elbow. Luke knew exactly what she was. She certainly wasn't there to gamble in the traditional sense, but her profession was a gamble in itself at the best of times.

She had glossy lips and an inviting smile as she watched a couple playing, laughing, and winning at the nearest roulette table. Luke had never seen the woman before, but he knew her, and he knew she wasn't a guest or a player. She was a Vegas icon.

Las Vegas, the limelight of Clark County, was ironically one of the few counties in Nevada where prostitution was *illegal*. Sin City, implied by its name, was known for sex. If you wanted to get laid, this was your town. Las Vegas had more whores than cops, but being a whore was illegal.

That didn't mean you couldn't be a whore, or find one, but it did mean you were violating the law, especially in the big dog casinos lining the Strip. In addition to holding a negative image for most tourists, prostitution often resulted in theft, robbery, disease, and divorce. If you had prostitution in your casino, you probably had a pimp or two as well. Pimps were not known for their smiles or their upstanding rating with the better business bureau.

Pimps were liars, thieves, and crooks. They wanted only one thing: money—yours. And they wanted all of it. Those who paid for sex—straight or kinky—were often blackmailed with the simple question, *You wanna buy this picture or shall I just send it to your wife back in Fort Payne?*

Luke decided to test-drive his intuition. He pushed onto a barstool beside the blonde. The bartender appeared, offering no hint of recognition. The new guy syndrome. Luke ordered a drink. The blonde finally glanced at him and offered a smile. He returned it.

"I'm waiting on the Miranda Lambert show," Luke said after a taste of his drink.

"She's good," the blonde agreed, turning her attention and body to Luke. She allowed a look that took her green eyes from his shoes to his hair before she spoke again. "But I'm betting you don't have to stand in line, do you?"

"Stand in line?"

The blonde picked up her own drink, sipped it, then looked at Luke again. "Takes one, to know one," she said with a smile. "Tell you what, Officer. You tell me what you want, and I'll tell you what I want."

Luke was surprised, yet pleased. He gave her a congenial nod. "Ladies, first," he said, no longer certain where the conversation was going.

"You metro or house?" Her question was candid and accurate.

"House," Luke said. "My name is Luke."

"And I'm Pam." She offered a hand.

She wore three gold rings and a bracelet. Her hand was soft, warm, but firm. "I'm actually going to see Miranda. My date is meeting me here. All I know is his name is Saul Shoop, a fifty-nine-year-old meat packer from somewhere in Idaho, and he has a streak of gray in the front of his hair."

"He won't have any trouble finding you," Luke said.

"I'll bet you say that to all the girls."

"No, just the ones loitering in our card room." Luke knew the blonde wanted to talk about anything but why she was there. "You have any *friends* working here tonight?"

Pam slid the tip of a polished nail around the rim of her drink. "There're three girls with me. One's having dinner with her date. The other two are playing black-jack. Their money, of course. We're from Palm escorts. We get paid to babysit, let's say, older men, lonely men, homely men. You know, the ones who show up in Vegas alone. Meat packers who want a fun night with someone holding their arm, but not their wallet. You get an *A* for spotting me, but I'm not going to take my clothes off. I get paid one fifty an hour, and my night is over at one a.m. We checked in with Dan Payne when we got here an hour ago. I gave him our usual five percent. Now, honey, who are you?"

Luke was surprised at Pam's mention of Dan Payne. Especially her saying she paid him. Paid him after Luke ordered Payne to halt his collections. He hid his surprise and tried to match Pam's candor. "What did you do before you became an escort?"

"I booked helicopter flights to the Grand Canyon. I made eighteen dollars an hour and I worked six days a week. And no, I've never been to the Grand Canyon. Now, what do you make an hour, Luke?"

"More than eighteen bucks, and I haven't been to the Grand Canyon either."

"And you became a Palace guard, when?"

"I'm a new guy."

Pam shrugged. "Were you here when the girl tried jumping off a balcony? I saw it on the news."

"I was here."

"So you pegged me as a whore. Nice compliment. Can I say I thought you were gay?"

"I never said whore," Luke said. "All I saw was an attractive woman, sitting here, alone, at the bar. Do you really think I look gay?"

Pam emptied her drink and pushed the glass aside. "Must be a tough job, looking for women in bars."

A man in a plaid checkered sports coat and tie appeared. He was fifty-plus with a gray streak in the front of his bushy hair.

"You must be, Pam," he said, obviously pleased with what he saw.

"And you must be Gus," Pam said, swinging her stool toward the man. She offered him her hand.

Luke tried to look disinterested. Gus took Pam's hand in his, raised it and kissed it gently.

"How sweet," Pam said, professional smile in place. "Gus, this is Luke. We used to work together."

The meat packer reached to take Luke's hand. He shook it vigorously.

"You got good-looking friends, Luke."

"I do," Luke said. "I hope you enjoy your show."

"Luke's waiting on his wife," Pam said, snaking an arm around Gus's. "They're going to the show too."

"Well, hot damn," Gus said. "Maybe we'll see ya inside."

"Maybe," Luke said as the two moved away. "But I don't think so," he added when they were out of earshot.

Pam and the meat packer disappeared into the crowd. Once they were gone, Luke headed upstairs to his office. He was not happy.

At his desk, Luke keyed his radio on the security network. "Gatekeeper Thirty, this is Gatekeeper Ten. Ten-nineteen my twenty and bring your senior sergeant with you."

"Roger, Ten," Payne's filtered voice answered on the radio.

A few minutes later the uniformed Daniel Payne and a uniformed sergeant arrived At the open door to Luke's office. The sergeant was a muscular Hawaiian named Anakoni Stone.

"Come on in," Luke said, inviting them with a wave to sit in front of his desk. "Daniel, we met a couple of hours ago."

"Correct," Payne said.

Luke looked to the other man. "Sergeant, did your watch commander tell you anything about his meeting with me?"

The sergeant looked at Payne and then to Luke. "No. I didn't even know there was a meeting."

"Listen, it's important…" Payne began to speak.

"Yes, it is important," Luke cut him off. "Important because I said there would be no more cash soliciting."

"New policy takes time. Change takes time," Payne tried to defend himself.

"You're going to have lots of time to think about this," Luke said. "You're suspended. Insubordination and failure to follow a direct order. I want you off the property. The badge and gun you're wearing belong to The Silver Palace. Sergeant, take his weapon."

"What! This is bullshit," Payne protested, gripping the arms of his chair.

"Sergeant, take his weapon."

Sergeant Stone hesitated, looking first at Payne and then at Luke before standing and moving to the back of

Payne's chair. He then reached down, unsnapped Payne's holster, and lifted the automatic pistol from it. Payne stiffened but made no attempt to stop him.

"You're going to regret this, Mitchel," Payne growled, stiff with indignation as he stood up.

"Sergeant, I want you to stay with him until he's off the property. You're now in charge of the shift. Call someone to join you until he's escorted out," Luke ordered.

"Yes, sir."

"Where's the cash the girl gave you?" Luke asked as Payne turned toward the door.

Payne paused and dug in a shirt pocket. He pulled out a wad of folded bills. He deliberately threw the money on the floor. Luke decided Payne's suspension had been promoted to a termination.

"Let's get the fuck outta here," he said to the sergeant moving for the door. Sergeant Stone looked at the money on the floor. Then to Luke. He stooped to reach down and gather the cash from the floor. Stone looked at the bills, then dropped them onto Luke's desk.

"Fuck both of you," Payne growled as he marched out. Sergeant Stone followed. He didn't look intimidated.

Luke watched as the two men walked to an elevator down the hallway. Luke expected to feel better. He wanted to feel victorious, but it escaped him. He was apprehensive, worried. He hoped he hadn't started something he couldn't win. He hoped the GM and HR would back him.

Vegas was complicated. It was a town that ran on tips and gratuities, but he had just suspended a man for accepting a gratuity. But this was far from being a tip or a gratuity—it was flat-out extortion in defiance of a direct order.

He was still worried. The Mojaves would have dealt with this quickly. He hoped Greg Lawson was part Indian. Luke gathered the money from his desktop and dropped it into a drawer without counting it. He knew he needed documentation. He dialed surveillance.

"Surveillance, this is Harmon."

"Candice," Luke said, remembering the attractive blond. Gayle Turner had introduced the woman as her right hand. "Luke Mitchel, here. As we speak, Dan Payne is being escorted off the property."

"Yes, we saw it," Candice answered, surprising him.

"He's been terminated for extortion. I want you to reach back to when he came on the property today. I want everything you got with him on it up until he was marched out tonight. When you have it, please put it on a CD I can play for HR."

"You got it," Candice purred in his ear.

Luke spent the next several hours searching for security officers. He wanted to meet them, know them, their posts, their performance. They also needed to know their new boss—especially as he'd just kicked their watch commander's ass.

He'd started on the casino level. There, he spotted a uniformed officer whom he watched for a few minutes, assessing performance, and attention to duty, then he approached and introduced himself.

He was careful about the words he chose to explain Dan Payne being terminated. The officer politely cut him short. Apparently, the casino's rumor mill was in high gear, and everyone already knew.

Luke talked to two more officers near the front entrance, then two near the cash cage, another in the card room floor, two working a growing line at the showroom, and another at the elevators where it was registered guests only.

He watched a young officer be polite but firm, dealing with a couple of customers who were one drink away from fall-down-drunk. Luke was pleased.

He finally met the two men who had handcuffed him on the night of the jumper. One was on duty in employee dining. The other was at the back of the house at the employee entrance. Both recognized him and were awkwardly apologetic. Luke smiled and said he didn't remember either of them. They both knew he did, but appreciated his gesture. Both also welcomed what seemed to be his sincere interest in their duties.

The AM watch came on duty at twenty-two hundred— ten p.m. to the majority of the *straights*, who weren't even aware of the clock ticking. The officers assigned to the shift met in the security squad room for a briefing before they would relieve the PM watch and assume their posts.

The AM watch lieutenant's name was KC King. He was a fit forty-year-old, an iconic-looking security officer. Luke liked the man's professional persona. At the start of the briefing, King introduced Luke and invited him to speak.

"I'm Luke Mitchel, your new director," Luke said to the gathered officers. "That's new, not naive."

Luke surveyed the collection of faces. There were both men and women. Ages ranged from midtwenties to early forties. They looked fit. Luke was pleased he had their attention and hoped he would have their support.

He talked about Lieutenant Payne's termination, knowing he was telling them what they had already heard. He hoped the message they got from it was a positive one.

"How many people are working security tonight?" Luke asked, choosing to go in a different direction.

"Twenty-two," came an answer from a male voice amid the officers.

"Twenty-two of you in uniform tonight," Luke said. "Plus about four thousand other employees working tonight. Point being, they all part of security. They're going to see dope in the rooms, the guns, the knives. They're going to hear the domestic disputes. They'll report the missing television set, the pillows, the towels. The pickpockets in slots. The prostitute who found her way into a back-of-the-house elevator. The car clouts in the parking structure.

"They see it all, and unless they know they can trust you, you're never going to hear any of it. You need them. Try this tonight, make a friend of a housekeeper who doesn't speak English, or the tech in slots, or the chef who never gets a break. They all need to know we're aware of them and appreciate them.

"This job is much more than a badge and a gun. Show them some care, be someone who opens a door, picks up a piece of trash, be someone who smiles and says hello. Our nights are long and challenging. So is theirs. We're all on the same side, and they need to know it.

"And there's another very important group we haven't talked about. A group who seldom calls us, they're young, they're old. They're here for Miranda's show, a chance at twenty-one, maybe a couple hundred lost in slots, some drinks, maybe breakfast in bed. I'm talking about our guests. Tonight, we're at ninety-eight percent occupancy.

"We've got guests who paid a handsome price to spend a night with us. They won't give much thought about their safety or their security. Why? Because their safety and security is our responsibility. They trust us. A lady downstairs tonight called me a Palace guard, and she was right. I am a Palace guard, and I'm proud of it."

Luke heard the hand clapping as he turned with a smile and headed for the door. At first, there was just a splattering, but the sound grew as more hands joined in. He was pleased. He had touched a nerve.

He spent the next hour on the casino level watching the cash cage and the mantrap leading from it to the count room.

A steady stream of winners, losers, dealers, and employees came and went. The employees in the cage never allowed a line to form. The women in the cash cages were attentive and proficient. The surveillance cameras watching their every move reinforced their performance. Every move included nose-picking, crouch adjustments, butt rubs and more.

Luke knew behind the protective glass, man trap, and the array of surveillance cameras, were millions of dollars in cash. His thoughts took him to the other side of the mantrap and a stack of gold bricks valued at almost three million dollars hidden there.

How in the hell did a thief carry away three two-pound gold bricks? Maybe the missing gold bricks were never in there. Maybe they had been. Either way, three gold bricks were missing.

Or was more gold gone? He only had Larson's word on the amount, and he hadn't earned Luke's trust yet… Luke

knew what people said, what they claimed was the truth was always their perception of the facts.

He needed to get the facts for himself, and they were waiting behind the mantrap he was watching.

Another hour passed before the count team—a group

of five armed uniformed security officers in bulletproof vests, including Sergeant King—gathered at the side of the card room. Two of the officers pushed a nondescript four-wheeled cart with a spring-operated metal drop door on top. Items could be dropped, but not retrieved. The team were tagged the *drop team* for a good reason.

Occupancy was up at The Silver Palace. The drop— the monies collected from individual card table lock boxes, roulette, slots, and other cash points—averaged between six and eight million dollars per night. The drop team coordinated with surveillance as close-ups, wide shots, fixed cameras and PTZs watched and recorded their every move.

Guests might catch a glimpse of the drop team as it moved through the casino, but they didn't see another hidden team of security officers armed with long guns. This team was stationed strategically while the drop was in process in order to prevent the risk of snatch-and-grab or a standard straight-up robbery. The drop times were coordinated with the card room manager whose decision was usually based on the number of players in the casino. This meant the drop often occurred during late night or early AM hours when all but the skilled players—or those who had lost their ass and were determined they could win it back—still hung on.

Luke watched as the drop team worked its way through the maze of tables, unlocking each drop box to dump bills, house tokens, and coins into the cash cart. When they were finally finished, they wheeled the now million dollars plus in the wheeled cart to the cash cage where a cashier buzzed them in.

Luke knew behind the cash cage, the money-laden cart would be pushed through the man trap. First, buzzed through a thick, heavy metal door with a remote

electronic lock into the gray harsh lighting of the trap—
where hidden cameras watched everything—to be
followed by the thud of the first door closing. When the
first door lock buzzed shut with a thud, and all looked
well in surveillance, an electronic lock on the second
reinforced heavy metal door would be opened to give
access to the hidden count room.

The armed drop team finally emerged from the cash
cage to wander off toward the back of the house—it was
Luke's turn. He badged the manager of the cash cage
through the heavy glass façade. Once inside, he pointed
at the mantrap. Again, the electronic lock buzzed, and
the first door opened. Luke stepped in. The door closed
behind him. He waited. A second lock buzzed, and he
was in.

The Silver Palace's count room was designed to do
two things. Hide money and protect it. There were no
break-ins. All entries were noted, and every sound
recorded. Luke knew this, but he still felt uneasy. The
gray walls were spotless. The floor glistened. No one
dropped anything that couldn't be found. The now heavy
drop cart sat waiting with its soon-to-be-counted
millions locked inside.

On a rear wall, stacked neatly atop a row of wooden
pallets reaching from floor to near the ceiling, was row
after row of tightly bound paper currency. Luke looked
at it. As a veteran of casinos, he thought he'd seen big
money. He was wrong. He had never seen anything like
this. He was looking at what had to be hundreds of
millions.

Luke turned from the wall of stacked currency to the
count room table. It was covered with a white sheet
bearing The Silver Palace logo. He stepped closer and
lifted a corner of the neatly placed sheet. Beneath, he

found row after row of neatly stacked paper-wrapped bars forming the solid base of the table. The vertical and horizontal lines formed by the wrapped bricks were perfectly aligned. Luke wondered how anyone could determine anything had been touched let alone stolen. The GM advised the head of cash operations to report three bars were missing from the stack.

The thief reportedly replaced the missing gold bars with paper-wrapped bricks. Luke knew from what he was seeing, the theft hadn't taken place in the count room, but he knew he had to look. Before reaching, Luke keyed the radio on his belt. "Surveillance, eyes wide. I'm going in for a look."

"You're covered," a filtered male voice answered almost immediately.

Luke kneeled, pushing fingers into the folds of paper between the bricks to work one loose three rows down. He pulled. The paper-wrapped brick was heavy, but it yielded slowly to his effort and sweat.

Luke sat the paper-wrapped brick near the center of the count room table. He walked around the table, studying it from all sides. Pausing, he wiped his sweating hands on his pant legs and reached to carefully unfold the near-colorless nondescript paper to reveal the unmistakable glitter of a gold bar inside.

"Damn," Luke said in a near whisper. He reached carefully with a finger to touch the surface of the gold gently. It was cool. He pushed more paper aside to reveal the entire glistening brick. Chiseled in its surface was *999.9. FINE GOLD. Net Weight 2.2041 Kilos.*

Luke struggled to rewrap and replace the gold brick in its place in the solid gold table camouflaged with its Silver Palace king-size sheet and a stack of paper products. Luke decided it looked as if it were made in China.

The value of the table had him breathing hard. He wanted very much to be out of the count room.

"Surveillance, I'm out of here," he said, keying his radio.

————

IT WAS LATE when Luke finally reached his room. He tossed his jacket to the couch, gathered a Diet Coke from the fridge and walked to the suite's wide-windowed view of the Strip. The usual steady stream of cars and head-lamps below were now mainly cabs, buses, and limos, as well as weary pedestrians.

Luke drew in a breath. It was beautiful, intoxicating. Almost like a nude. A gold nude. You were compelled to look, but asked what you were looking at, it was difficult to find the words. It was Vegas. An eclectic mix of hopes, dreams, winners, and more often than not, losers. You could see Vegas, but you couldn't touch her. You had to wait until Vegas touched you. Luke felt very much like he had just been touched. Touched by Vegas gold.

Luke thought about the challenge of finding the gold thieves. He knew one thing. The gold wasn't stolen from the count room. The theft may have been discovered there, but the gold sure as hell wasn't taken from there. If the theft occurred away from the casino, was it time to reach out to the police? This would mean the press would be all over them.

He walked to the bedroom, kicked off his shoes, and pulled his T-shirt over his head. The GM told him the lavish suite was his as long as he wanted it, and he knew he had to find a home, but he wanted a house, not a condo or an apartment. You couldn't call Vegas home if you lived in a guest room at The Silver Palace, and you couldn't be anything but the new guy until you got out. He remembered Gayle Turner mentioning Candice in surveillance was a realtor. Maybe she would help.

Luke picked up the bedside telephone and dialed guest services.

"How may we assist you, Mr. Mitchel," a sultry female voice asked.

"I'd like a wake-up call at six."

"My pleasure. Six a.m. Is there anything else we can help you with, sir?"

"Not tonight, thank you." He hung up.

Turndown service had been to his room. He turned out the lights and climbed into the king-size bed, thinking of the sultry voice on the phone. His head found a pillow. He was building a house in his head when sleep took him. The house was built with gold bricks. Three were missing.

————

SIX MILES up East Sahara Boulevard, in the glitter and light from the Strip were the locked gates of the Lakes. Behind those gates, fortunate millionaires enjoyed security and privacy while sitting in their lavish, sprawling six-million-dollar homes.

The hour was late, but the lights in Greg Larson's man cave were still on. Larson sat in a recliner in front of a wide theater-sized screen with *The Late Show* playing. However, his thoughts were not on host Steven Colbert or his shapely guest, Margot Robbie. He was thinking about divorce. He had been married twenty-three years. Not all happy, not all unhappy—just married.

He knew everybody had problems. This was Vegas.

Millions started their married lives here, and many ended here. But if anyone in Vegas had it all, including sex, it was the man who couldn't sleep sitting in front of *The Late Show*. There were several paths, several possible outcomes. None good. Charlotte Johson was gone. If she revealed their affair, he was finished. The Chinese would fire him.

He could easily say *screw them*, as he had plenty of money. But he was at a point in his life where he had learned there was more to life than money. There was love.

The problem with love was who you gave it to. He had given it secretly to Charlotte, but fate turned it into a snake. A snake whose bite could result in death. Death to a career. Death to a marriage. Death to love.

The choices crowding Larson's sleepless mind yielded to a painful reality. He was usually the man in charge. The man with all the answers. This time, it was different. He was in charge of nothing. He had no power. Someone else was going to decide what tomorrow held. Charlotte Johnson or his wife would decide. All he could do was wait.

"Dad," a feminine voice said behind him.

Startled, Larson dropped his feet from the recliner, set his drink aside and looked to his daughter. She was dressed in PJs and a robe.

"It's late, Dad. Go to bed."

"You're right," Larson said, pushing out of his chair. "Good night, honey."

He turned off the TV. The irony was his daughter was deciding his day was over. Larson walked to a switch and turned the room to shadows. His daughter was another factor, another reality. Which woman he chose, the head of The Silver Palace's HR or the head of his household—

where his daughter had just told him to go to bed—weighed heavily on his mind.

In the master bedroom, Larson could hear his wife breathing. She was asleep. He did his best to be quiet. He undressed in the master bath and returned to the bedroom. His wife stirred when he climbed into the bed. She moved a foot to touch his. Was she awake? He hoped not as he adjusted a pillow.

He stared at the darkness, wondering when he stopped loving this woman. This was his daughter's mother. This was his wife. Had he stopped loving her, or was Charlotte Johnson just a fantasy? He cursed himself as he struggled to find enough courage for the day ahead. Sleep remained a bird fluttering around the room, lost in the shadows, afraid to land. That fit, Larson decided. He was a bird afraid to land.

TWELVE
TRUTH OR CONSEQUENCES

Greg Larson awoke several times covered with sweat. Finally, he surrendered near dawn. He got out of bed and left with his wife still sleeping. His drive to The Silver Palace at the early hour took only minutes. Driving into the employee area of the multi-level parking structure somehow melted away the insecurity haunting him. In his home, he was a troubled husband and a doubting father wrapped in secrets. Here, at The Silver Palace, he was one of the big dogs in Vegas, here he was a mover and shaker, here he was in charge. Here he was the GM —at least for now.

Larson could smell the kitchen as soon as he entered a back hallway. A group of eight hundred fast food franchisers were in-house and scheduled for a morning banquet. The aroma assured Lawson they had come to the right place. He offered the usual nods and short-lived smiles to those he passed—a security officer, a Hawaiian-looking kid, two housekeepers, an engineer, and a front desk staffer. The tempo of the Palace in the morning was somehow invigorating, encouraging. Here, his secrets were safe. Here he was the boss. He welcomed the comfort of his office. Although, he had to turn the lights on himself.

Larson sat at his desk, turned the computer on, and read the daily reports from his department heads. Occupancy was at eighty-eight percent. Revenue was up. The daily drop increased by seventeen percent. The heater for the Palace River had failed—again. He would order it to be replaced.

He fought an urge to call Charlotte, but he knew she was angry. He felt powerless. He couldn't remember if he had ever said he loved her. He wondered if he did love her or was it just sex with an attractive Black woman. He knew it was more than just the sex. It was the excitement, the danger…and it was over.

The feeling that came over him wasn't fear—it was an empty, painful ache.

———

CAROLINE SUMMERS, the head of cash operations, arrived at her office just after eight. She wasn't surprised to find Luke Mitchel waiting in the reception area with her assistant. Greg Larson had told her the theft of the gold had been reported to the new security director.

Luke stood when she walked in. He was younger than she thought he would be.

"Good morning, Miss Summers," he said. He was holding a cup of coffee her assistant had provided.

"You must be the new security director?" Caroline said as she walked by and into her office. "Come in."

Caroline turned on the lights and moved behind her desk.

"Please give me a minute to check my messages," she said as she turned on her computer monitor.

Luke sat down, coffee in hand, in front of her desk, studying her. She looked the high side of fifty, but life in Vegas had been kind. Her hair was dark, cut in a stylish shag. Her makeup looked as if she had stopped at a salon on her drive in. Her aging figure was masked beneath a blouse and a jacket. Her breasts were impressive and held where they should be. Wearing pants with heels, she looked like a business professional. Luke hoped she wouldn't be annoyed with his questions.

Caroline scanned her monitor, made notes, and then called out to her assistant, "Alexa, coffee, please. And hold my calls and close the door." She turned to Luke. Thanks for waiting."

Luke sat his coffee on a small table between the chairs and stood to extend his hand. Luke had long ago learned a handshake was sometimes important in an interview or an interrogation. Interrogations, however, no matter the subject, were a challenge for the individual being questioned.

Questions were words reaching into the human physics. Not all were welcome. Skilled investigators underscored their questions by learning to read faces, fingers, hands, as well as the cadence and rhythm of answers. It really was show and tell. The interrogator had to remember truth was a fleeting shadow.

Caroline's handshake was firm and quick. Too firm and too quick. Luke now knew she was apprehensive, but this was not surprising.

"Thank you for fitting me into your schedule this morning," Luke said.

Her assistant entered to set a cup of coffee in front of Caroline. She closed the door quietly on her way out.

"This must be concerning the missing gold bars?" Caroline said before she sampled her coffee.

"The GM told me you discovered three gold bricks missing from the count room."

"Yes, I found them missing yesterday. I check on them randomly. Usually, every two or three days. I'm sure you can see it on camera. As soon as I suspected tampering, I notified the GM. You must have all this on tape…"

A prepared answer, Luke decided. Maybe even practiced. "What was it you saw that aroused your suspicion."

"The gold bricks are paper-wrapped. Stacked precisely, brick on top of brick. Blake Mancini and I put the gold count room table together three months after the grand opening. Yesterday, I noticed a line along the bricks—top to bottom—which was slightly off. I'm a very precise person. I pulled the paper away and discovered a clay brick. Alarmed, I looked for more. I found three missing. You must have all this on your recordings."

"I'm sure we have."

"I immediately called Greg. Each kilo, depending on market value, is about $61,910.76 That means someone stole one hundred and eighty-four thousand dollars without you and all your cameras seeing it."

"We're still reviewing," Luke said, noting her answer included a swipe at his authority. "You mentioned the missing gold bars were replaced with clay bricks."

"Yes."

"Do you have any idea who may have done it?"

"No. You said you were still reviewing recordings?"

Luke ignored her. "Have you talked to anyone other than the GM about this?"

"No."

"Are you confident you weren't deceived when you bought the gold bricks?"

"I buy from reputable dealers. Director Mancini always assigned an officer to accompany me when I made a pickup."

"And you both examined the gold bricks when you accepted them."

"Always." Caroline was annoyed.

"Do you know the officer's name?"

"Of course. Payne, Daniel Payne."

Luke took that tidbit and squirreled it away. He thought about telling the woman he had fired Dan Payne but decided against it. Was it coincidence?

"Any others?"

"No. It made sense to use the same officer every time."

"And how many times did Officer Payne accompany you?"

Caroline's fingers drummed the desktop as she considered the question. Her expression was serious. "Your department keeps records. Perhaps you should check them. There were many pick-ups. I want to be accurate."

"Pick-ups. Could you be more descriptive? An address where you received the gold bricks?"

"Price dictates who we buy from. One of our merchants is here on Russell. Another in Reno. I'll email you the names and addresses."

"Why Reno?" Luke asked.

"As I said, price. The motive for the Chinese to buy the gold is their mistrust of the US dollar. I am prohibited from giving you the value of the gold in the count room without the GM present."

Luke nodded agreement and then deliberately took the woman back to her comment about Reno.

"Did Daniel Payne make the trip to Reno with you?"

"Yes, it's a day trip by air."

Luke nodded acknowledgment, then added, "A day trip. Was there ever an occasion when you stayed overnight?"

"The inference you're making is not appropriate or appreciated," Caroline said.

"I'm not inferring. I'm investigating," Luke said, matching the chill in the air. "I think you'll agree our thief is not likely a stranger."

Luke knew the ice was growing thin. The question in his mind was *why*. Was he dealing with an annoyed executive or an individual who was giving him as little information as possible because of her criminal knowledge?

"Now, I'll ask again. Did you ever spend the night in Reno when picking up gold bricks.?"

Caroline's discomfort with the question was obvious. She gave him a look of contempt before answering.

"Several months ago, we flew to Reno in the morning, but the weather deteriorated. Our flight back was canceled and we were forced to spend the night."

"*We* meaning you and Officer Payne?"

"Yes," she replied quickly. "As well as the crew of our company aircraft."

Luke sensed he had gone far enough for his initial interview. He stood knowing it sent a message that he was deciding the questions were over for now. "Thank you, Miss Summers. I know bringing this to our attention must have been difficult. I must ask you to *not* discuss the loss."

"You'll keep me informed?" Caroline said. It was almost an order.

"The GM will make that decision," Luke said.

He left the office feeling uncertain. Was he dealing with a woman who had six pounds of gold hidden in the trunk of her car or a widow nearing the end of her career?

He hoped he could find a way around her because she had clearly demonstrated she wasn't going to be his tour guide. He did, however, have a takeaway from their conversation—security officer Dan Payne.

Three missing gold bars weighing two pounds each. It was an audacious theft, and Luke knew he wasn't any closer to unmasking the thief or thieves. As it stood, snatching the gold had been a clever theft, but it was impossible to tell how dangerous those involved might be when cornered.

If surveillance found nothing then the theft had to have happened outside the Palace. Luke knew there was a lot on the line, not just for Greg Larson, but also for himself. Either he found the gold before the Chinese learned of the theft, or there would be a new GM and a new director of security.

Luke's cell phone vibrated as he left the cash ops office. He pulled it from his jacket pocket, glanced at it, then answered.

"Mario, what's up?"

"Morning, Chief. You available for a look-see at the employee entrance?"

"On my way."

As he headed for the employee entrance at the back of the house, Luke thought about Caroline Summers's attitude. He couldn't decide if she was offering Vegas candor or a smoke screen. She was quick with answers and all of them seemed logical, but this was Vegas, and he was learning the hard way that a poker face wasn't easy to read. The woman's answers hinted at a masquerade. He wasn't ready to say she was lying, but he couldn't say if she wasn't lying.

Security maintained a 24/7 post at the ground floor employee entrance at the rear of The Silver Palace. Luke found Mario Lopez and a Black female security officer waiting there with a backpack sitting on the floor between the two.

"What have you got?" Luke asked as he reached the two.

"This is Casey Winston," Mario said.

Luke's eyes went to the Black officer. She was attractive, and younger than Lopez. He offered her a nod of acknowledgment.

Lopez continued, "Casey did a routine backpack check." He kicked at the backpack sitting on the floor. "This one belongs to Lucy Torres—she works housekeeping. There's eight rolls of unopened toilet paper, nine bottles of shampoo, and twelve bars of soap inside. When Casey found it, she called me."

Their eyes went to the open backpack on the floor. Bulky rolls of white toilet paper were stuffed into the backpack, along with a mix of bottled shampoo and bars of soap.

"Where is Lucy?" Luke asked.

"She's outside," Casey said. "Her backpack looked heavy. She told me housekeeping policy is if these items have been used or moved by a guest, they should be replaced. And anything used is considered trash."

"That doesn't look like trash," Luke said.

"Employee dining has a note on the bulletin board," Casey said. "It states Lucy is having a garage sale tomorrow. Just so happens, I love garage sales."

Luke exchanged a glance with Lopez then looked to

Casey. "Okay, after roll call tomorrow, you two change into plain clothes and go see what she has for sale."

"What do you want to do about these items?" Casey asked.

"Nothing," Luke said. "But effective immediately, we have a new policy. I'll put out a memo today stating we can search any employee we want—back door, front door, anywhere and at any time. We already do this with the count team. We not only search them, we make them wear pocketless jumpsuits and send them through the mantrap."

"What if an employee refuses a search?" Mario asked.

"Then they're suspended—immediately." Luke eyed the backpack. He did a quick calculation in his head. "If we lost this amount every day, it adds up to fifty-eight rolls of toilet paper, sixty-three bottles of shampoo, and eighty-four bars of soap every week."

"You sure you don't work accounting?" Casey smiled.

Luke shot her a look. "We all work accounting. Send Lucy on her way with no hassle. Plan A is you'll see her tomorrow."

Luke returned to his office. He wrote the new search policy memo and sent it to every security supervisor with a note that it was to be read at every roll call.

Then he did what he did every morning—read the daily security logs. The shift supervisors kept detailed digital logs of calls for service, employee conduct, and guest contact. He also received count team reports which provided a gross accounting of monies as well as its source—gaming, food services, or entertainment.

In the security log for the PM watch, there was a note stating two guest vehicles—a new Mustang and a Tesla—were stolen after being valet parked. Luke checked the

number of guest vehicles valet parked the night before.
There were 2,013.

Dealing with the challenge of thousands of car keys
at any given time, valet services took a practical
approach to the issue. When they parked a guest's vehicle, they locked it and then set the keys atop the left front
tire. On most vehicles, the keys were out of sight but
quickly available for any valet staff. If the keys were
visible on a front tire, the valet would simply place them
atop a rear tire. In the instance of some four-wheel-drive
vehicles where leaving keys on a tire was not possible,
the keys would be hidden beneath the right front
bumper. It was simple but practical.

The problem was word of mouth. Not only did valet
services know where the keys were hidden, but an
uncountable number of others also knew. Luke knew
cameras were a deterrent, and there were hundreds of
them. No car could enter or exit The Silver Palace
without appearing on video. Luke sent a note to alert
surveillance of the thefts and let them know he wanted
quick results.

During the PM watch, when it seemed Las Vegas
really came to life, there had also been five domestic
disputes in guest rooms, six ejections based on the facial
recognition system, three illegal handguns recovered
from guests, eleven counterfeit bills detected in the cash
cage, a guest medical emergency in slots, an assault on a
twenty-one dealer in gaming, and an employee slip and
fall in the kitchen. From his experience, Luke knew it
was a more or less routine night, considering they had
six thousand eight hundred and fifty-two guest rooms,
with seventy-two percent occupancy, and three thousand four hundred and nineteen employees on duty.

Luke cautioned himself on deciding anything was

routine about being on the job at The Silver Palace. Balance was an important factor, and Luke was discovering he had lost his. He felt he was being consumed by a city where the majority came to play and relax. Ironically, he hadn't really relaxed since jumping off the balcony to save a woman he didn't know.

He leaned back in his office chair and took a deep breath. The six pounds plus of missing gold bars were constantly in the forefront of his mind adding to the pressure he was feeling. He tried to think of what would bring him sanity, peace of mind, and a little comfort. Two things quickly came to mind. A home and love.

He was living in one of The Silver Palace's VIP suites. It was nothing short of luxury. Housekeeping and room service had not only met but exceeded his expectations. His view of the Strip was breathtaking, yet it wasn't home. He was living where he worked. He could close the door to his room, but Las Vegas was still on the other side. He was sleeping and living where he worked. That had to change.

The other issue was love. He wondered if he had given it up for a job. He'd been happy with his life at the Wild River Resort. But at the bigger, more opulent Silver Palace, he felt incomplete. As he thought about it, he realized Barbara was the missing piece. She had made him whole, made him happy.

He rocked forward in his chair and picked up the telephone on his desk. He punched the button for surveillance.

"Surveillance, this is Turner."

"Gayle, it's Luke. Do you still have people looking for the gold?"

"We're looking, but I wish we had a more specific time reference. We've been using Caroline Summer's discovery in the count room as a starting point and working backward from there, but so far, nothing."

"I know it's not easy, but don't give up," Luke said. "Your team is the best chance we have of finding something. Also, I need you to be in charge tonight. I'm going to be away from the resort."

"Are you taking your phone?"

"Yes, but no calls unless you find the gold."

"Got it."

"I'll be back in the morning."

THIRTEEN
CHASING DREAMS

BARBARA NICHOLS FINISHED HER HAIR. She wasn't satisfied with it, but she walked away from the mirror in her bathroom anyway. She wasn't satisfied with what she was wearing either. *Screw it*, she thought, *there was nobody who would care*.

She was heading to another fun-filled night behind the bar at the Wild River Resort. All she needed as a uniform were faded jeans, a form-fitting blouse unbuttoned down to there, and a thin bra showing just a hint of nipple.

She had to put up with too many men, insulting pricks who came in every night. She had a feeling it was time to get out of Wild River and get out of serving liquor. There had to be life beyond mixing drinks, wearing a smile, and hoping the tips would be worth it— and the tips were always linked to tits. *Your tits are like a mirror. I can see myself in them*—everybody had a line they thought was original and would help get them into her pants.

Maybe she'd go back to nursing and get her certifi-

cate. Nurses made good money. But there were also
assholes in hospitals and nurses didn't earn tips and had
to eat the same shit every day.

Sitting on the edge of her unmade bed, Barb put on
her sneakers. She was tying the second one when she
heard what had to be a motorhome pulling into the
space beside her coach. She knew it was the prick from
across the street. Like everyone else around Wild River,
she knew Luke was gone and never coming back. As far
as she was concerned, he had abandoned her. Now, she
didn't have to worry about what color panties she wore,
but it didn't mean the old guy from across the street was
going to park his freaking motor home in her space.
Ready for a fight, she bounced off the bed to go tell him.

―――――

LUKE WASN'T sure what he was going to say. He had one
hundred and seventy-seven miles to think about it, but
he still didn't have the words. His heart was in his throat.

Barbara opened the door. She stared in shock. Luke
wasn't the only one without words.

He returned Barb's look. His anxiety plain to see. His
first thought was her eyes were much bluer than he
remembered.

"Luke…" Barb said softly in disbelief.

Words were no longer an issue. Luke stepped
forward, closing the space between them, and pulled
Barb into his arms. He kissed her neck, her face, and
then her lips. She moaned as her arms snaked around his
back. A tear traced down her cheek. Luke kissed it away
and pulled her even closer.

"I've missed you so much," he said to her neck. "The
days are too long and the nights too empty without you."

She gave a small gasp.

"I want you in Vegas with me. We'll buy a house. We'll be together."

"You want me to move to Vegas?" Barb cupped Luke's face in her hands. She wanted to believe him. She kissed him again and moved her hands to his shoulders. "I have to be at work in forty minutes."

She led him into her double-wide. They sat on the couch, holding hands. She whipped another tear away, but her smile remained.

"The answer is, *yes*. But saying you surprised me is an understatement."

She quietly reminded him she had a life and friends at Wild River—not a happy one without him, but one that deserved care. Her feminine compassion was showing.

Luke loved her more because of it. She wanted to follow him, be with him, share it all, but first, there was today…tonight.

The reality was they both owned mobile homes in Rio Vista and Barbara still had her job there. She promised Luke she would give notice at Wild River, but then there was the logistics of moving. Two coaches to sell and a life to move two hundred miles.

Luke had thought of it all during his drive. He had a plan. The Silver Palace assured him they would move his belongings and market his coach. All Barb had to do was move everything and anything into his coach and let the Palace worry about it.

She hugged and kissed him again. It was the answer Luke wanted.

Luke followed Barb to work. He ignored being banned from the casino by the tribe. He didn't know it, but the tribe was ignoring the ban as well. He sat at the bar while Barb poured drinks for the few patrons able to break away from the slots or gambling tables.

Luke drank a Diet Coke as they talked. A fleeting hour into their smiles and excitement, Luke knew it was time to go.

"We'll remember today," Barb said when Luke finally slid off his stool at the bar.

"Today and all our tomorrows," Luke said.

They moved to the end of the long bar. There, they kissed, hugged, and kissed again, surprising the three patrons at the bar who all smiled. One even raised his drink in encouragement. They knew love when they saw it.

Luke's return to Las Vegas was a much shorter drive than the one to Rio Vista. The seat beside him in his Telsa was empty, but Barb's promises were riding with him.

The lights were comforting when Vegas finally came into view. Luke thought they looked brighter, but knew they were simply shining brighter after his reunion with Barb.

The Strip, as always, was crowded, and traffic was slow. It brought Luke back to reality. Somewhere here, amid all the glamour and excitement of Vegas, were the gold thieves. Luke knew they were here. He just didn't know where. He was back and so was the knowledge he had to find them.

There had to be more than one. No one could steal three gold bars weighing two pounds each without help. Nor was it likely the gold was carried away from The Silver Palace's protected inner sanctum. It wasn't likely the surveillance review was going to reveal anything other than the head of cash ops discovering the missing gold bricks, but still, it had to be done.

Luke wondered if Caroline Summers was a liar. As the head of cash ops, it was hard to accept she was a thief. But all things were possible in Vegas. Luke was on the edge, and he felt his pulse quicken as the lights of The Silver Palace came into view.

————

Greg Larson was also chasing lights. His night had not gone well. Sleep was troubling, filled with grim reality, lies, unfaithfulness, and Charlotte Johnson—Black, beautiful, naked, and cursing him. Several times, he feared his wife lying beside him, breathing in deep sleep, would somehow hear the angry cursing.

His uneasiness finally yielded to the fact that sleep was eluding him. He got up, dressed, and drove down the hill toward the Silver Place. There he wouldn't be a husband haunted by guilt, there he wouldn't have to worry about the lies being uncovered, there he wouldn't have to worry about truth lying beside him in bed. There, he would be Greg Larson, the GM of one of the most profitable gaming resorts in the world. There he was *the man*. He was the one with the full authority and all the juice—unless, of course, they discovered his lies.

————

Returning from his unannounced four-hundred-mile round trip drive to Arizona, Luke was waved into the employee parking by an attentive female security officer. She recognized both Luke's car and face. He offered a nod of appreciation from behind the wheel as he passed. The drive had been long, but he had no regrets. His reunion with Barb had proven successful. She accepted

his invitation to move to Vegas. Their meeting invigo-
rated him. He wasn't tired. He was excited. For him, it
was a new day.

A set of headlamps followed Luke into the employee
level of the parking structure, filling his rearview mirror
with light. He had a reserved space, but he avoided using
it. Being the director of security had more than enough
challenges, and he didn't want broken car windows or
spray paint to add to them.

The headlights following him passed to pull into
another reserved space he was familiar with. It was Greg
Larson.

"Either you're getting to work early or coming home
late," Greg Larson said as he climbed from his car and
spotted Luke.

The radio clipped beneath Luke's jacket stole any
answer.

"Gatekeeper twenty, Gatekeeper six is requesting
back-up, code three. Female in fifty-six-oh-seven is
threatening suicide with a handgun."

Greg had heard the broadcast and gave Luke a *get-to-
it* nod. Luke bolted toward a nearby elevator.

If anything happened near dawn in Las Vegas, it was
usually not much. The winners were asleep, the lonely
had found companions to share their seven-hundred-
dollar beds, and the losers were watching Netflix, but
there were exceptions. There were those who came to
Vegas to win. They didn't win every time. Vegas was full
of losers. Their losses were hidden behind big stars in
big shows, gourmet dinners and less-than-subtle tits and
ass. It was no secret that Vegas was built by the losers,
whose unspoken reality became *what happens in Vegas,
stays in Vegas.*

Most losers drove away in silence. Not all their losses

were in slots, twenty-one or roulette. Some won gambling but became losers at checkout when they saw what they had spent on room service, the headliner shows, and more.

The words *loser* and *Vegas* had the same number of letters, and many times, the same painful reality. Winning sixteen hundred at roulette could be bragged about in the morning, but charges of thirty-eight hundred on a Citibank Visa became a compulsion to bet bigger next time.

————

LINDA MORRISON DIDN'T NEED to see her Visa card balance. None of what happened was her fault. The money spent on a four-hundred-dollar dress, a two-hundred-dollar haircut, the massage, and the spiked heels were not what caused this. Nor was it the cocaine they bought and snorted during Lady Gaga's show. Linda knew her drunken husband was downstairs playing slots after rummaging in her purse for the one hundred and eighteen dollars she had hidden. After losing all their money playing blackjack, he cursed at her in front of everyone. He yelled that it was her loser attitude causing the turn of bad luck. Fate ran trucks over fear. When fear sat down at a table, it lost. You had to have balls to win.

There were more guns in LA County than there were people, and Brad Morrison owned three of them. He had carried one of them to Las Vegas. He had figured everyone did. Linda Morrison had found the gun covered with a sock in one of her husband's dress shoes.

She wanted him to know what he had done. He had killed her hopes, her dreams. He didn't do it all at once.

Seven years of marriage. Seven years of waiting, feeling, crying. Piece by piece, the son-of-a-bitch did it until there was no more. Linda was determined to make him pay.

Gun in hand, she sat down on the carpeted floor of their guest room to lean back against the bed, awaiting his return. When Brad opened the door, he would see the gun to her head. The look on his face would be her ultimate revenge.

Alcohol had its way of leveling the playing field. Before their argument, over who lost what and Brad's angry departure from the room, he had called room service to order a pint of Crown Royal. The pint of liquor, coupled with a twenty-two percent tip, resulted in a charge of sixty-eight dollars and seventy-two cents to their Strip view luxury suite fee of four hundred and seventy-six dollars per night.

Linda, gun in hand, fell asleep sitting on the floor of their luxury suite. Liquor, cocaine, and lost love had all contributed. She nearly dropped the gun when a knock sounded on the guest room door, jolting her awake. Why in the hell was he knocking?

"It's open," she called, pushing the muzzle against her temple.

The server, dressed in a jacket and tie, silver tray in hand, adorned with a carefully folded towel and the pint of Crown Royal along with two iced glasses, opened the door. Both Linda and the server were shocked. The server gasped, dropped his tray crashing to the floor, and ran. Linda decided to keep the gun to her head. The door was now open.

Four minutes passed before the female, uniformed security officer arrived. She was younger than Linda Morrison. The moment the officer saw the open door and Linda sitting on the carpet with the gun to her head, she backed away, keyed her radio, and asked for help.

There were five uniformed officers in the quiet guest hallway when Luke's elevator door opened on the floor. Two were beyond the open guest room door, and three more waited with their backs to the wall, guns and radios in hand, on the side closest to Luke.

As he approached cautiously, a hand grabbed him by the shoulder, and a body tried to move by. It was the AM watch commander, Lieutenant KC King.

"Wait here, Chief," King said, getting in front of Luke. It was a surprise, but Luke paused near the cluster of uniforms.

Lieutenant King looked to the female officer who had put out the call. "Tell me what you got?"

"She's on the floor," the nervous, uniformed female whispered. "Just inside the door. Gun to her head. Server found her while making a delivery."

"Get the hallway secured," Luke ordered from behind the officers.

"Done," King said. "The elevator won't stop on this floor until I clear it. Both ends are covered. Anybody else seen her or speak with her?"

Negative nods answered him.

"Okay," King said. He glanced toward the open door and then the officers. "I'll take a look. You cover me."

"Wait," Luke said impulsively. "Don't do that until we get a shield up here."

"I'm wearing a vest," King said. His attention was on the open guest room door. "Here we go."

Luke tensed as the lieutenant's shoulders raised as if he were in a parade. He marched casually to the open door. The silence in the hallway was heavy. Guns were in hand, all pointing to the floor. Luke wished he had his own. He stood behind the three officers, realizing he had deferred to the lieutenant. He was mad at himself. This could get ugly, but the thought was lost as he watched the lieutenant step boldly in front of the open guest room door and then kneel in front of the woman.

"Ma'am, my name's LC King. I'm in charge tonight and I want to help you."

"Go away or I'll shoot," the high-strung woman said.

"I know you didn't come to Vegas to do something like this. Tell me what's wrong?"

The woman pushed the barrel of the revolver harder against her temple as she spoke. "It's none of your business."

"You've got a gun. That is my business. Now tell me why you're doing this?" It sounded like a confident order. Luke knew they would soon hear the shot. He hoped the lieutenant wasn't going to die.

"The son-of-a-bitch lost all our money," the woman said flatly. "He blamed me."

"So, you're going to hurt yourself to get even with him?"

"He'll regret it."

"For a while, but he'll get over it," King said candidly. "But you won't. All his friends, and yours too, will pity him. Not you. You're the one, you did this. They'll be waiting for him when he drives home, all thinking what a poor bastard he is."

"They'll know he caused it," the woman said. Her tone was less than convincing.

"No, they won't. He'll lie. Plus, it looks like you were going to do this when he came back to the room. I'm sorry, but he's not coming. I can't let anyone up here while you've got a gun. I don't want you hurt. You know he doesn't, either. Is this man your husband?"

"Yes."

"Good times and bad," the lieutenant said. "For better or worse. None of it gets solved this way. Let me help. Put the gun down. Give me his name and I'll have a couple men go find him. We'll talk. You know he doesn't want anything like this to happen. You going home tomorrow?"

"Yes."

"What's his name?"

A long, chilling silence followed. Luke held his breath and waited.

Finally, she spoke, "Brad. Brad Morrison."

"Okay, we'll find him, but first, you gotta give me the gun."

It was again a firm, friendly order. Luke and the others stood silent and tense. They had heard every word. So had the lieutenant's deliberate open radio and his body cam. All was being recorded.

The woman sniffed as a tear ran down her cheek. The hand holding the gun to her temple trembled. LC King watched the barrel as his hand moved discretely to his holstered weapon. The woman sniffed before lowering the two-inch thirty-eight. She looked into King's eyes and then offered him the weapon.

King took the gun, opened the cylinder, and dumped six cartridges to the carpet. "Let's talk inside," he said, extending a hand to the woman. Linda Morrison lowered her head and began to weep. The others closed on them.

It was three-twenty AM when Luke picked up the telephone in his room. He dialed Larson. The number only rang once before he answered. "Tell me she's not dead."

"She's not," Luke said. "She and her husband are in an

ambulance on their way to Sunrise Hospital. We kept the gun. I'll get a copy of the report to you in the morning."

"You did good," Larson said.

"This one belongs to Lieutenant King."

"Give King my regards," Larson said.

Luke thought about KC King as he kicked off his shoes in the bedroom of his suite. He had shaken King's hand and congratulated him. The guy was young and in great shape. Luke now felt silly over his insecurities about letting King run the show. It all turned out right, and it was King's watch.

Luke promised himself he'd quit acting like a jealous girl scout. KC King had proven himself. Barb was coming to Vegas. He couldn't remember a better day in a long time.

He thought about his return to The Silver Palace and the chance meeting with the GM. Luke pitied the man. The shouting match he and the GM's assistant heard was going to become an issue if they hadn't already. Luke wondered if that was why Larson was on the property at such a late hour.

He turned off the bedside lamp and fell into his pillows. Had he returned five minutes later, he would have missed the guest with a gun. It underscored his determination to buy a house. He wondered how much money he had in the bank. He thought about staying in town, sleeping at home, sleeping with Barb—and then sleep and exhaustion found him.

———

GREG MAY HAVE THOUGHT The Silver Palace—standing like a massive, towering, illuminated, mirrored candle amid the bright lights of the Strip—would offer him refuge from his troublesome night at home, but he was wrong. It brought anxious thoughts of Charlotte Johnson.

He was tempted to go and look at her quiet office again. At least there, he could smell her scent, feel her spirit. She had always been so beautiful. But she was gone.

Luke knew the full story, and had even helped fend off the prick, Blake Mancini. He wondered if Jackie Fallon knew the truth. As his assistant, it was more what didn't she know. He wondered if he should talk to her.

Tomorrow was already today, and Greg wondered if it would be his last. He damned himself. He knew what he would have to do if someone on the inner circle of the senior management team was discovered screwing a female subordinate. There was no choice—he'd fire their ass.

As GM, Greg kept a comfortable room on the third floor reserved for himself. Sometimes, it was used for Saudi princes and their multi-million dollar bets, the would-be jumper, the big-name star who developed stage fright, or the vice president, who although he claimed to be an avid Christian, seemingly welcomed any excuse to come to Vegas—especially The Silver Palace.

There were a thousand reasons for the room, but Charlotte had never been in it. Still her spirit haunted everywhere else by her absence, by thoughts of her onyx nude beauty, and it all drove him tonight to be in a room where she had never appeared.

On his way to the back-of-the-house elevator, Greg passed an attractive female uniformed security officer. He wondered if she knew anything about the guest with a gun. He supposed not. He offered the woman a smile even though it wasn't likely she knew who he was.

He shared the elevator with a server and a cart filled with what had to be breakfast for two. Clearly, someone was up late. A uniformed housekeeper joined them as the elevator worked its way down to the third floor. Neither seemed to recognize him. It added to his smile. He felt invisible. Maybe it wouldn't be a bad day after all. The elevator finally reached the third floor.

"Good night," Greg said to the two and stepped off.

The room had a view of a big humming evaporator on a wide roof just below. Greg walked to the curtains and closed them. The room was small but smelled fresh. He checked the fridge. From its well-stocked shelves, he selected a bottle of Starbucks and sat down in a bedside chair to turn on the TV.

On the screen, Joel Olsten was smiling as he paced on a raised platform in front of a massive audience. "God is much bigger than the mess you've made. He's waiting on your call." Greg recognized the evangelist from a meeting at the Las Vegas convention center a month or so earlier. His appearance resulted in a sellout weekend.

Greg turned off the television. He didn't believe God would be interested in his problems. God probably didn't make many stops in Vegas. If God appeared at all, Greg was certain it was to listen and laugh at all the prayers whispered in slots or at the poker tables.

He drank his Starbucks in silence, wondering what his wife was dreaming. He also wondered where Charlotte could be, what she was thinking, feeling. Greg felt lonely and abandoned. There were over one hundred thousand guest rooms in Vegas, but on this night, this room felt empty, and so did Greg Larson.

FOURTEEN
WIPED CLEAN

THE RINGING SOUNDED like heavy rain falling on his poncho. Marine Corporal Luke Mitchel was sitting in the muddy ditch as it filled with cold rainwater. He pulled on the poncho to discover it was a bedsheet in his suite covering his legs but not his back. The ringing rainwater was really the bedside telephone. Luke reached for the telephone before it rang again.

"Hello."

"Good morning, Mr. Mitchel, this is the hotel operator. You requested a wake-up call this morning for six thirty a.m."

"Yeah, thanks," Luke said and hung up. He reached for the pillow and bedsheet, burying his head in both. He laid motionless before he growled, jerked the pillow aside and swung his bare feet to the carpeted floor. "Hell," he muttered as he stood and glanced at the illuminated bedside clock.

Six thirty was a harsh reality, but sleep had to wait. He had a plan, which he had thought of during his return drive from Rio Vista. Finding a thief with three two-pound gold bars was an unrealistic challenge with a predictable outcome—zero, zip, nada.

Starting the investigation where and when the chief of cash operations said she discovered the gold missing might be exactly what the thief, or thieves, wanted. He needed to turn the theft upside down. The reality was the thief stole the gold to turn it into cash.

The three gold bars had an appraised value of almost nine hundred and fifty thousand dollars. The key word Luke knew was *appraised*. Stolen gold wouldn't be appraised at its true value. The price would be speculative. Lower. Not only by someone who knew gold, but by someone who would know the gold was stolen. That conclusion made the number of players on the field much smaller, and Luke knew where he had to start, and it wasn't in The Silver Palace.

Forty-six floors below, day-watch commander Mario Lopez stood in front of the twenty-six men and woman from The Silver Palace's day-watch security team. They sat in rows in the security briefing room while Mario went over the events of the past night as provided by the AM watch. It had been a routine night.

"In addition to the woman with the gun to her head, we had another death in Rolet," Lopez said, glancing at his notes. "A natural. A senior with heavy losses. Eight firearms were recovered from guests at the front entrance. Two were ghost guns. Metro was notified and took possession. An arrest at the cash cage after a guest tried to pass three counterfeit house chips. The fifty-six-year-old resisted and assaulted the officers. Six more counterfeit chips were recovered from his pockets." Lopez paused, allowing several who were taking notes to catch up.

"Housekeeping found drugs in three different guest

rooms," Lopez continued. "Photos were taken, the drugs were left undisturbed." Lopez looked directly at the two men. "Jacobs and Carter, you're working the parking structure today. Here's a challenge for you. We lost two guest vehicles last night. One was a four-wheel-drive Jeep, the other a Mercedes. Both were stolen from valet parking. Something's wrong there. Find us some answers."

Lopez ended the briefing with an emphasis on the revised employee search protocol. "We now search any employee, anytime, anywhere on property. Anyone who doesn't cooperate will be suspended. We're The Silver Palace, not the Dollar General. Paulson is going to act as watch commander this morning while I'm off property. Don't give him fits. He's a sensitive guy. Let's get to work."

———

AFTER ROLL CALL WAS DISMISSED, Lopez found Casey Winston, dressed in civilian clothes, waiting for him. Lopez was pleased. He and Gayle Turner had vowed to take the burden off Luke while he investigated the missing gold.

A day earlier, Casey had discovered a housekeeper trying to leave the property with a variety of supposed partially used rolls of toilet paper, soap, and shampoo stuffed into her backpack. They knew the same house-keeper had scheduled a garage sale with a note on an employee bulletin board. Casey and Lopez were going to go have a look.

"You ride a motorcycle to work. We're going to a garage sale. Let's take my truck," Casey said, talking Lopez into allowing her to drive.

Lopez accepted. Casey drove a muddy four-wheel-drive Ford F-250 pickup. Her husband was a fireman. "He likes dirt," Casey explained.

Lopez tried relaxing on the passenger's side, but Casey's weaving in and out of traffic lanes, coupled with a mix of side streets and parking lot shortcuts, mixing with the truck's loud muffler, had him on edge.

"Lucy lives in Henderson," Casey said as they merged with traffic on the freeway. "We'll take the two-fifteen down to the Charleston exit."

When they finally slowed and exited the freeway at Charleston, Casey glanced at the pickup's dashboard monitor. A digital on-screen map with an arrow showed every turn. "Around the next corner, on my side," Casey said.

"How's a housekeeper afford a place out here?" Lopez asked, looking at the expanse of expensive homes sweeping by. "I have to drive in from Boulder every day."

"I reached out to a snitch in housekeeping," Casey said. "Sophia's old man's an engineer at the Grand. Figure, they're up there."

"It shows," Lopez agreed as Casey slowed and pulled the pickup to the curb. Across the street from where they parked, a BMW sat in the driveway of the comfortable-looking home. Beside the car, a variety of items sat covering the driveway. Toilet seats, light bulbs, big-screen television sets, a mix of men's and women's shoes, folded towels with the MGM Grand and Silver Palace logos, a clothing rack with a variety of men's and women's suit jackets, shirts, blouses, and a large cardboard box bulging with rolls of toilet paper. Beside the toilet paper stood a card table lined with bottles of small shower-sized shampoo and fresh bars of soap.

Five women and a disinterested-looking thirty-year-old male holding a child's hand browsed the inventory.

Sophia, the Hispanic housekeeper, detained the day before by Casey, stood watching shoppers and talking on her cell phone.

"You think she'll recognize you?" Lopez asked as they crossed the street.

Casey slipping on a pair of sunglasses, offered Lopez a smile. "Recognize me? You know we all look alike. Come on, let's do some shopping."

"Remember, we're just here for a *look-see*. No questions," Lopez said as they joined the other shoppers. Sophia, dressed in faded stylish jeans that were too tight and an MGM Grand sweatshirt, glanced at them, and offered a quick smile, but seemed to pay no attention. Her look went back to others.

Casey and Luke paused near the box stuffed with rolls of toilet paper. They looked, knowing where it was from.

"You could say she's wiping us out," Casey whispered with a smile.

They looked at the soap and towels. The logo brands made their source obvious. It was the same with light bulbs, shoes, and clothing from lost and found and just about everything else. Lopez pulled out his iPhone and began taking pictures. Casey posed, acting as if she were the subject of the photos.

Sophia noticed and immediately protested. "No, no pictures allowed," she called, waving a hand.

Lopez offered acknowledgment with a shrug and pushed his iPhone into a pocket. They looked through the clutter before Lopez had an idea.

"Watch this," he whispered. Casey followed as Lopez rounded the front of the BMW in the driveway to walk down the driver's side. Reaching the driver's door, he tried the handle. It was unlocked. He opened the door and reached inside. His hand slid along the sun visor until his fingers found a garage door remote. He pushed the button.

"You can't do that! Get out of there," Sophia called with alarm as she rushed toward them.

The garage door hummed, folding upward to reveal a garage jammed with clutter matching the array in the driveway. Boxes stuffed with toilet paper, soap, towels with logos, shirts, jackets, shoes, a printer, and more.

Lopez aimed his cell phone and took a series of pictures. Casey watched. Sophia burned them with a look as she rushed into the cluttered garage to find the button for the door.

"I think our work here is done," Casey said and smiled at Lopez as the garage door came down.

————

LUKE WAS DOWNING a near-empty bottle of chilled Starbucks and eating a Fig Newton as he rode the employee elevator to basement parking when his cell vibrated. He pulled it from a pocket to read the text. It was from Lopez. *Sometimes a picture tells the story*, Lopez had texted. Several photos were attached. The first showed Sophia's open garage, filled with an array of resort toiletries and other branded items. The second showed shoppers browsing in the driveway, and the third showed Sophia Torres, the soon-to-be ex-house-keeper, bolting frantically toward the garage door. The pictures brought a smile to Luke's face. The troops had done good. Perhaps even more important was the fact they had done it without him.

A trash can on the employee level of the parking structure accepted Luke's empty bottle as he neared his car. He'd spent a couple hours at the desktop in his office searching the employee files on Caroline Summers and his recently fired PM watch commander, Daniel Payne. Both had been *hands-on* with the missing gold. As head of cash ops, Summers had decided where the gold was purchased. Records supported the fact she price-shopped. Payne, then a security lieutenant, was assigned by Blake Mancini, the former head of security, to accompany Summers. Payne's job was simply to provide an armed escort and vehicle for Summers.

The review of HR digital files revealed the recently fired Daniel Payne had worked security at the Hyatt, Treasure Island, Signature, and the Wynn prior to signing on with The Silver Palace while it was under construction.

Caroline Summers also had a lengthy line of former Vegas employers. New York New York, Luxor, Mandalay Bay, Ceasars, and finally, The Silver Palace.

Neither subjects showed any record of termination. Payne's Facebook account still claimed he was a watch commander at The Silver Palace.

Luke then pulled up Google Earth to study the homes of both employees. He called up a street view. Both homes were nice, but Caroline Summers's house made her the clear winner. Her home was impressive. Luke did an evaluation of her property. The assessed value showed it was worth nearly two million.

Daniel Payne's home was less ostentatious, a second-level condo near the airport. Its value was estimated at four hundred thousand. Luke returned to Payne's Face-book account. He studied the details. Payne was divorced. His posts were usually pictures of his car, a

new Dodge Charger, or himself. He dressed extrava-
gantly. He had four hundred and thirty-six friends. Luke
paged through them. He found four who were clearly
digital *dial-a-whores*.

Luke had made notes, which were now in a jacket
pocket. He needed more than an online look. He needed
an up close and personal view of the woman who set all
this stuff in motion. Pulling back the curtain would
either find Caroline Summers was no more than a
responsible director of cash operations, or a thief.

After climbing into his car, Luke instructed his sultry
female digital guidance system to take him to Caroline
Summers's street address. Luke followed the instruc-
tions. The Strip was slow-moving. Luke had no clue why
all these people were up so early or if they were arriving
or leaving.

The crowds were becoming part of Luke's perception
of Las Vegas. Sexy women, new cars, sunshine, good
food and alcohol—and gambling. Luke, however,
couldn't gamble. As a member of the management team
at The Silver Palace, he was prohibited from gambling
anywhere in the State of Nevada by the state gaming
commission. He wondered if that was why the thieves
stole the gold. If they were employees and couldn't
gamble, maybe they found another way to take a chance,
gamble, play the odds. Luke figured in this instance the
odds were in his favor.

The voice of his navigation system took Luke onto
Mountain Avenue and beyond as the Strip faded behind
him, yielding first to a mix of liquor stores, fast food
outlets, bars promising nudity, and then a Las Vegas he
had not seen before—houses. Lots of them. Tract after
tract.

At first, the homes were no surprise, they looked like

the neighborhoods he'd patrolled in LA, but as he drove on, Mountain Avenue started to climb uphill, and the streets took on a different look. Individual homes became tracts with curved sidewalks and plush landscaping. Trees and expansive strips of grass erased the grip of the desert.

Luke listened to the voice of the guidance system as he wormed his way from one winding street to another, his attention on the Las Vegas he'd never seen. He realized this was the hidden secret where the city's near one million lived. This was their hiding place. This was the Vegas most never saw. This was what he had been missing.

Two joggers passed by. Then, a senior on a bicycle. The houses were all different, but in some ways, the same. They were all neat and clean with polished cars in their driveways. Sunshine added to the allure.

Luke took out his cell phone. He sent Barbara a text. He was excited. *You're going to love this*, he typed. At an intersection, the sultry GPS voice instructed him to turn left. He passed a busy grocery store next to a hair salon, a drug store, a pizza place, and more.

Mountain Avenue was named appropriately. As Luke drove, the incline of the street grew. Something else changed, too. Retail disappeared. So did the rows of inviting, attractive, comfortable stucco homes, yielding instead to long stretches of wrought iron fence with sharp spikes at the top in front of thick hedges and trees masking what was behind. An occasional gated entry swept by. All had uniformed guards and formidable gates, with stylish retreats.

"Your destination is ahead on the left," the female navigator warned. He slowed and looked for an entry. The entry to Shadow Mountain Estates came into view.

The iron gate standing across the two lanes leading to the entrance could not be ignored. Luke slowed to a stop as the guard, an overweight uniformed senior stepped out to meet him.

Luke noticed the man was armed and decided to take the initiative.

"Good morning," he said, pulling the gold badge from his belt to hold it up for the guard to see. He allowed the man only a quick glance. "Coming in for a meet with one of our managers."

"Give me his name," the senior suggested soberly. "I'll give him a call." His attention went from Luke to his car. His eyes swept over it. "Is this one of those EVs?"

"You got it. Three hundred miles plus," Luke said with a nod. "And she's quiet."

"But you got to pay for charging it?"

"You do know the price of gas, don't you?"

"Yeah," the gray hair answered with a glance at the car's interior. "My wife likes these."

"We're giving away an EV at The Silver Palace Saturday night. All you have to do is be there. What's your name?"

"Bud Frazer."

"Bud, you come down and ask anyone to find me. They will. Saturday night or any night. Name's Luke Mitchel."

The gray hair smiled. "Luke Mitchel. The Silver Palace, huh? We might do that. Okay." He stepped back, reached and pushed a button on the door frame of the guard shack. "Have a good day, Luke."

The iron gate across the entry lanes rumbled and rolled aside. Luke offered the man a smile of appreciation and drove through. The open gate fading behind him brought Luke another reality. His navigation aid had done all it could. The residents of Shadow Mountain Estates not only had iron gates protecting them, but digital mapping was also prohibited. Luke had no idea where Kings Lantern Drive was, but he was in, and it was still early. He knew Caroline Summers drove a silver Mercedes. The car might still be in her driveway, and he was enjoying looking for her street.

The sprawling homes of the rich were impressive. Each set on a landscaped half acre. Gardeners were already at work to beat the heat. Luke drove slow, reading street names. The driveways were full of BMWs, Bentleys, Ferrari's, and a lonely Cadillac.

"Kings Lantern," Luke said aloud as the street name came into view. Caroline Summers's expansive ranch-style home sat hidden behind a line of trees, scrubs, and flowering bushes. Luke saw her silver Mercedes at the head of the curved drive. A black BMW was parked next to the Mercedes. Luke slowed and pulled to the side of the winding street across from the house. He looked at the BMW. It had a Nevada license plate.

"Lincoln, George, Tom, six, six, seven," Luke said aloud again, reading the plate while making a note of it with a pen on the palm of his hand. Cop habits were hard to forget. Luke drove further into the curve of the street until he could see both cars in the driveway in his rearview mirror. There, he parked and reached for his cell. He dialed Gayle Turner's number. She answered on the second ring.

"This is surveillance."

"Gayle, it's Luke. Get me the registered owner of Nevada Lincoln, George, Tom, six, six, six."

"Got it. Stand by."

Luke wished he had another Starbucks. He thought about the supermarket he passed before reaching

Shadow Mountain. Maybe he's stopped there on his way out. He glanced at his rearview mirror. The two cars were still there. Seeing Caroline's home didn't give him much, but it was a starting point. She reported the theft. She was the point. It might not end here, but here was where it started.

"Luke," Gayle Turner's voice said on his cell. "You ready?"

"Ready," Luke said, clicking his ballpoint.

"The registered owner comes back to Daniel Payne, 9630 Starlight Drive, Las Vegas, Nevada."

Luke was shocked. Daniel Payne was the prick he had just fired for insubordination and extortion. His eyes went again to the rearview mirror. He was shocked. Dan Payne was in the driveway, climbing into the black BMW.

"Luke, did you hear me?" Gayle's voice questioned on his cell.

Luke silenced his phone and lay down over the center console. He held his breath. A long, silent moment passed. The pieces fit. The head of cash operations and a fired security lieutenant who was the escort when they bought gold. He listened as a car drove by. Luke waited a few seconds before sitting up. The black BMW had passed and was driving away.

Luke's cell phone vibrated. Gayle Turner was calling.

"Got it, Gayle," Luke answered, hardly able to contain his excitement.

FIFTEEN

A HOUSE IS NOT A HOME

THE EXECUTIVE BOARD of The Silver Palace was meeting in the resort's board room. As GM, Greg Larson sat at the head of the long, polished table. He was surrounded by the department heads who turned the towering resort into more than just an architectural miracle. Engineering, housekeeping, guest relations, cash operations, food & beverage, reservations, entertainment, and eight other departments changed The Silver Palace from a Timex into a Vacheron Constantin.

They were the best Vegas could offer. Their skill sets and experience made them independent and capable, but much of their work united their forces like an NFL team and ensured a win. Most around the table brought with them an inventory of needs or wants to be addressed. The meeting, although routine, was mandatory as well as beneficial. Those in attendance did notice a new face. The face belonged to James Bergman.

Some on the executive committee knew James Bergman. Most did not. Lawson filled in the blanks from the head of the table. "

Ladies and gentlemen, I'd like you to meet our new human resources director." Larson gestured to Bergman who sat three chairs away.

The thirty-five-year-old with dark, close-cut hair offered a nod and a smile to the GM as he took off his glasses. His position as the new director of HR was only three hours old. He suspected the only reason he'd been promoted—other than he was both capable and deserving—was to cover Charlotte Jonhson's untimely departure.

Bergman had read the tea leaves the day before. Charlotte's call to the GM's office. The isolation in her office for hours after she returned. Her untimely and unannounced absence in the office. No answer to his calls on her private cell. The two of them were close, but he understood what he was seeing wasn't something she was ever going to share. This was private, and big enough to cause Charlotte's departure. Bergman knew Larson wasn't promoting him as much as he was covering his own ass.

"We all wish Charlotte the best in her new endeavors. She did a remarkable job for us, but James has been with us since the day we decided to build. First in a rental office down the street and then right here for our grand opening." Larson looked at the others around the big table. "He's done a spectacular job in not only supporting Charlotte's programs, but by also demonstrating his own value and initiative. He was an easy answer to a challenging question. Please join me in welcoming James to membership in our exclusive club."

Larson started the applause by clapping his hands. He was quickly joined by the others around the table. James Bergman's smile assured Larson his suspicions would remain unspoken. The secrecy had been traded for a title. And he had a secret of his own—he was gay. He wondered whether Larson knew or if it would have made a difference if he didn't.

———

CAROLINE SUMMERS LOOKED at the other faces around the table. One was missing—Luke's.

She had found him waiting in her office when she arrived the day before. No surprise there. Her report that three gold bricks were missing from the table in the count room had undoubtedly prompted it. Luke had many questions. She had answered promptly and candidly. She hoped he believed her. She also hoped she had sent him in another direction, but his absence from the executive meeting was worrisome. She wondered where he was, if her secrets were safe, or had she been betrayed?

———

KNOWING he was missing the meeting, Luke was heading back to The Silver Palace from Mountain View. He was convinced Barbara would share his excitement over having a home in the area.

A text from Gayle Turner caught him on the hop— *HR is trying to reach you. New guy says it's important. He doesn't know you're off property.*

Luke was surprised. Larson hadn't said anything to him about a new guy. It must mean Charlotte Johnson was gone. It explained her attitude when he spotted her the night before near the employee elevator. Now he knew what the argument he and the GM's assistant overheard was about.

Luke wondered if this meant the end was near for Larson. Charlotte Johnson clearly had him by the balls, but none of it explained why the new HR guy wanted him to see him. He was ten minutes away. He'd know when he got there. He turned down the hill toward the Strip. Mooning over a dream house would have to wait.

————

THE SCREEN on his desktop told the new director of HR that Luke had arrived and was waiting. James Bergman was straightening things on what was now his desk. He put on his jacket and straightened his tie before buzzing his assistant in the outer office.

"Send him in," Bergman ordered over the intercom after sitting back down in his high-backed executive chair.

Luke was escorted in by an assistant who looked like she needed time to finish high school. Bergman stood and gestured with a hand to two chairs in front of his wide desk. He did not offer his hand to Luke.

"Please, have a seat, Mr. Mitchel."

Luke chose one of the chairs. He read the atmosphere in the room. It was not good. The young assistant exited, closing the door behind her.

"My staff tells me you reached out," Luke said, wanting the annoying meeting over. He was almost certain there was going to be questions about Charlotte Jonhson and Larson.

"Yes," Bergman answered, carefully placing his fingers together in a near prayerful manner as he rocked back in his chair. "I'm sorry if today's questions cause you any discomfort but there is solid, shall we say, corporate policy reinforcing the issue."

Luke was now near certain it was going to be about the Larson and his affair with Charlotte.

"Uncomfortable questions are part of our security operations," Luke said. "How can I help?"

"Well, we often use a professional moving company in Havasu, Arizona to accommodate moving our new hires. You are still, for your first ninety days, considered a new hire. This moving company is available to facilitate your move from Rio Vista to a yet-to-be-determined address here in Las Vegas—or storage if you prefer. The company provided an estimate of their cost after you approved their inspection of your home, a fully furnished double-wide manufactured home."

"It was furnished when I bought it," Luke said.

"If I may continue," Bergman said after a glance at notes on his desk. "They found a living room, kitchen, two bathrooms, three bedrooms, a crowded double car garage and a vintage 1986 Chevrolet pickup truck without an engine."

"The engine is in parts in the garage."

Bergman made a note before going on. "Nevertheless, your agreement with The Silver Palace subsequent to your hiring was that the company would pay for your move."

"And that's changed?" Luke asked.

"Yes, ironically by you, or someone you know."

"I haven't changed anything. You're being vague."

"Allow me to be direct," Berman said, leaning forward in his chair to rest his elbows on the desktop. "A van was sent the other day to pick up your vintage truck, with no engine. While there, a woman arrived driving a U-Haul. She had a Native American with her. They began moving a significant inventory of personal property, to include multiple boxes as well as furniture into your home. You will recall I stated an estimate was provided earlier and a contract signed. The question is, is this woman your wife? I believe you claimed you were divorced. Is she a companion, perhaps a relative?"

Luke stiffened in his chair. He resented Bergman's attitude.

"Let me tell you who she is—she's none of your business."

Bergman didn't seem intimidated. He pushed on his glasses with the hope it made him look more executive. "I'm afraid it is our business. A contract, much like winnings in a casino, can't be changed after the terms are set. You owe us an explanation."

"Owe?" Luke said, standing. "Owe you what? You've been a director now for how many hours? I don't owe you anything. Forget moving me. I've been screwed by bigger dicks than you."

Bergman pushed to his feet. "A bigger dick! Don't bring name-calling and sexual innuendo into this."

"Sexual innuendo," Luke laughed sarcastically. "I don't see anything sexual about you. Except maybe the fact you don't like me having a female companion."

"You better watch your words," Bergman cautioned emotionally, pulling off his glasses. "You're on thin ice suggesting what my sexual preferences are."

"I'm surprised you have any."

"You're saying I'm gay."

"Are you?"

"Yes, I am, and I'm not ashamed of it."

"Yeah, well, I'm straight and I'm not unashamed of it. Now, what the fuck does all that have to do with moving me and my soon-to-be wife to Vegas?" Luke was angry at Bergman's referring to Barbara as the woman in a U-Haul. He expected being called to HR was going to be about the Larson's affair. He was angry that it had become about him and Barbara.

"Tell you what." Luke deliberately lowered his tone. "Take your moving contract and shove it up your ass."

Luke turned and marched out, slamming the door behind him.

Bergman sank into his high-backed chair. Luke Mitchel had shaken him, stolen his confidence. He picked up his glasses and pushed them on. He'd get the sonofabitch fired.

————

THE SILVER PALACE'S executive management meeting had lasted its usual two hours. Somehow, the sleep-deprived Greg Lawson got through it. The fact the managers and department heads did most of the talking helped. Larson concluded the meeting by expressing his appreciation for the united effort by all that had led to a new high mark in The Silver Palace's monthly earnings.

Once said, he gathered his notes, tactfully passed on questions from several department heads, and headed for his office. There, he found his assistant, Jackie Fallon, at her desk in his outer office. She looked up from the screen on her desktop when Larson entered. "Morning, boss."

The door to Larson's office stood open, and the lights were on. Larson glanced at Jackie and offered her a pretend smile. How the hell could she look so good, so early? He was envious of her smile and her age. He felt old and tired. Haunting Larson was an emptiness welling inside over the unexplainable and damning vacuum caused by Charlotte's absence. She was gone. It was as if part of his soul was missing. He allowed the thought that maybe it was.

"Housekeeping told me you were in early," Jackie said, reading Larson's weary expression.

Larson paused beside Jackie's desk. It was as if his assistant had connected the dots. How could she not? The girl was paid to be his shadow, his conscience, and many times, his voice. She was his safe place to fall at the Palace. But then there was the unspoken secret they both knew, standing like a tall, thick, cold glass between them. They both knew the ice was thin, but the truth had to remain unspoken, silent, and hidden.

Jackie parted the shadows and brought them both back to the moment. "While you were in your meeting, you had six calls. Three need your attention. Mayor Bray called regarding our plan to hold a veterans-only day next month. He would like to be included. Larry Edwards, executive producer of *60 Minutes,* wants to talk regarding a behind-the-scenes segment, and Mei Kum, secretary to the directors, would like to talk about the proposal to give a hundred thousand dollars to our best-dressed guest every month. She called from a Hong Kong number. You can return her call at any hour. All of this is on your desktop, and there's a fresh coffee on your desk."

Larson studied Jackie. She had deep blue eyes and a sincere expression that assured him that, at least for the moment, the Titanic hadn't hit the iceberg. He could almost feel her support. Larson surprised her by reaching out to take her hand. "Thank you, Jackie."

———

She was surprised at how warm his hand was. She couldn't recall if he had ever touched her before. His thank you was deep with emotion. She could almost feel the power he carried. Charlotte Johnson may have wounded him with her departure, but he was still at the wheel.

On the surface, promoting Bergman appeared to be something that had been on the drawing board. A smooth transition. At management and department head level, tradition dictated one did not talk about why those who moved on, resigned, or accepted a new position.

Instead, managers were expected to offer their support to those joining the team. Especially if they were stepping up. At the management meeting all had wished James Bergman the best. Charlotte Jonhson, who was no longer on the team, was hardly mentioned and would soon be forgotten.

At least, that was what Jackie hoped. Larson's action clearly indicated he was hoping the same. However, both knew it was Charlotte who held a match near the fuse to the bomb that would empty the GM's office in a flash.

———

Luke surprised both Larson and Jackie when he opened the hall door to the GM's outer office. Larson released his awkward hold of Jackie's hand, which she quickly pulled into her lap. Luke had seen it. He looked at Jackie, then Larson. He was the one feeling awkward. He was uncertain whether to step in, speak, or withdraw. Larson saw Luke's reaction. He filled in the blanks, "Been expecting you. Come on in."

Luke offered Jackie a quick glance and a smile before following Larson into his office.

"Close the door," Larson said, walking to the chair behind his desk. He gestured Luke to a chair.

"I was just down in surveillance," Luke said after sitting down. "They've finished their review of activity around the gold in the count room, including the placement of the last four bricks. Nothing suspicious. They also looked at the arrival and departure of the safe car, driven by Dan Payne with Caroline Summers, who was the purchasing agent for the gold. When the safe car returned from their gold pickups, they were met by two security officers who provided escort to the stack in the count room. Again, nothing suspicious."

It had been a long night for Larson. He wasn't in a mode for bad news. "In other words, you don't have shit." His words were confrontational.

"Actually," Luke said. "I brought some shit with me."

He was still on the edge from his shouting match with James Bergman. His tone matched Larson's. "I was a little uncertain about putting you in the loop, but then why should I be the only one up to my neck in shit."

"Okay," Larson said placatingly. He wiped a hand on his pant leg, "Cut to the chase. What's got you so tense?"

Luke hesitated, considering telling the GM about being summoned to HR over the issue concerning Barb being included in his moving expenses. He chose not to. Bergman didn't deserve the time. The little prick.

"You going to tell me or what?" Larson asked.

"Blake Mancini assigned Dan Payne, the then PM watch lieutenant, to accompany Caroline Summers every time she went off property to buy gold. It's all on tape. No issues there, but allow me to remind you that I fired Dan Payne for insubordination and extortion."

"Was that related to the theft of the gold?" Larson was puzzled.

"Not related at all, but this morning, I drove out to Caroline Summers's house. I went because she discovered the three gold bricks missing from the count room, and I didn't have anything else."

"I don't see where Caroline lives means anything. Where's the connection?"

"I'm staked on Caroline's house when who walks out? Dan Payne. The same prick I fired. The same man who went with Caroline when she bought gold. I fired him for extortion. What's he doing with Caroline Summers? Was he there overnight?"

"Son-of-a-bitch," Larson said. "Last night I was thinking, three gold bricks, who gives a shit—I'll just replace them. Tell Caroline to find the money. Hell, it won't break us. The Chinese know nothing. We tighten things up, so it doesn't happen again. Hell, things get swept under the rug all the time."

"This one could leave a big fucking lump in your rug."

"Yeah, okay. I didn't say it was a good idea. So, what's next? You haven't found anything that happened on the property. Maybe it's time to call Metro, let them put it all together?"

"That's your call. I'll do whatever you want. But I think if this goes to the police it's only a matter of time until it makes the evening news. Last I heard the Chinese do watch the news."

Larson was troubled. He looked to his wide window as if the panorama of the Strip would somehow allow him an escape. First, Charlotte took him to the edge and now another woman—a woman he'd known and worked with for years—was wrapping him in a maze with no answers.

Ironically, she too, was involved with another employee. It was a painful realization. How could he pass judgment on her when he was guilty of the same thing with Charlotte.

He drew in a breath and returned his look to Luke. "You know Caroline deals with millions of dollars every day. She's got people looking over her shoulder, but if she wanted to steal from us, she'd find a way. You've seen her house. Hell, her old man was an investor. He left her comfortable. She doesn't have to steal."

"I've seen her house," Luke said. "She may be comfortable, but who's been sleeping in her bed? Dan Payne? I saw him walk out of there this morning and he's a thief."

Larson nodded agreement. He was troubled, but he knew what he had to do.

He drummed his fingers on the desktop. "In Vegas it's not all about winning. It's about beating the odds. Kicking your opponent's ass. If you know he's a cheat, you're going to take your money elsewhere. Point being, we can't cheat, we can't hide, we've got to play the hand we're dealt. We're The Silver Palace. Odds are we'll win, but it will be because of the odds, not because we've stolen it. So, go find this sonofabitch. Do what you have to do. Get it done."

———

LUKE STOOD. He wanted out of the GM's office. He got what he came for, and none of it was pleasant. He thought about speaking to Jackie on his way out but decided against it. He was still wondering what the hell the hand-holding with Larson was all about, but he wasn't looking for any more drama.

As Luke stepped into the hallway, his cell phone vibrated. It was Barbara.

Luke welcomed her call. Finally, a good moment. He'd texted her after seeing the housing tracts on his drive to Mountain View.

"Hey, gorgeous," Luke said to his cell as he walked the hallway to the employees' elevator. "Sorry if my early text woke you."

"It's okay. I was up. Had a meeting early this morning at the casino."

"Everything okay?" Luke questioned, pausing short of the elevators. He didn't want to talk there. Privacy was an issue.

"No," Barbara answered candidly. "There's good news and bad."

"Let's start with the good news," Luke said. Her tone worried him.

"I've been offered a position as head of food and beverage. Tom Young left last week. Ironically, he moved to Vegas. The GM offered me the position...along with a serious raise."

Luke leaned on the wall. He ignored the stream of employees passing as he pushed the cell phone closer to his mouth. Barb's words twisted his stomach muscles tight.

"I don't understand. What are you saying?" Luke knew, but he didn't want it to be true. It wouldn't be true until she repeated the words.

"If you haven't heard about me taking things over to your place for the move up there, you will. The moving crew I ran into was less than cordial."

"I heard, but I don't give a shit about them, what about you? What does this F&B thing mean?"

"I'll be in charge. I'd be a director, working days. In charge of the whole department. I'm excited. I'll have a career instead of just a job. They picked me, Luke."

Luke was breathing hard. She had said the words.

"I picked you too, Barb," he said, deliberately pushing her into a corner. "Does this mean you're not coming?" He knew the answer. He had heard the words.

"Luke, this is a good thing. Can't we have both? Somehow, some way?"

She was pushing back. She wanted it to be his problem. Love was the problem. Wasn't it always? A thousand thoughts raced through his mind, but none were good. The cell phone was silent in his ear. It felt like he was holding a hot rock.

He drew in a breath and let it out slowly. Life had taught him doing the right thing was important. He spoke like the man he hoped he was, knowing it was now his words that were looking for an escape from what was the probable end of a dream. "Sure," Luke lied. "We'll find a way. I'm happy for you. Congratulations, Miss Director."

"I love you, Luke. Thank you."

The lie continued. Didn't they always?

"I'm on my way to a meeting. We'll talk later. I wanna hear your plan about how you'll serve a better steak for less money."

"Promise?" Barb said, reading his tone.

"Promise," Luke said, lying again. He ended the call.

SIXTEEN
PICTURE THIS

THERE ARE CAMERAS EVERYWHERE. In houses, in cars, in supermarkets, in the pockets of everyone carrying a cell phone. It was rare for a human being to live through a day without being photographed, recorded, or watched digitally. There were front door cams, body cams, drone cams, and more. Cameras had become a vital and critical part of the human experience, both at home and on the job. Getting through a day without appearing on camera or watching what a camera had captured had become impossible. Watch the evening news, drive on a public street, you appeared and were recorded on camera.

There were places, cities in the world with more cameras than Las Vegas, but most were in China or Southeast Asia. In Las Vegas, cameras greeted you when you drove into the city. They watched where you parked. You walked through facial recognition when you entered the casino, and there were more at the front desk, a wide shot as you crossed to the elevators, and more on the elevator. And finally, hallway cams followed you to your room, but even there, if you opened a window or walked onto a balcony, they found you again.

Vegas had proven to be an innovator with its use of cameras. Especially the subtle, hidden ones. How could they not? Where else could you walk by a poker table with fifty-nine thousand dollars in chips and cash, lying open, waiting on the next bet? It was a digital camera world in which Luke lived. The Silver Palace had so many cameras that nobody knew the exact number.

It was this digital image world that gave Luke an idea. If his casino had cameras to look for cheats and thieves, it was likely that gold merchants had them, too. Luke needed to find out.

After his initial interview of Caroline Summers, Luke sent her an email request for the names, addresses and dates of where she bought the two-pound gold ingots used to build the million-dollar table the Chinese wanted in The Silver Palace's count room.

The list provided no surprises. He was certain Larson was aware of the names as did the cash operations support staff. Who sold the gold to The Silver Palace was no big deal. Who stole it was.

Las Vegas had more than its share of alleged gold dealers. Vegas was a town where gold was often traded for cash. Cash for those who had little cash of their own left. Cash for gold wedding rings topped the list, but there were also gold necklaces, gold earrings, gold bracelets, gold piercings, and more, but these were minor gold dealers.

Las Vegas also had its serious gold merchants. The one used most by Caroline Summers was located on Russell Road a few blocks off the Strip. They did business as the Southern Nevada Mineral Merchants—which was better than hanging a *come rob me* sign out front emblazoned Gold Merchants—shoppers with sawed-off shotguns were not the desired customers.

Gayle Turner watched Luke drive away from the casino after his meeting with the GM. His visit with her earlier had been unusually short. Gayle and Mario Lopez had pledged to cover daily security challenges, allowing Luke to focus on the theft of the gold, but he still wanted a daily briefing to stay in the loop. Today, however, had been different.

Charlotte Jonhson had left without explanation. Luke had met with the GM after being away from the grounds when he requested the DMV on Dan Payne's BMW—a man he had fired and ordered off the property. But while surveillance let you see it all it didn't mean you understood it all.

————

CHARLOTTE JONHSON WAS ALSO UP EARLY. Her hair was pulled back in a style that complimented her natural beauty. She was dressed in her best suit and heels. A briefcase was propped at her feet as she waited in the comfortable outer office of the GM at the Cosmopolitan Casino and Resort Hotel. Charlotte was feeling smug. The call from the Cosmopolitan had come shortly after she'd arrived home yesterday. The Vegas rumor mill was obviously alive and well. Word was out that Charlotte was suddenly available. The call had lit up her private cell from the GM of Cosmopolitan himself at the other end. She was invited to come and have an informal chat at the Cosmopolitan. Informal or not, Charlotte knew she'd take whatever they offered just to rub it in Greg Larson's face.

———

In the GM's office at The Silver Palace, James Bergman told Jackie Fallon he wasn't going home until he talked to the GM. Bergman was upset. His emotions were written all over his face. Jackie tried explaining to him that the GM had a resort and a casino to run. He was on a long- distance call to Asia, and he had a face-to-face meeting pending. She told the emotional Bergman to make an appointment for later in the day. He refused and sat down to wait. When Jackie saw the GM had concluded his long-distance call, she knocked on his office door and stepped inside.

"Sir, Jim Bergman's out there. He's insisting on seeing you."

"I got three more calls I have to make. One of them to the governor," Larson said. "What's he want?"

"I have no idea, but he's a man on the edge."

"All right, get him in here. Five minutes. Then get him the fuck out."

Jackie nodded agreement and returned to Bergman in the outer office. "He'll see you, but five minutes is it."

Bergman was quickly on his feet. He pushed by Jackie as she closed the door behind him.

"This has to be quick, Jim," Larson said. "I've got a lot on my plate." He gestured to the two chairs facing his desk.

"I want Luke Mitchel fired," Bergman said as he sat down in a chair.

Larson flashed on his earlier meet with Luke. There had been no mention of a problem with HR. Had Bergman learned of the role Luke played in black-mailing Blake Mancini or maybe about his affair with Charlotte Jonhson? Larson did his best to mask his anxiety. "Jim, I have no idea what the hell you are talking about."

"He called me gay," Bergman said, tightening his grip on the arms of his chair. "That's sexual discrimination as well as employee harassment under corporate guidelines as well as harassment defined by the US Equal Employment guidelines. His blatant bigotry cannot be permitted."

"All right," Larson said cautiously. "There's no need to shout. Tell me what the hell happened."

"I'm sorry," Bergman said. He tried to calm himself. "I called Mitchel after our moving services found his girlfriend, his live-in, whatever she is, trying to move stuff, specifically boxes and furniture not included in the agreement, into his property in Alta Vista, for shipment to Las Vegas. He got angry and asked me if I was gay?"

"He asked," Larson said. "How's that an insult?"

"Trust me, I know when it's an insult," Bergman said, pushing on his glasses.

"Listen, James," Larson countered. "I'm the GM. You know an accusation like this has to come to my desk. I decide, and so far from what I'm hearing, you called this man to your office to point a finger at him for something his girlfriend did a couple hundred miles away. Is that accurate?"

"I was tactful."

"What is the big deal if we move some of his girlfriend's belongings? We move new employees belongings as a perk, don't we?"

"Yes, but…"

"The conversation you had with Mitchel was in your office in private. Is that true?"

"What does it matter where he insulted me?"

Larson leaned into the desk and laced his fingers

together. "Jim, when you're insulted in public it's everybody's business. When you're insulted in private it's *your* business. Not mine. All yours. Nobody but you. This isn't something you want a committee investigating. If Michell insulted you in private. You gotta fix it in private."

Bergman took his glasses off, folded them, and slipped them into his jacket pocket. He felt defeated.

Larson saw Bergman's expression. He added more. "Today's your first day as an HR director. Mitchel challenges you. *How dare he?* I'm betting he's pissed over what you said. The point is none of this is my business. One-on-one personal shit happens. It's your job to fix it, not mine."

Bergman studied his shoes. He started to take his glasses from his jacket pocket but changed his mind. He raised his eyes and looked to the GM. "Thank you."

"Yeah, now get your ass outta here. Get back to work."

———

TWO POINT seven miles away at the Cosmopolitan Casino and Resort, Charlotte Johnson sat in the GM's office. She was psychologically prepared to accept an offer to join their HR staff. She knew Howard Morrison, their current HR director. He was an older man, perhaps three to five years from retirement. Charlotte knew the game and knew it well. She would work herself into position and wait. The GM surprised her with his strategy.

"Charlotte, we've been watching. We like what we've seen."

"Thank you, sir."

"Before you became an HR director you were a housekeeping manager?"

"And before that a housekeeper." Charlotte smiled.

"So, you know firsthand the importance of guest rooms."

"From the bottom up."

"Well, we have nothing available in HR that might match your skill set, but we do have something else I'd like you to consider."

Charlotte tried to mask her disappointment. She thought she was about to be offered a position as the assistant to somebody or a role in guest relations.

"We'd like to ask you to take over as director of our rooms division."

Charlotte's breath left her. The offer was better than she could have imagined. She would have over thirty-three hundred rooms and a staff to manage. She had landed on her feet. She didn't care about the money. Wait until Greg Larson heard about this. The prick. She hoped he would be jealous. She tried to fight the thought he might really care.

———

LUKE WAS eager to get away from the property. He wanted air, air he didn't have to share with anyone. Right now he was feeling that Barabara, James Bergman, Larson, and The Silver Palace itself could all go to hell. However, once in traffic on the Strip, stuck behind a slow-moving van pulling a large two-sided sign for the stage show *Menopause Meadows*, he knew he had to get it together.

Barbara was foremost on his mind. The thought he'd lost her to the Wild River's food and beverage division really irked him. He knew it was a big deal as she'd be in charge of everything to do with the Wild River's restaurants, snack shops, and room service groups. She would buy the stock, supervise the preparation, formulate menus.

She was right when she said it was a career. He knew she'd earned it. He also knew she was only two hundred miles away. He'd deal with it. He had to. He would move ahead with his plan to buy a house and get out of the Palace.

The slow-moving traffic finally reached Rusell Road. Luke gladly made a turn to leave the Strip behind. He started looking for the Southern Nevada Mineral Merchants where Caroline Summers had bought most of The Silver Palace's gold bricks. He had little doubt the Chinese would want somebody's ass for the loss of three gold bricks. He had to wonder what his future was if he couldn't solve this mess.

Daniel Payne's involvement had cracked open the door on who was doing what to whom by walking out of Caroline's house earlier in the day. She had to know he'd been fired. He wondered if Payne had been in her house overnight or if he was maybe there every night. Luke knew he needed answers.

Spotting the sign he was looking for on a storefront in a strip mall on his right, Luke slowed and wheeled his car into the parking lot. There were other cars. His would draw no attention.

The gold merchant's windows were glazed dark. On the right of the gold merchant was a sign announcing *Las Vegas Realty*. Beyond the realty office was a shoe store. To the left of the gold merchant, a bold digital sign read *Four Minute Tattoos*. The shop was busy. Luke could see two artists working on a man and a woman. Vegas would not be forgotten.

Beside the tattoo parlor, another colorful digital sign blinked at passing traffic—The Red Rooster, Drinks, Nudity and More. The door to the Red Rooster stood open. Next was a nail salon and a busy supermarket. Luke lowered his window. He could hear the faint sound of music from inside the Rooster. Some were finding it an inviting place, even at an early hour. Luke reminded himself nobody cared what time it was in Vegas.

His attention went back to the Southern Nevada Mineral Merchants storefront. It was quiet. It wasn't much. Luke had pieces of the puzzle, but he needed more. He reached for his iPhone and dialed into Google. He needed information. He learned the Southern Nevada Mineral Merchants dealt in precious metals. They were owned by a company called SandMan Inc. Luke searched the net to find them. He found SandMan Incorporated was a Delaware Corporation LLC. He knew he wouldn't find much else.

Shifting gears, he looked for cameras. He was midblock, so the city wasn't going to help. It wasn't likely the realty company spent anything on security. The tattoo shop, however, proved different with a camera showing above their front door. Luke hoped it was a wide-angle camera that would also capture images of whoever went in and out of the gold dealer's storefront.

He then looked to the Red Rooster. What he saw made him smile. If you had a liquor license in Clark County, Nevada, you did your best to protect it. The Rooster had three cameras. One on their main entrance and two more aimed at the parking lot. Shit that started in a small club always spilled into its parking lots. Luke

knew the digital images would also capture the front of
the gold merchants. Getting access to the recordings was
another issue, maybe a big one, but it was a start.

Surrounded by empty cars, Luke sat behind the
wheel and watched the activity in the parking lot for
nearly an hour. The realty office had business, so did the
tattoo shop, the salon, and market, but nothing
happened at the Southern Nevada Mineral Merchants.

The biggest business was being conducted by the Red
Rooster. Single men seemed to find the blinking sign
promising nudity inviting—especially middle-aged men.
He made a mental note to dig up whatever he could on
the Red Rooster when he returned to The Silver Palace.
He wanted to know who owned it and who was running
it. The answer could tell him what access to their digital
recordings was going to cost. He would need clean cash,
which was something Greg Larson could solve.

Luke was about to leave when the man walked out of
the Southern Nevada Mineral Merchants' front door.
Luke straightened in his seat, trying not to overreact.

The man was Luke's age, dressed casually in a short-
sleeved light-blue shirt, faded blue jeans, and cowboy
boots. Not unusual for Nevada. He smoked a cigarette as
he walked. Luke was two rows away from him. He raised
his cell phone casually and punched the camera record
button, videoing as the man walked by the tattoo parlor
—slowing to glance inside—then passing and walking
through the open front door of the Red Rooster.

Luke knew he needed more than pictures of this
man. He pushed his cell phone onto his belt beneath his
jacket and climbed out of the car, welcoming the relief.

The music was loud, and the lights were dim in the
Red Rooster. A muscle-bound bearded bouncer greeted
Luke just inside the door, "Welcome." He smiled at Luke

exposing a gold front tooth. "Sit anywhere you like, and no touching."

Luke glanced at the near-nude thirty-year-old shapely girl dancing on the bar top in front of three smiling men. She wore near knee-high, soft boots and a dark bikini bottom which had several bills stuffed in it. Her bare breasts and smooth stomach were of Vegas standards. A cluster of battery-powered candles lit small round tables that filled the shadowy room.

Luke spotted an empty table on the far side of the room. As he crossed to it, he recognized the light-blue shirt of the man from the Southern Nevada Mineral Merchants who was sitting nearby. A waitress, dressed much like the dancer on the bar top except she wore a loose-fitting—but not to be ignored—shirt over her ample breasts, was setting a drink in front of the man in the blue shirt. It was obvious the girls were multitasking.

The waitress spotted Luke.

"What can I get for you?" She smiled.

"Jack Daniels and Diet Coke."

"Be right back," the waitress said, moving for the bar.

Luke did a quick body count. There were eight men at the small tables. All sitting alone and all watching the dancer on the bar. Luke watched as a gray-haired man to his right laid out a spread of bills on the tabletop. It was bait.

The man in the blue shirt was to Luke's left and a few feet in front of him. The waitress returned with drinks balanced on a small tray. She stopped first at *blue shirt's* table where she sat a burger and french fries in front of the man. Luke watched. The man was having lunch. Nothing like tits and ass with your bacon and cheese burger. The waitress then moved to Luke, delivering his drink.

"You can keep a tab open for a while," she said with a glossy-lipped, seductive smile. "You may want something else."

Luke answered with a nod and a smile. The girl moved away to a table where a man held a drinking glass in the air. Luke sipped his drink. He didn't want alcohol getting in his way, but it was cold and inviting. He split his attention between the topless dancer on the bar and *blue shirt* eating the sandwich. Luke needed to know much more about *blue shirt*. He needed to find out if he was man who sold gold bars to Caroline Summers—if he was, then Luke needed his help with dates, times, and the number of transactions.

If he was the gold merchant, he might also know where the thieves could turn stolen gold into cash. Luke decided on a direct approach. They were in a bar so the approach needed to be soft. He test-drove his opening line under his breath, *Aren't you Carl Fraiser from the Cosmo?* That would get him started.

He would follow up with his own name and the ball would be rolling. He successfully interrogated thieves and cheats. He figured a gold merchant wouldn't be much different. He'd let him have four of five more bites of his burger and another french fry, and it would be time. Luke sipped his drink and watched the man.

When the music changed from one loud, profane rap group to another, the set of nipples on the bar got down with the bartender's help. *Blue shirt's* burger was gone, and he was eating the last of his french fries. There was an illuminated restroom sign near the bar. Luke stood and walked toward it. When he returned, he'd play the recognition game.

In the restroom, he stepped toward the urinal and unzipped. He heard the door open. Whoever it was chose to wait behind him. Luke finished finding relief. He zipped up and turned to find the sober, bearded, muscular bouncer standing behind him. Luke offered the man a look and tried stepping by him. The bouncer raised an arm to block Luke's movement. Luke's eyes went to the man's face.

"I'm gonna walk you to the front door, dude. You're done staring at guys in my house. You can play find a dick to suck somewhere else. Your time pretending to watch girls is up."

The bouncer's words surprised Luke. He pushed the bouncer's arm aside forcefully. The bouncer was ready, he grabbed Luke's jacket with both hands and slammed him against the wall.

"This isn't a gay bar, dude. You're out."

Luke grabbed the bouncer's arms to pull them away when something metallic rattled to the tile floor between the two men. It was Luke's gold and silver badge, pulled from his belt.

"Shit," the shocked bouncer said, seeing the badge. He released Luke. "You should have told me, dude. How was I to know?" It was a plea.

The bouncer's question was to go unanswered as the man in the blue shirt opened the bathroom door. The bearded gold merchant stopped and stood frozen. He looked first at Luke, whose jacket was still pushed high, exposing his belt, and the holstered automatic pistol strapped on his side. His eyes went to the muscular bouncer.

"Sorry," *blue shirt* said quietly, stepping out to let the door close.

Luke straightened his jacket and gathered his badge from the floor. The bouncer, who was convinced he had assaulted a police officer, offered another plea, "I'm sorry, man. I didn't know."

Luke looked in the mirror to smooth wrinkles from his jacket, "My fault," Luke said. It wasn't but it was better to make a friend than an enemy. "We good?"

"Yes, sir," the bouncer said in an apologetic tone. "Thanks…"

Luke knew from the moment he saw *blue shirt* enter the restroom, the game was up. He washed his hands, dried them, and headed for his car. On the way out, he noticed the bouncer was no longer at the front door.

SEVENTEEN
FAMILIAR FACES

GREG LARSON'S day was proving to be much better than his night. His busy schedule was proving therapeutic. The answer was simple. Being the general manager of The Silver Palace carried with it incredible responsibilities. It was his task to get 10,206 employees to come to work every day. Not only to show up, but do their best to please guests who could number as high as 13,704— and that wasn't counting casual visitors who came in to gamble, dine, or shop.

Larson learned early in his career it wasn't first-time guests who held the key to success in the dynamic world of hospitality, it was the guest who returned a second and third time. And the key to bringing a guest back was to make sure they enjoyed their first visit. Guest contact was vital. This concept ruled the day's schedule.

Larson showed up at the morning housekeeping briefing where he encouraged the staff to think of the guest rooms they serviced as a room they would like to spend a night in with someone they loved.

His visit to housekeeping was followed by a tasting in

the kitchen where he watched the room service staff prepare trays for delivery. He tasted scrambled eggs and oatmeal before moving on to engineering—who had just received a new shipment of flat-screen smart TVs that provided guests access to the internet, free streaming, and a port enabling smartphone connections for their photos and videos. Larson left engineering after they promised one of the new sets would be installed in his office.

Back at his desk, he looked at the food and beverage order inventories. After reviewing it, he penciled in an additional order for Starbucks coffee. Meetings with guest services and valet followed.

The *get lost in your work* bandage came loose in the early afternoon when Larson went into his private bathroom to put on a fresh jacket for the Big Ten monthly meeting. The Big Ten comprised the top ten casino managers who contributed the biggest pull for the weekly average influx of Las Vegas's six hundred thousand guests.

The Big Ten met quietly and briefly. They were competitors, but competitors who cooperated in the coordination of citywide events such as the Formula One race, the rodeo, the electronics show, and a hundred other venues. When your rooms were sold out, you needed a place to send guests, and when you needed to get three hundred and twelve high rollers in to see someone else's headliner, you needed their help. There were an uncountable number of things to coordinate, and the cooperation between the Big Ten held the answers.

Today's meeting was scheduled at the Bellagio. Larson would be accompanied by his guest services director. He would also be accompanied by the smarting, haunting guilt Luke had laid on him. Caroline Summers, a mature, aging woman, was having an affair with a younger former employee—a security officer fired for extortion. The same employee who escorted Caroline on her gold-buying expeditions. It was ugly any way you looked at it, and Larson knew he would eventually have to be their judge—a judge haunted by the fact he was guilty of the same thing, guilty of screwing a subordinate who had recently quit in anger.

All manner of possibilities chased around and around in Larson's head—did she want revenge, was his marriage at risk, was it a marriage worth saving? He felt like a scumbag—a man he no longer liked. A man he didn't want to be, but painfully was. He wondered if any of the others at the Big Ten meeting were liars or cheats. He supposed there would be some, but he still felt alone —very alone.

———

LUKE'S IDEA was born from the recent hacking at the MGM Grand. The iconic Grand had been shaken to its foundation by a covert hacking of its extensive electronic network. Room keys, reservations, resort-wide heating and cooling, and more, had all been compromised. The result had been major bad press, a worldwide outcry on social media, hundreds of unhappy guests, and major losses. The big lion was wounded but not dead. Its roar warned others. Now, Luke was about to turn hacking into a two-way street.

Back under the roof of The Silver Palace, he found it felt much like a protective shield compared to how he'd been treated out in the world. Luke deliberately turned his thoughts to finding the missing gold as he made his way to an employee elevator.

A smile from an attractive young housekeeper boarding the elevator was reassuring as Luke headed up to surveillance. Gayle Turner was at her desk when he arrived.

She offered a smile. "We caught the car thief in valet parking."

"Tell me about it," Luke said, sitting down in a chair beside Gayle.

"First, are you okay? You looked tired," Gayle said.

Luke straightened in his chair. "Nice to see you too."

"I ask because I care."

Luke shrugged. "It's been a long day. Now tell me about our car thief."

"Caught him in the act. It was a male housekeeper hired five months ago. He was pushing a laundry cart through guest parking. We watched him pay particular attention to a valet attendant parking a Mercedes. He was a row away, and the valet didn't see him when he put the keys on top of the right front tire. It struck us as suspicious, so we watched the guy until he got off duty. Be he left property and we thought we'd been mistaken."

"But…" Luke prodded.

Gayle punched a button on one of her monitors. An image of the guest parking garage appeared on the screen. It showed rows of cars and SUVs parked unattended in the shadowy garage. There was no movement for a few seconds, and then a dark hooded figure appeared. The figure looked around. Distance and shadows hid his identity as he walked through a line of parked cars to reach the Mercedes where he paused and looked around. Feeling secure, he went to the car's right front tire and snagged the keys. He then unlocked the driver's door and climbed in. The Mercedes's headlights flashed on, and the car pulled away and out of the camera's frame.

Luke and Gayle watched as a second image appeared on the monitor depicting the illuminated crossing guard exit of the valet parking garage. Standing in the path of the approaching headlights was a serious-looking uniformed Sergeant Stone. He held a long rifle at his side. Two other uniformed officers stood on either side of the sergeant. Both were armed with long guns. Light from the approaching headlamps brightened the men. They raised their weapons. The Mercedes came into view, stopping short of the armed trio.

"Get him," Stone could be heard to order.

The other two officers went to the driver's door, pulled the hooded man from behind the wheel and pushed him against the car.

"His name is Jose Mullins, twenty-two," Gayle said, as they watched the man be handcuffed. "He said he was paid by a former valet to steal our cars. We know where to pick him up as well after I play this for Metro."

"Nice work," Luke said.

Gayle turned off the monitor and looked at Luke. "Is this visit official, or is it my good looks that bring you here?"

"I need help. Are your IT guys on duty?"

"They're both here—hiding in their closet as usual."

"Can you call them in? The gold circle is about to get wider."

Luke tried to relax as Gayle left the room. She was an attractive woman. A former line dance leader. It still showed. Line dancer to director of surveillance—only in Vegas.

Gayle returned with the two IT specialists.

Gayle introduced the two men. "This is Haruto and Riku, our network specialists. Gentlemen, this is Luke Mitchel, our security director."

As the three shook hands, Gayle wheeled in two chairs and invited the two men to sit down. The two men were in their late twenties. They looked eager and attentive.

Gayle closed the glass door to the primary surveillance suite and sat down with the others.

"Gentlemen," Luke began, "what I'm about to share with you is confidential. It stays with the four of us. Agreed?"

Nods from the two men assured they understood.

"There's a gold merchant on Russell Road just off the Strip. They're doing business as the Southern Nevada Mineral Merchants," Luke told them. "They've sold a number of two-pound gold bullion bricks to The Silver Palace. These purchases were legitimate and approved by management. They were made by Caroline Summers, the head of cash operations. For security, she was accompanied by Lieutenant Dan Payne, who has since been terminated for an unrelated cause."

Luke noticed both men beginning to look excited. He was pleased. "I've no doubt the gold merchant has cameras all over his operation. Nearby is a tattoo parlor, a salon, a bar with nude dancers called the Red Rooster, and a supermarket. I saw some exterior security cameras and I'm sure there are more. We need to get into those cameras and look for the dates and times Caroline Summers and Dan Payne appear."

"We know who they are and the car they drive," Riku said. "We covered their departures and their return from the bullion buying trips."

"Great," Luke said. "What I'm looking for is three

gold bricks. Someone stole them. They're obviously worth big money. Whoever stole them had to know where we got them, how we transported them, and where we store them. In other words, it was an inside job. There is good cause to believe there is an ongoing illicit relationship between Summers and Payne. I need to see their arrival at the gold store on Russell Road— date and time, their departure, and what they carry out. If they put it in the trunk of their car, who put it there and—since you saw them return—who took the gold out? Can you do it?"

The two IT men exchanged a look then Haruto spoke. "Most security cameras on commercial properties have Internet links. The owners and managers want to see their properties or employees, just like we do."

Haruto's comparison made Luke smile, but it was true. He could dial into any security camera in The Silver Palace from the comfort of his suite. There was no doubt the GM and others had the same privilege.

"Many make an effort to protect their network connection, but it's not likely a tattoo parlor or a nudie bar can afford to do the same. This means we might be able to get in and check out their feed."

"What about recordings," Luke pressed. "I'm looking for something that has already happened."

"Once we find a way into their net," Riku said, "we can access how long they keep their images. Sometimes, the company installing the equipment keeps recordings on the cloud, waiting for a vendor to ask for a look back."

"And we can view it?" Luke asked.

"Depends, but maybe."

"This becomes priority one today," Luke said. "And I want it done quietly. Understood?"

"Understood," Haruto answered for the two.

"I'll get you the address of the gold merchant on Russell Road," Luke said.

"You already have." Riku smiled. "Google will take us there, up close and personal."

Luke stood up. The others followed.

"Keep Gayle informed. She'll reach out to me."

Luke shook hands with both men again. He noticed a slight bow from both when they shook. When the two were gone, Luke exchanged a look with Gayle, "Where did you find those two?"

"On the Internet," Gayle said.

———

THREE BLOCKS AWAY, riding in the back seat of The Silver Palace's glimmering limousine, Greg Larson admired the towering water fountains of the Bellagio Resort Casino as they jetted high in the hot afternoon air. Riding with him was JoAnne Burns, an attractive thirty-eight-year-old, shapely, head-turning brunette who was head of guest relations at The Silver Palace. Larson told her she would play a role in coordinating issues with high rollers. The real reason for her being with him was as a *play trophy*.

The uniformed driver pulled into the front entrance for their arrival at the Big Ten meeting. Larson's limo was met by several Bellagio executives offering smiles and handshakes. Tourists and guests, held back by red rope and stanchions, could only wonder who and what they were seeing as they crowded to stare and take pictures. Larson's ego enjoyed the moment as he and his attractive aide followed a stylish uniformed escort leading the way to a guarded conference room.

The conference room was plush. A busy full bar with two bartenders and banquet tables filled with an appetizing array of finger foods and desserts, while a string quartet filled the room with soft, comforting music. Larson, with JoAnne Burns holding his arm, entered. His glance estimated there were twenty-five plus guests already gathered. He was among the last to arrive. This added to his enjoyment as the others took notice. He accepted two glasses of champagne from a shapely waitress with a tray of drinks. He gave one to Joanne.

"Please go and mingle," Larson encouraged with a whisper.

It was her first visit to the Big Ten, and she was awed. Joanne moved away to do Larson's bidding.

Larson sipped his champagne while looking for the familiar faces of other GMs who could help with the big-ticket items which needed the cooperation of nearly every casino on the Strip, including the Formula 1 Las Vegas Grand Prix, the Monster Jam, and the National Rodeo Finals. They all meant millions of dollars, which meant pushing aside competition while seeking much-needed coordination and cooperation. He was still skimming faces when he saw her. He coughed in his drink and spilled some from the glass.

Across the room, standing with a cluster of Las Vegas movers and shakers, was the tall, Black, and beautiful Charlotte Johnson. She looked even more gorgeous than he remembered. Larson stared as his heart raced. What the hell was she doing here? He downed the remainder of his drink, gave the glass to a passing server, took a deep breath, gathered his composure, and gave in to his impulse. He crossed to where Charlotte stood.

"Charlotte," Larson said in what he hoped was a friendly tone as he reached her and the trio of men standing with her. Larson recognized them all. The GMs of the Cosmopolitan, the MGM Grand and Caesars Palace. He offered all a nod as he reached out to take Charlotte's arm.

"If I may please have a moment?" he asked her.

Charlotte's eyes found Larson's. If she was surprised, she hid it well. She glanced at the hand on her arm. He withdrew it. Waiting, hoping, not breathing. Charlotte offered a smile to the trio of men. "Gentlemen, please excuse me."

The two stepped a few feet away. Several in the trio gave Larson *go-to-hell* looks. Larson wet his lips and hoped he could find the words. Charlotte maintained and waited. Seconds dragged by.

"I don't know what to say other than fate put us here," Larson said quietly with effort. The persona of strength he had marching into the room was gone. He felt powerless. "I've been fucking miserable without you."

"Watch the language," Charlotte cautioned with a forced smile.

"Charlotte, I love you. Marry me. Please?"

Charlotte's hand went to her heart as she stiffened with shock. "What…"

Larson ignored looks from the trio standing nearby, reading their body language.

"I'll get a divorce. I'll move into our condo. I have nothing without you. I need you, Charlotte like I need my next breath. Please, forgive me. Come home."

Charlotte's eyes filled with tears. "You bastard," she whispered, reaching out carefully to touch his hand. Larson gave in to it. He pulled Charlotte into his arms.

"Come home, please," he whispered to her neck and then taking her face in his hands, he kissed her. Charlotte's arms went around Larson's shoulders as she surrendered to the kiss. One of her legs lifted into the air. A heeled shoe fell away.

At first, those in the room stared in shock. The quartet fell silent. Larson and Charlotte, still locked in an embrace, were unaware of any of it. First, there was an approving cheer from the GM of Mandalay Bay and then the other cheers followed, giving way to a solid round of applause. The movers and shakers were there for important business, but love came first, and they were seeing it.

EIGHTEEN

WHAT GOES AROUND

LEAVING SURVEILLANCE, Luke found he was hungry. He remembered watching the blue-shirted man from Southern Nevada Mineral Merchants eat his burger at the Red Rooster. The employee cafeteria was open twenty-four-seven. He had a hamburger cooked well with bacon and cheese. He headed for an employee elevator.

Luke shared his elevator ride with a server returning from a guest room delivery who bragged about his twenty-dollar tip. Luke smiled along with an engineer carrying a new toilet seat, and two housekeepers with a pushcart loaded with soiled sheets. All got off on the bottom floor.

Luke remembered a tip he received from an old, Black homeowner in south LA after he spent an hour chasing a kitten around a crowded, dusty attic. It was a five-dollar bill. Luke had accepted after much protest. He smiled remembering it. He reminded himself he was living in a city fueled by tips. He heard the valet staff at the Palace earned almost a hundred thousand a year in addition to their salaries. There was a fine line between tips and extortion. Luke was glad he'd discovered Dan Payne's scheme and put out his memo prohibiting forced collections for security services. The smell of the cafeteria reached him, putting an end to all his thoughts except the hamburger.

After capturing his hamburger with fries and a Diet Coke from the buffet line, Luke looked for a table in the busy dining room. He saw only one seat vacant, and it was next to James Bergman, the HR director with whom he'd clashed earlier in the day.

Well, screw it, he thought. He was tired, and his burger was getting cold.

Luke worked his way through the maze of tables to Bergman's table.

"Anybody sitting here?" he asked.

"No," Berman answered. He gave a forced short-lived smile.

"Thanks." Luke sat down. Uncertain what to say, he took a bite from his burger. He was taking a second bite, when he decided he had to say something. His conscience decided for him. He had been wrong when they had their confrontation, and he knew it.

"Earlier today, we talked about being gay," Luke said after he swallowed.

Berman took a swallow from his iced drink before answering, "Yes, I hadn't forgotten." His tone was almost a challenge.

"So, after our meeting I went out in the world on business and a big bodybuilder guy accused me of being gay."

Berman smiled. "And how did that feel?"

"Awkward and embarrassing," Luke confessed,

sampling his french fries. "Didn't matter if it was true or not."

"Been there, done that," Bergman admitted.

"It reminded me of our meeting this morning. If my words were insulting, I owe you an apology. I'm sorry."

"That's kind of you," Bergman said, looking at Luke. Luke read the surprising sincerity in the tone.

"So, can we start over?" Luke asked, pushing a french fry in his mouth. "Can we say all is well between security and HR?"

"Well," Bergman said, pushing back in his chair to look around at the other diners to ensure they weren't listening, "There is some other business we have to deal with."

"I'm listening," Luke said, taking another bite from his burger.

"Dan Payne came in midmorning."

Luke stopped chewing and looked at Bergman. He wasn't happy with what he was being told.

Bergman continued. "He filed an appeal for his dismissal. He's claiming you fired him unfairly for a policy established by your predecessor, Blake Mancini." Bergman's tone was businesslike.

"He wants to come back?" Luke questioned after a look at his half-eaten burger.

"He didn't say. I think he's after cash. Damages. Big dollars and a clean resume to take with him."

"He's a prick. He collected extortion money from casino staff as well as a whore after I told him no more. He's a piece of…well, he deserved being fired."

"Right or wrong, policy dictates he has a right to appeal, and the right to a hearing."

"What kind of a hearing," Luke questioned, taking another bite.

"Since the basis for his dismissal is monetary, his hearing, which has yet to be scheduled, will be heard by the GM, myself, and you since you were his supervisor. Plus, since it involves alleged extortion, the head of cash operations, Caroline Summers, also needs to be there."

"Alleged extortion," Luke said in disbelief. He wondered if Bergman knew of the relationship Dan Payne had with Caroline Summers. Could he know about the stolen gold?

Bergman read the concern on Luke's face. "Don't worry," he said, taking his glasses from an inside pocket to slip them on. "The hearing will be fair."

"This guy is dirty," Luke said. He decided Berman didn't know about the missing gold.

"Again, back to policy," Bergman said, adjusting his glasses. "I can't discuss the details of the appeal with you, but you can be assured it will be fair and impartial."

"And who makes the call?" Luke asked. His anxiety was showing.

"Majority rule," Bergman answered. "After the hearing, the GM, Caroline Summers, and I will discuss the facts in private, and then vote,"

Luke pushed back in his chair. The words were troubling. Did Bergman know about the GM and Charlotte Johnson? Did he know he saw Dan Payne come out of Caroline Summer's house? His role as director of security was becoming a complex web of lies. He could feel his authority and power slipping away.

"I'll send you official notice of the hearing," Bergman added carefully, reading Luke's mood. "It will come as an email as well as an official in-house written notice."

Luke nodded his understanding. "I'm glad I sat down with you."

Bergman raised his hand and took off his glasses. "I

saw you come in. I wondered if you would come over here. I'm sorry I mentioned Dan Payne, but if I didn't, it would be more difficult later. I didn't want you to think I was sandbagging you."

"I'm glad I did," Luke said, hoping it sounded sincere. He pushed at the leftover french fries on his plate. "Dan Payne is my problem, not yours. I'll be glad to fill in the blanks for you."

Bergman nodded appreciation. "This morning we talked about your move. Is the young lady still joining you? I got clarification on the protocol and costs," Berman said as he stood and picked up his tray.

"Unfortunately, no," Luke said. "She got a promotion and is staying at Wild River for a while."

"Well, we'll do what we can to make your move comfortable. Have a good day." Bergman smiled and turned to walk away.

"Thanks," Luke called after him. Then he looked at the remains of his hamburger and fries. He was no longer hungry. The day sucked.

Dumping his tray, Luke tried looking ahead. He had to make a plan. Maybe he could make Dan Payne late for his hearing. He decided to stake out Caroline Summers's house when it got dark, and this time, he'd film the sono-fabitch. But would that help? It could turn on him if it looked like revenge.

Payne was no longer an employee when he saw him, and how the hell could Greg Larson judge him when he was guilty of the same fucking thing. Luke could feel the walls closing in on him as he walked to the employee elevator.

On the elevator, two room-service employees talked and joked in the midst of the usual cluster of Hispanic Housekeepers, and two front desk agents. Luke paid little attention to any of it until he heard Greg Larson's title mentioned. It was one of the room servers.

"Yeah, the GM kissed her. Our GM. Right in front of everyone. His ass is toast." The two men laughed while everyone on the elevator listened.

"A couple days ago she was the boss in HR. Charlotte Johnson. Good-looking woman. Black."

"Who said this is true?"

"Friend of mine. He's a barkeep over there."

"So, did they get a room?"

They laughed again. A couple of the housekeepers whispered to each other in Spanish. Luke listened for more.

"He's a GM. Nobody will do anything."

"Yeah, well, my money says we get a new one."

The two servers got off when the elevator made its first stop. The security officer pushed through the housekeepers to follow them. "Hey, guys, wait up."

The doors closed, and Luke wished he had followed them. What had they heard, and from who? The elevator resumed its climb. Two more stops, and Luke was alone. He considered calling Larson, but what would he say or ask.

He wanted answers. What he heard worried him. What the hell had Greg Larson done? Maybe it was just gossip. Employee gossip paved the streets of the Strip. Once in his suite, Luke tossed his jacket to a chair and dialed Surveillance on his cell. Gayle Turner answered. "Gayle, it's Luke, have you heard the rumor?" he questioned, walking to his bedroom.

"Rumor," Gayle answered in a businesslike tone. "Who needs a rumor? Surveillance at the Bellagio sent us a video."

"A video! What's on it?" Luke questioned apprehensively.

"Greg Larson and Charlotte Johnson, kissing like they were at the prom."

"At the Big Ten meeting?" Luke said in disbelief.

"The one and only."

"What happened afterward? Did they stay there or…"

"After the kiss, and it was an impressive one, the GM took Charlotte's hand, and they walked out."

"Where is he now?" Luke questioned.

"We've been looking. Waiting on him, maybe them, to come back. He hasn't. Surveillance at Bellagio tells me they left in a cab."

"A cab."

"Now you know as much as we do."

"I heard talk on the elevator."

"Color that talk true."

"You'll keep me informed. I need to know when he returns."

"Bet on it."

"Anything from our Asian duo looking at the gold merchant?"

"They're still in their closet looking. Nothing yet."

"Thanks, Gayle."

Luke tossed his cell phone and collapsed on the bed. He smiled with a thought of admiration. Greg Larson obviously had balls. More than balls, he obviously had made a choice. Demonstrating his love for Charlotte Johnson in public erased all the rumors and suspicions. Seemed he not only loved this woman, he'd just shown the world he didn't care who knew. It was good news and bad news. News of his public declaration was sure to reach the investors. What would the Chinese think of love? He wasn't sure. He knew they liked women. Especially Vegas women. Women and missing gold. Greg Larson and Charlotte Johnson may have had their moment. Luke hoped it wasn't the end for both. He was silently wishing them well when the bedside telephone rang. Gayle was calling with news on the GM. Luke rolled on the bed and had it in hand on the third ring, "This is Micthell."

"Mister Director, this is Candice Harmon. Remember me? I'm one of those who works all day to make your life easier."

Luke remembered the woman from surveillance—blonde hair, attractive, and a firm handshake. He swung his feet to the floor. "It's been one of those days, Candice. What's up?" He was disappointed it wasn't news on the GM.

"Gayle told me you were looking for a place. Well, I've found it. You wanna go for a ride? Take maybe an hour at the most."

Luke rubbed his eyes and looked at the shadows gathering in the plush suite. Although comfortable, it was large, and it was empty, "Why don't you give me the listing? I'll take a look at it on the net."

"On the net," Candice's friendly voice mocked. "Have you tried online dating? Trust me, online listings are worse. This place just came on the market. In Vegas, that means it will be there as long as your money would be on a sure bet. Either you like housekeeping talking about the aftershave you wear or not. Come on, we're talking about going outside. It's a beautiful day in the neighborhood."

Luke warmed to the friendly tone as well as her skilled sales pitch. He had time. His plan was to go back to Caroline Summers's house after dark thirty with the hope of finding Dan Payne there again," Does house-keeping really talk about me?"

"Do ducks fly south? Come on. I'm downstairs at the employee entrance in the yellow Charger.

"How did you know I would do this?" Luke questioned.

"Maybe because you wear Gio. Don't put any on. It drives me nuts."

"All right, ten minutes." Luke smiled. She had made him smile, she had a great voice, she was attractive, and he wanted a home. No, he needed a home. He needed to get out of The Silver Palace. He looked forward to being a slob and not worrying what housekeeping might think or say. Were they really talking? He washed his hands and face, sprayed Gio on his neck and his face and headed for an elevator.

Candice, waiting in the yellow Charger, was easy to find. She was listening to a Taylor Swift CD with the windows down when Luke arrived. She turned off the music as he opened the door to climb in. "Welcome aboard." She smiled as she brought the powerful car to life.

Luke looked at Candice as she pulled the car in gear and drove toward the exit of the underground garage. He wasn't sure he would have recognized her. When he met her in Surveillance, she was attractive but dressed conservatively and businesslike, but now she was a blonde in sunglasses with shaggy hair, a sleeveless button-up blouse revealing the swell of her breasts and a pair of jeans with tears exposing both knees.

"Welcome aboard." She smiled at Luke as he strapped himself in.

"And where is this place I have to see?" Luke questioned as the Challenger's tires screeched on the smooth pavement, turning toward sunlight and an exit.

"Henderson, just a couple miles away," Candice answered, slowing for a stop sign as they emerged onto a busy side street. "Relax, you'll enjoy the drive."

"Henderson," Luke questioned. "Sounds like a guy's name."

Candice glanced at him as they roared into traffic. "No, this Henderson is our sister city. She's big, second to only Vegas but with a small-town heart. You'll like what you see."

They made small talk as Candice wormed her way through the traffic on the Strip until she found a freeway onramp.

Luke learned she was divorced. Who wasn't in Vegas. The mother of a twelve-year-old who moved to Vegas from Orange County, California where she could no longer afford to live. Once in Vegas she found work as a waitress, then more money as a model in a clothing store at the Wynn. It was there she met Gayle Turner. "I helped her find a pair of jeans," Candice explained," and she helped me find a job in slots at The Silver Palace. The tips were good, and I learned more than you want to know about slots. I worked there until Gayle invited me into surveillance. I knew I'd found a home. You can learn a lot from watching people. I didn't know what I had been doing all my life. What about you, Luke Mitchel? Who are you."

Luke admitted he was also divorced, as well as the father of a twelve-year-old. "I send her money and I remember her birthday." The confession made him feel guilty.

"Do you see her?" Candice questioned, passing several trucks.

"I lived in a doubled-wide on the river down in Alta Vista. Brought her out a couple times," Luke explained. "She seemed bored. It was awkward. She talked about her mom and stepdad. He's a cop in LA. Living in a suite at the Palace has made it difficult to invite her up here."

"We might just solve that problem today. You get along with your ex," Candice probed.

"If the question is, did I want the divorce," Luke answered, "it solved the problem at the time, and no, it's none of your business if I'm seeing anyone now."

"You know we see your every move at the Palace, don't you?" Candice countered with a smile.

"I haven't forgotten where you work," Luke added with a smile. He liked her perfume as well as her car and jeans. She was a subordinate, and he wasn't totally comfortable with that.

"I got into this reality thing through a guy I dated a couple of years ago. He told me what he was earning in commissions. I got rid of him and started studying. Now, I'm a licensed realtor in the great State of Nevada. The extra dollars are nice, plus, when I meet someone, I don't have to say I work surveillance. I'm a realtor."

"Your cover fits you nicely," Luke agreed.

They exited the freeway at Eastern avenue. Luke studied the passing neighborhood. It was a mix of gas stations, retail, and tract of comfortable-looking homes. Not so different than what he had seen of Vegas earlier in the day.

"Welcome to Green Valley," Candice announced as she followed several major streets and then turned into a neighborhood near a sprawling grassy park with mature trees. The desert was hidden. Luke made a mental note of that. He liked what he was seeing although he didn't allow himself to forget he was riding with a realtor.

Candice slowed the Challenger and pulled into a drive behind a two-story building. "Welcome to Valley Crest Condominiums," Candice said, pulling into a parking space between other cars. "Don't worry, we're coming in the backdoor."

They followed a gated sidewalk leading to an inner court. In its center was a large, contoured pool with blue water surrounded by a sprawling green lawn and towering palms. Luke saw several tanned couples lounging beside the pool beneath the shade of umbrellas.

"We're going upstairs," Candice announced quietly. Luke followed, looking around. He spotted two tanned, shapely women near the pool.

"There's a nice workout room on the first level," Candice said as they climbed the stairs to the second floor. There, she paused in front of a door and punched numbers into a lockbox hanging on the doorknob. Gathering a key, she unlocked the door, and stood aside, gesturing Luke inside, "Welcome home." She smiled.

Luke's first impression was comfort. There was a cushioned sectional coach greeting him. Two recliners added to the allure. A large flat-screen TV was positioned to accommodate the sitting. Decorative lamps, wall décor, and a glass coffee table decorated with a flower arrangement brought a smile to Luke's face. The living area fronted a dining table with chairs, which opened to a kitchen beyond.

"Check out your balcony. I've heard you like them."

Luke walked to the living room glass slider, unlocked it, and stepped onto the balcony into the afternoon heat. There were two comfortable chairs with a table between them and a Bar-B-Que oven. Luke looked at the view. The pool surrounded by its deck and the swath of grass made it inviting.

"Two bedrooms, and the master has an en suite," Candice advised as she led the way to the bedrooms. The master had a king-size bed with inviting pillows and a spread as well as two bedside tables with lamps and a comfortable chair near the window. Another wall-mounted flat-screen added to the masculine theme. Luke looked into the bathroom. It had both a tub and shower. Candice leaned on the doorway, waiting as Luke opened the door to a large walk-in closet.

Closing the closet door, he looked to Candice. "We talked a lot coming down here, but we didn't talk price."

"The property is listed at $435,000. I recommend offering another ten or fifteen thousand to blunt other offers, and there will be others."

"That's a lot of money," Luke said as he followed Candice back to the living room.

Candice sat on the sectional coach as Luke looked around the kitchen, opening the dishwasher, the microwave, and the refrigerator.

"Did I mention it comes completely furnished with assigned covered parking for two."

"That doesn't sound free," Luke said, returning to the living room to sit down in one of the recliners facing Candice.

"HOA, homeowners Association, costs $210 a month. Included in that is the pool, the gym, a sauna, parking, and all outside maintenance. You won't have to worry about mowing the lawn or cleaning the pool. All you have to do is move in."

"If I wanted this how long before I get a key?"

"Depends, we'll have to verify employment, income, how much you want to put down, and find a lender. If you're interested, your title and position have weight. I suggest we put up impressive earnest money, and propose a rent to own. That we could do it in a matter of days instead of weeks."

Luke looked around the living room again. He tried the recliner. It folded back comfortably. He straightened the chair and gave Candice a sober look. "Okay, it fits. Make it happen."

Luke was quiet on their drive back to the Strip. He was apprehensive about his decision, but he had followed his gut. It had worked for him in the past. He hoped it would this time. They were on the freeway when he asked, "How did you know it was a fit? I've only seen you two or three times."

"I work surveillance," Candice said with a glance and a smile.

"And as my realtor, how do I thank you?" Luke questioned.

"My three percent will cover it," Candice answered.

"Can we add a dinner for two?" Luke questioned with his eyes closed, head back on the seat cushion, enjoying the hum of the tires on the freeway.

"Thought you'd never ask." Candice smiled.

NINETEEN
A KISS IS JUST...

THE CAB TOOK the infamous couple to their condo where they sat, uncomfortable, awkward, uncertain what to say, and how to get back to the real world. Greg Larson tried alcohol. He was on his second Bloody Mary. Alcohol didn't help. Neither did staring into his glass, but that's what he was doing as Charlotte Johnson paced from kitchen to bedroom to living room, again and again, with her arms folded over her breasts. Finally, she said, "You know calling me would have been a little more subtle. I just got that job."

"I agree," Larson admitted, shaking the ice in his glass, "I didn't know you'd be there."

"So, you see me and decide to just flat out, come take me by the arm, and kiss me in front of a gathering of some of the most powerful men in Vegas."

"I think I remember you returning the kiss."

"Okay," Charlotte agreed sitting down in a chair facing Larson, "so the world now knows it's more than a rumor. We're lovers. What's next?"

"Wanna move to Europe, South America? I've got a couple bucks."

"I like Vegas. This is home. I just became the rooms director at one of the busiest resorts in the city…at least until you decided to play kiss and tell."

"Charlotte, I'm not sorry." Larson reached to take her hands. She gripped his and offered a smile.

"Me either," she confessed. "But what's next? What do we do?"

Larson released her hand, finished his drink, and looked into her eyes. "I do love you."

Charlotte returned his look. "But there is tomorrow. Since we missed the meeting, what do we do. I hope they made notes."

Larson got up to mix himself another drink. "Wasn't the shouts and applause a surprise?"

"Yes, but then."

"Then we do what we have to do," Larson said returning to sit down across from Charlotte without his drink. "I'm still the General Manager at The Silver Palace. You're still the Rooms Director at the Cosmo. No one's taken that from us. We're two people in love. You used to work at the Palace but now you're at the Cosmo. No problem there. I'm married but that's hardly a first in this town. I'll tell my wife today. I'll get a divorce, we'll move in here. What the hell can they say, we shouldn't have fallen in love. Sad day for them. Babe, all we have to do is go on, together."

Charlotte studied Larson for a moment and then literally lunged at him. "It's my turn," she said before kissing him passionately as they fell back onto the coach, wrapped in one another's arms.

———

LUKE MITCHEL RETURNED to his suite full of hope. Candice had given it to him. A good-looking blonde, a flirt, a surveillance professional who worked for him, but she also had a real estate license. Luck, chance, fate— they were all talked about in Vegas. Now he was swimming in the middle of them of them, and they felt good. He would soon sign away his financial well-being to become the owner of a condo worth nearly a half million dollars. At least, he hoped it was worth it. It seemed a staggering amount, but the nighttime drop in the casino was higher. He reasoned he was making a bet. He was betting he could do it, and he was betting it was the right thing to do, and he was betting he'd be happy there. He looked around his suite. His view of the Strip was worth a fortune. The furnishings were the stuff of dreams. Housekeepers and Servers added to the ambiance. Few could afford an extended stay, but he had lived there free. Why was it then he wanted out. In Luke's mind, it was simple. It didn't fit. It was like looking at one of the scantily clad beautiful showgirls. They were great to look at, but don't touch.

Every morning in his suite, Luke would straighten his pillows and bed, make sure the bathroom was clean, flush the toilet, gather trash from the living room, put all his clothes on hangers and make sure his shoes were in the closet. He learned it was all futile. His clothes may be neat hanging in the closet, but they now talked about the cologne he wore. He wasn't a guest, he was a transient employee. *Was*, was the word Luke clung to. He was soon out of there. His hope was invested in Candice Harmon, a surveillance officer-slash-realtor, who could not only see things with cameras but also had an intuitive feminine ability to read character and personality like a book. Somehow, this blonde in faded knee-less jeans had known what he wanted. If that was true, she knew what he really wanted when he invited her to dinner, and it was to be much more than fine dining. Luke cautioned himself about going down a path Greg Larson had chosen, only to find himself in quicksand. He thought himself smarter than that, but Candice was a good-looking girl, and he hoped maybe she might provide him more than a key.

Slouching in a living room chair, Luke watched the last rays of sunshine cast long shadows over the towering facades of the Strip. Plan A was back to Caroline Summer's home when it got dark. He had two thoughts haunting him. Should he call Barbara and ask how she was doing with her new responsibilities, and second, where the hell was Greg Larson, their GM. Leaving the Bellagio hours ago, in a cab with Charlotte Johnson, after they kissed for all the world to see, they had simply disappeared. Luke had Larson's private cell number, but their kiss had *do not disturb* written all over it. He fell asleep in the chair, wondering if Candice's tits were really bigger than Barbara's.

———

NAOME LARSON WAS in her backyard herb garden when her Rottweiler began barking. The dog bolted to a wrought iron gate beside the garage. Naome emptied her watering can and followed after the dog. Given the time of day, she thought a car in the driveway meant her daughter and boyfriend were arriving. She had talked to her daughter about her relationship with Doug, a junior at UNLV. He was five years older, and they had been dating for nearly three months. Had they become inti-mate? Did the sun set in the west? They had been gone all day. Red Rock Canyon Doug announced when they left, but Naome didn't believe him.

Naome was surprised to find the car in the driveway was a cab. She was more surprised to find her husband climbing out of it.

"Greg, are you all right," she called, pushing through the gate as the cab pulled away.

The Rottweiler bolted to Greg Lawson and jumped at him. "Hello, Sparky." Then, with a look to Naome he said, "We need to talk."

His sober tone and expression, coupled with an arrival by cab, chilled her. "Greg, you haven't lost your job?"

"No, such luck. Now, where do you want to talk?"

"The kitchen," Naome said, leading the way. She was worried. She could read her husband's moods, and this wasn't a good one.

Naome went to the kitchen sink to wash her hands while Larson sat down at a breakfast nook.

"Coming home in a cab tells me you're not bringing good news."

"Depends on your point of view," Larson suggested.

"And what's your point of view, Greg?" Naome questioned, as she dried her hands on a towel. Her apprehension was turning to annoyance. She was eight years younger than Larson, an attractive Burnett and former blackjack dealer. They had met at Caesar's Palace where Larson was once the assistant manager. They had shared good times and bad. Naome was an asset when it came to sharing her husband's business persona. She was a trophy when relating to investors at The Silver Palace, the employee appreciation party, and the seemingly endless string of *dress-up and drink* events Vegas presented, but Naome was savvy enough to know things were not well. They hadn't been in years. Without comment, they had parted directions. Greg's hours at work grew longer. His absence, not coming home some nights, was explained as a necessity to know and be part of the business at all hours. As the nighttime absences increased, their sex life decreased. Naome wasn't stupid, but the money was good. She drove a Rolls Royce, lived in a house worth millions, enjoyed being a member at Las Vegas's top Country Club, and she had finished tennis lessons with Andre Agassi at the Red Rock Tennis Club. She bought what she wanted when she wanted.

Other than having a sixteen-year-old as a daughter, life was good. She hoped her husband wasn't about to fuck it all up.

"We've been together a long time, Greg," Naome said, leaning her back against the kitchen sink and folding her arms. "Let's not play twenty questions. Why did you come home in a cab."

Greg nodded agreement. If this woman could read him, he could read her. He had, and she wanted answers. Money usually solved most problems in Las Vegas, and he was about to put money on the table. "I want a divorce," he said soberly. "You can have the house, your Rolls, and half of what we have in savings. It's a lot. I'll pay for Raquel's education as well as a monthly allowance. I'll give you sixty-five hundred a month in alimony unless you fuck with me. Do that, and I'll see you in court every month for the next five years."

Naome stiffened her stance as she listened to the words. She was silent as she studied her husband. Her arms were still folded as she answered angrily. "Fuck you, Greg. I saw this train coming down the tracks a long time ago."

"Is that a yes, or a no?"

"That's a no," Naome said, tightening her folded arms. "Screw your sixty-five hundred a month. I want eighty-five hundred, the house and everything in it, my car, Raquel's support, her education, and you can walk away."

"Done," Larson answered without hesitation. "But I've got a lot of things here I want."

"Take what you want. Like I give a shit if you can't get it all. It will be in the garage when you come back."

The Rottweiler came in, wagged its tail, circled, and laid down at Naome's feet.

"You've thought about this haven't you?" Larson questioned.

"Screw you, Greg, you heard what I want," Naome answered soberly.

"You'll tell our daughter?"

"You no longer have a right to tell me what to do," Naome cautioned.

Larson nodded agreement as he pushed up out of his chair. He stood for a moment, looking at Naome, the woman he had shared so many years with. The bond between them was gone. It felt monumental, large, life-changing. It was too easy. The words had been said, the lines drawn. Now, it was no longer a marriage, it had dissolved into a financial agreement. Larson had expected shock, sadness, tears. There were none. It seemed he was not the only one who knew they were living in a house divided.

"I'll get some things together and call a cab."

Naome marched to the kitchen door, opened it, and went out, slamming the door behind her. Larson did not see her tears. The Rottweiler got up, looked at Larson and then crossed to a doggie door, pushed it open to follow after Naome.

Larson bit a lip until pain stopped him. He looked

around the kitchen. It was empty. He felt much the same. He drew in a breath and headed for the master bedroom.

———

WHEN LUKE MITCHEL AWOKE, the bright digital lighting and the flashing videos from the Strip were illuminating his suite. He pushed out of his chair, stretched, yawned, and turned on several lights. It was dark, and it was time to go to work. He hoped the prick Dan Payne would cooperate and be at Caroline Summers's house. He considered dinner but that could wait until he got back. He was curious about the IT team in surveillance. He dialed surveillance on his cell, knowing if they had made any progress, Gayle Turner would have called him. He was surprised by the voice that answered.

"Surveillance, this is Harmond."

"Candice, it's Luke. What are you doing?"

"I'm working. Remember, this is my real job."

"Showing me the condo could have waited until you had a day off."

"That's not regret speaking, is it?" Candice questioned.

"No, no regrets, thanks for taking me to Green Valley. Have you got me a key yet?"

"Not yet." Candice smiled. "Be patient."

"Speaking of patience, how's the IT team doing?"

"They're still in their closet. One of them, I can't tell them apart, came out when they had food delivered a while ago. He didn't speak."

"Okay, just checking. I'll be off property for a while, but if they…"

"Got it," Candice assured, "call you with any news. Don't worry, I got your number."

Her confidence made Luke smile. "Thanks. Give you a head's up when I'm home."

"Bye."

Luke collected a can of Diet Coke from his fridge to take with him and moved for the door. He was stepping out when he heard a guest door close on the other side of the wide, carpeted hallway. He glanced, expecting to see a guest. He was surprised. She was blonde, busty, and attractive and they had met her at the bar in the card room several nights before. He remembered her name was Pam. She was the woman Dan Payne collected extortion money from. Luke knew she was more than a guest. The blonde walked toward him, moving for the elevator at the end of the hall. She returned Luke's look and smiled.

"Pam, if I remember right," Luke said as she reached him.

The blonde paused, remembering him. "And you were, well, you know."

Luke looked at her. She was dressed sexy in a short skirt and heels. "I'm betting that room isn't in your name."

"Save your bet for downstairs," the blonde suggested, turning to move on.

Luke took her by the arm. She paused, looked to him, and he said, "The other night you told me you were an escort. Looks like you've graduated to something else."

The blonde sobered and pulled her arm away from Luke.

"I know that's not your room," Luke continued, not liking his words, but knowing they had to be said. "I can check and see how long you were there. While I do that, you're going to get on the elevator, go downstairs, and get out of our hotel. You're no longer welcome in The Silver Palace. Do you understand me?"

The blonde studied Luke's sober face. She adjusted the bag on her shoulder and moved on for the elevator. Luke watched as the car arrived. The doors parted and the blonde stepped on. She and Luke exchanged a final sober look as the doors closed.

Thoughts of the girl haunted Luke as he drove from the underground parking lot onto the crowded, busy Strip. He didn't like the accusation he made. The blonde he met in the bar was attractive and witty. He enjoyed talking with her. He was disappointed to discover she was more than an escort. She was a whore. Whores were a problem. Prostitution in Clark County was illegal. That didn't mean it didn't happen, it just meant it was illegal. Why? Because prostitutes wanted money. Lots of it. Money they usually shared with a pimp. Pimps encouraged their girls to get all the money they could, anyway they could. Rings, watches, wallets, cell phones and anything else that could be hocked or used to blackmail a wayward married client from Fort Payne. It was an ugly business and Luke felt sorry Pam was part of it. He'd call surveillance later and have them pull the tape on his meeting with her. Her face would soon be joining others who were banned from The Silver Palace.

The Strip was its usual self. Full of slow-moving cars, inching from one red light to the next, block to block. The sidewalks were filled with voices and smiling faces, cell phones held high, drinking beer, waving, smoking joints, with their jeans hanging low while looking at the light show they could not believe. Luke knew them, hell, he'd been one of them. They were refugees, running from somewhere to something in Vegas. There they would have fun, there they would gamble and lose.

There, for a fleeting moment they could live, have fun, laugh with strangers, get lost in the crowd, and pretend they were someone else, and for the moment, Luke was there, among them.

GPS on his cell provided Luke with a feminine voice telling him when to turn and how far it was to the next intersection. He was glad to leave the glowing, busy nighttime Strip behind as he climbed the shadowy night-time streets into the estates of Mountain Shadows. The voice on his cell told him he was now six blocks from his destination. Luke thought about what might be found at Caroline Summer's house. Even with the chance Dan Payne's car might be in her driveway didn't prove a fucking thing. Facts were scarce. All he had was the fact they bought gold bricks with management's approval. The fact Dan Payne might be screwing Caroline Summers was just a suspicion and didn't prove shit. He needed more. Maybe it was frustration. What a fucked-up day. Barbara hadn't called. A bouncer thought he was gay, Candice Harmon called, and now he was buying a condo in Green Valley for nearly a half million dollars, and Pam, or whatever the hell her name was, turned out to be a whore.

"You have arrived at your destination," the feminine voice on Luke's cell phone announced. "Your destination is on your left." Luke slowed and looked. Dan Payne's black BMW sat parked in front of Caroline Summers's garage, basking in the light from a towering lamppost. Luke drove by slowly, smiling. He went to the end of the block, turned around, and returned. This time he drove slower, passenger window down, cell phone camera recording, aimed at the parked BMW. Luke made sure his video shot was wide enough to show it was at Caroline's home. He imagined walking to Caroline's front door and ringing the bell. When she opened the door, he would say, "Got you." But none of it was going to be so easy. Luke drove away with a smile on his face. Crooks always made mistakes and when they did, he'd be waiting.

Luke drove back to The Silver Palace. He considered going to his suite, but the idea reminded him how big and empty it was and how lonely he felt there. He decided surveillance was a better choice. There, he would be closer to the IT team and Candice Harmon who was working the PM watch. She seemed surprised when he arrived.

"Going to hang for a while if you don't mind," Luke said, announcing his intent. He sat down in one of two chairs at the watch commander's desk flanked by a row of monitors with live-rolling video shots from locations in The Silver Palace.

Luke sat and watched the big monitors in surveillance's main room. Candice had a team of five on duty. All were scanning monitors, watching dealers, chefs, guests, slots, twenty-one, sports book, a growing line for the showroom, and more. If casinos had taught Luke anything, it was, *a picture was worth a thousand words*. Video didn't lie. It presented facts. All you had to do was know what you were looking at. Cheats were good. Surveillance was better.

"Gayle mentioned the surveillance team at Bellagio sent over images from the Big Ten meeting," Luke questioned.

"You mean the one where our GM stuck his tongue down Charlotte Johnson's throat." Candice smiled.

"Yeah, that one."

"Gayle showed it to me. After we looked at it, we locked it up."

"I need to see it," Luke said soberly. "Everyone's talking about it. I need truth. Not gossip."

Candice gathered a set of keys from her belt and unlocked the desk she sat at. She opened a drawer and lifted out a CD. She pushed out of her chair and shoved the CD into a player beneath the monitor in front of Luke. "Fasten your seat belt," she warned.

Luke pressed the play button and watched the video in silence. He was silent until one of the GMs shouted and the applause began. Luke smiled and pushed the stop button. "You and Gayle have seen it. Anybody else?"

"Not that I know of."

"Good," Luke said, ejecting the CD from the player. He pushed it into an inside pocket. "Tell Gayle I have it, and we don't talk about it, with anyone. Agreed."

"Agreed," Candice answered. "Why do you think he did this," she added soberly.

"I think the GM is in love," Luke answered. "You know Charlotte walked out. I heard she signed on at the Cosmo as rooms director. After their kiss in front of the world, they rode away together in a cab. Key phrase there is, *together*."

"Do you think he'll survive this," Candice questioned soberly.

"Above my pay grade," Luke answered, wondering where Larson and Charlotte were. Mancini's attempt at blackmail revealed the GM and Charlotte had a condo somewhere. That was information he wasn't about to share with Candice or anyone else. He and Jackie Fallon, Larson's assistant, had heard what had to be a lover's quarrel, an exchange where they heard only a few words, loud profanities, and then Charlotte's angry departure. It was obvious Greg Larson's kiss was an announcement to the world that he loved the woman.

The clock was ticking. The time was coming, and he now had the pictures.

Luke considered knocking on the door of the closet where the IT duo was working, but he knew he shouldn't. Either they would work their magic, or he would have to reach out to the police and give them what he had. The police had more tools, but going to them was an admission he couldn't do it. The thought made Luke even more determined, but fate had put the gold thieves in the hands of two young Japanese men who had been locked in their fucking closet now for hours. Didn't these guys need to piss, talk to someone, see what day it was?

It was almost ten when Candice suggested dinner. Twenty minutes later, a server showed up with a push-cart and dinner for seven. There were hamburgers, pizza, and tacos, along with pastries for dessert. The server was tipped and sent away. Luke wondered if the Asian duo in the IT closet would think if they saw the feast that was going on, a feast they weren't invited to. Candice assured him the IT team didn't care. Their door was closed because they didn't want people in there.

Luke decided at twenty-three hundred, he was going to his room and go to bed. At least that was his plan after one more piece of pizza. Gayle Turner's arrival changed all that.

"What are you doing here?" Candice asked when Gayle arrived.

"What do you mean?" Gayle answered. "Didn't they tell you? The IT guys called me at home when they found it."

Luke bolted to his feet. "What!" He quickly connected the dots. "Who called you?" he questioned.

"Riku called me," the puzzled Gayle answered. "He

said they found Payne carrying bullion back to the gold merchant."

Luke bolted from the surveillance office to the closet where the two IT men were hidden. Reaching the door, Luke twisted the knob and found it locked. Gayle and Candice were at his side. Luke pounded on the door with an open palm. "Unlock the fucking door!" he shouted.

TWENTY
GLOD IS A FOUR-LETTER WORD

A MOMENT after Luke pounded on the door of the IT closet, a shocked-looking Haruto opened it. Luke pushed by him. "What did you find."

"Sorry," Haruto said. His words were lost as Luke, Gayle, and Candice crowded into the small, dim room where Riku, the other IT specialist, sat at a desk with four video screens and a keyboard.

"Tell me what you have," Luke ordered impatiently.

"We didn't know you were here," Riku apologized, scanning their faces. The two men and three women from the PM surveillance watch crowded the doorway behind the others.

The frustrated Luke looked to Gayle. "Gayle, talk to them. Tell them to lay it out."

"Riku," Gayle said to the worried-looking youth, "tell us what you found."

Riku looked to the illuminated screens on the desk. "Using a formula we found on the dark web, we enabled it and used it as a tool to unlock targeted iCloud memories. Then we…"

Luke cut him short. "Just tell us what you've got." It was another order.

Riku pulled the keyboard toward him and typed. "Watch the center screen."

All eyes went to the center video screen as an image appeared. "This was on a Thursday, three months ago."

A collective hush fell over the group crowded into the small room. They watched the screen as a black BMW pulled into a parking lot. Luke's heart raced. He recognized the lot near the Red Rooster. "The time," Haruto added, "is important. It is nearly six in the evening."

On the screen, a black BMW pulled into a parking space. A man got out of the car. Riku froze the image and zoomed in to enlarge the man's face.

"As you can see, this is Daniel Payne." He punched the keyboard, and the action resumed. Dan Payne, in civilian clothes, walked to the rear of the BMW, where he unlocked the trunk and lifted out a brick covered with paper. Riku again stopped the video and zoomed in on the brick Payne held.

"This looks much like the paper-covered gold brick he and Caroline Summers carried from the office of The Southern Nevada Mineral Merchant five hours earlier."

"Yes," Luke said with a clenched fist. He had the bastard.

"Why would he bring the gold back?" Candice questioned.

"Because the man that sold them the gold, five hours earlier, bought it back." Luke smiled, enjoying his conclusion and announcement.

"Yes, that's true," Riku agreed. "We found three different occasions, on three different dates, when this very same thing occurred."

"And we're short three gold bricks," Gayle added.

"Can you put all this on a CD for me?" Luke asked.

"Yes, but there may be issues of video ownership and rights," Haruto cautioned.

"I'll worry about that. You two are fucking genius," Luke said with delight. Pats on the back were made by all as laughter and sighs of relief filled the air in the IT closet.

The surveillance crew went back to work as Gayle, Candice, and Luke sat down with Riku and Haruto for a detailed briefing on the video stolen from the web.

"*Stolen from the web*, is a term we try not to use," Luke cautioned as they began the task of reviewing the images, frame by frame. Luke made detailed notes of dates and times as they watched Dan Payne, now in his lieutenant's uniform, arrive in the same parking lot in an unmarked sedan belonging to The Silver Palace. Caroline Summers was with him.

The two walked toward the building where the office of The Southern Nevada Mineral Merchant was located. Riku fast-forwarded the tape, as Caroline and Payne returned to the car. Payne now carried a package in a shopping bag which he put in the trunk of the car. They climbed in and drove away. Again, Riku hit fastforwarded to find Payne's BMW pulling into the same parking lot. He climbed out, opened his trunk, and lifted out a shopping bag. It was the same bag he had loaded into a different car earlier.

They were to spend hours looking at the tapes the IT crew had captured. Questions were answered, notes were made. Finally, Luke thanked the two men and shook their hands enthusiastically. Luke, along with Gayle and Candice, returned to the surveillance main office where they sat down. They chased away the AM surveillance supervisor and his crew who came on duty several hours earlier.

"Something's bothering you, Luke," Gayle suggested after she read the concern on Luke's face. "You're among friends. What is it?"

Luke looked at the notes in his lap, then to Gayle. "I was a police officer in another life. I know what circumstantial evidence is. It's evidence that paints a picture of guilt, but alone, circumstantial evidence is seldom enough to arrest or convict."

"What more do we need to get this prick?" Candice questioned.

"We need a look inside the Southern Nevada Mineral Merchants' office. We need to see Payne receiving payment. They've got to have cameras in there. Lots of them."

"So, we send the IT team after them again?" Gayle asked.

"Close only counts in horseshoes," Luke suggested.

"They've been in there twenty-four-seven, but I'll talk to them," Gayle said, pushing out of her chair.

"Maybe they could get into Payne's bank accounts. See if he's made any major deposits on or near the day the gold was returned. We're talking close to a hundred and fifty thousand."

"That should be enough to cover their overtime." Gayle smiled, heading for the IT closet.

When Gayle was gone, Candice looked to Luke as she covered a yawn with her hand. "I think I may go home. And you?"

"Thanks for the invitation, but I've got a room here." Luke smiled.

"Not for long, you won't. I hear you may move to Green Valley."

"Is the grass really greener in Green Valley?" Luke questioned.

"You know we'll be neighbors. Well, almost. I live six blocks from there," Candice added.

"You and your twelve-year-old son?"

"No, Jamie lives with his dad out in Boulder. He's a ranger out at Lake Mead."

Gayle returned from the IT team. "I told them to keep looking, Payne's bank accounts, credit debt, whatever they can find. They're on it. They ordered breakfast."

Luke pushed to his feet. "I'm taking the rest of the night off. They find anything—"

"I'll call you," Gayle promised with a glance at the clock. "I'm only a couple hours from the start of my watch. I'll stay."

Candice pushed to her feet. "I'm out of here. Circumstantial evidence says I'm tired. See you all tonight."

Luke followed after her. "Good night, Gayle. I'll be the guy upstairs."

Luke walked with Candice to the back-of-the-house elevators. "It's a good day when you find a place to live," Luke said.

"I'm glad you like it."

"You'll work on getting me in on a rent-to-buy," Luke questioned.

"You willing to write me a check for a non-refundable ten grand? Five for the first month. Five for a security deposit, and five a month until we close."

They reached the elevators. Candice pushed the down button. Luke punched an up button. "I'll write you a check. It will be waiting in surveillance when you come back this afternoon."

Candice's down car arrived. She stepped in as the

doors parted. "Our first date cost you nearly a half mill. Keep up the good work." They exchanged smiles as the elevator doors closed.

———

Six miles away in their condo on South Amblewood Way, Greg Larson and Charlotte Johnson lay in the bed holding one another. The new day was bringing with it an unexpected and unanticipated reality. Neither knew Don Marardino, the GM of the Bellagio, had gone to their surveillance unit after the Big Ten meeting where he looked at the video of Greg Larson kissing Charlotte Johnson. He smiled after looking at it and gave the order, "Erase the tapes. All of them."

"Sorry, boss, we already sent one to The Silver Palace."

Marardino smiled and nodded. "Larson will enjoy seeing it. Just make sure the others go away."

Larson and Charlotte had no way of knowing the GM of the Bellagio had taken action to protect them. They were worried. Sleep was fleeting as the hours passed. Charlotte lay with her head on Larson's shoulder. "I have to leave early. Go home and change clothes before going to work."

"I brought a clean shirt with me. I guess this is home."

"Home is where the heart is," Charlotte whispered, running a nail through the hair on Larson's chest.

"Wanna try Mexico? We could start with something big. You know, sort of an Airbnb or an upscale bed-and-breakfast."

"Sounds like too much work," Charlotte answered. "I'm a Vegas girl."

"Vegas might get really small today," Larson cautioned.

"And you, the big man who never does anything without a plan."

Larson pulled the nude Charlotte closer. Her body was soft and warm. "My plan has worked good so far."

"So, are you going in this morning?" Charlotte questioned. She was enjoying Larson's masculine scent.

"Yeah, I've got a meeting with rooms and engineering. We're switching to digital room lighting. Save us a couple bucks each month."

"Might try that at the Cosmo. Thronton will think I'm smart."

"You are smart. That's why you're attracted to me."

"Right," Charlotte agreed, reaching to run her fingers over his day-old beard. "It's you and me against the world."

———

LUKE MITCHEL MADE it to his suite. There, he tossed his jacket, brushed his teeth, and laid down on the bed, promising himself he'd take his pants off in a few minutes. In a few minutes, he was asleep.

A bell rang, signaling the end of the geometry class. Luke was glad, as he never understood the principle of the shortest distance being a straight line. Wasn't the line the issue instead of the distance? The bell continued to ring in successive annoying bursts until Luke opened his eyes to find sunlight filling the room and the annoying bell was the telephone. Luke knew who it was—Gayle Turner. The IT duo had done it again. She was calling with good news. Luke reached and grabbed the bedside telephone.

"Tell me it's good news," he said enthusiastically.

The caller wasn't Gaye Turner. It was a man, James Bergman, the new director in human resources, calling. "I'm not sure you'll think it's good news," Bergman cautioned.

Luke recognized the voice. He was now awake, feet on the floor. "Sorry, Jim. I was expecting a call from someone else."

"I'll be brief," Bergman promised. "As you know, Dan Payne appealed his dismissal. There is a hearing set for tomorrow morning at nine a.m. in the general manager's office. You will be expected to attend."

"Tomorrow. Why so soon?" Luke saw it as a threat to his investigation.

"Policy dictates if an appeal is filed, a hearing must be held within three to five days to preclude possible hardship on the concerned individual."

"Concerned individual. Good name for Payne. Who will be there?" Luke questioned.

"The general manager, myself, and as I mentioned yesterday, the head of cash operations, as well as the GM's assistant, Jackie Fallon. She will be taking short-hand notes. And you. I believe that's five. Unless you have any witnesses."

Luke's mind went to Sergeant Stone who sat in on Payne's dismissal. Stone heard it all, saw the cash Payne collected, and then, as ordered, escorted Payne off the property. "Yeah," Luke answered, "I'd like to bring a witness. Sergeant Stone from our PM watch."

"What's Stone's first name? I'll have to notify him."

"Damn," Luke confessed, "I don't know his first name. He's my witness. Let me notify him."

"All right, so there will be six of us present at nine

a.m. I suggest you schedule an hour plus. Will you be showing any video?"

"Yes, possibly." Luke's mind raced through the videos he'd seen of Payne. Which ones could he show, which ones *should* he show. "I may bring a CD." They had compiled a CD showing Payne and Caroline Summers every time they left and returned on their gold-buying missions as well as Caroline's subsequent addition of a brick to the table in the count room.

"All right, the GM has a flat-screen. I'm sure he'll allow us to use it. Unless you'd prefer something else."

Luke's thoughts went to the GM after Bergman's mention of him. "Have you talked to Larson?"

"Not personally," Bergman answered." I spoke with Jackie Fallon, his assistant. She assured me it would be put on his calendar. I must add this. We are all prohibited from talking to any and all of those taking part in the hearing."

"Welcome to witness protection." Luke resented Payne challenging him with the hearing. What if the sonofabitch won. Payne had Caroline Summers's vote. Probably Bergman's, too. Fuck, that was two out of three. It was over. How could he stay if his authority was overturned by a fucking extortionist? And with all that, Candice wanted a check for ten thousand. And Barbara still hadn't called. When was it they last spoke. Should he tell her about the condo?

"Unless you have any questions," Bergman asked after the awkward pause.

"I'll be there. Oh-nine hundred."

"Yes, nine o'clock," Bergman said, challenging Luke's translation to military time.

———

JACKIE FALLON, like most of the citizens of Las Vegas, learned of the kiss heard around the world. She got it from the security officer at the gate to employee parking. "Your boss called. He said he was kissing off the Big Ten meeting."

"What's that supposed to mean?" she questioned.

"Means he might be late. Sort of a kiss-off."

Jackie went away, annoyed with the security officer talking in riddles. Annoyed until she heard more on the elevator. Three housekeepers on their way down for breakfast, pushing a cart filled with soiled linen. If they knew who Jackie was, they didn't seem to care, or it was the truth.

"He kissed her."

"Where."

"At the Big Ten meeting. Right in front of everyone."

"Who says it's true?"

"My aunt. She works there in a gift shop."

"Did she see it?"

"No, but she knows people who did. Two servers and a barmaid."

"And I heard it from a girlfriend at the Cosmo."

"Why would he do that?"

"That's why she quit her job here. They're in love."

Jackie was worried when she reached her office. Greg Larson had not arrived. She turned on the lights and checked her messages. Two calls from the front desk, one from engineering, and three from local television stations, and four more from talk radio, all wanting a callback and comments, but nothing from the GM. Jackie was worried. How could she deal with TV stations? All she heard was gossip. What the hell happened? Who could she ask? She could almost feel the electricity in the air. Where was the GM? Was he late, or was he not coming in, and then she thought of Luke. He was there when the GM and Charlotte clashed. She didn't know him well, but she knew him well enough to trust him. She sat down at her desk and called his cell number.

"This is Luke."

"Luke, this is Jackie Fellon. Is it true? Have you heard?"

There was a pause, then Luke answered. "It's true."

"Damn," Jackie said. "I didn't want to believe it. What will they do to him."

"I don't know," Luke answered candidly.

"I don't know what to do," Jackie confessed into the phone as the door of her office opened.

Greg Larson walked in. "Morning, sunshine." He smiled, marching into his office.

"Cathy, I'll have to call you back," Jackie said, covering her tracks. She hung up.

"Cathy?" Luke questioned, giving his cell phone a puzzled look. Then he understood. He punched in the number for surveillance.

"Surveillance, this is Gayle."

"Gayle, it's Luke. Is the GM on property?"

"Yes, I tried calling you. Your line was busy."

"Thanks. Anything from the IT gang?"

"Nothing new, their doors still closed, but they have your CD ready."

"Good. Have a uniform. Bring it up."

JACKIE FALLON DID her best to regain composure, but she was still on edge. She dared going to the open door of the GM's office. "Would you like your morning Starbucks?"

"Yes, I would," Greg Larson answered from behind his desk. He pushed back in his chair and studied Jackie. "And yes, it's true. I kissed Charlotte yesterday at the Big Ten meeting."

Jackie's hand went to her chest. "It's true! You did that. Why?"

"My way of telling the world I love her," Larson answered with a smile.

"What's going to happen?" Jackie asked apprehensively.

"You'll be among the first to know," Larson said. "Now, about that coffee."

When Jackie disappeared from the doorway, the GM picked up his telephone and called Luke Mitchel.

"This is Luke."

"Luke, I need help."

"I'm listening."

"There's a lot of talk going around about what happened yesterday."

"Yes, I've heard."

"It was dumb. I don't regret doing it, but I do regret that it could hurt Charlotte."

"You're talking about the Big Ten meeting."

"I'm talking about all the fucking cameras. Bellagio probably has more than we do."

"You don't have to worry about videos. I talked to their director of security. He told me Don Marardino, their GM, ordered the tapes erased."

Larson closed his eyes and bowed his head, gripping the telephone tight in his hand. Luke wasn't surprised at the GM's reaction. He could hear Larson's labored breath. He considered telling him he'd seen the video sent over by Bellagio surveillance before it was ordered erased, but he thought there was nothing to be gained.

Larson drew in a deep breath before he spoke again. "Thanks, Luke. I appreciate you making the call."

"Don Marardino is the one you should thank."

"For sure," Larson agreed as relief swept over him. He wiped his face and raised his head. "Don's a big fan of Lady Gaga. I…I'll invite him over to meet her." He hung up abruptly.

Luke had a hundred questions for Larson, but he sensed they wouldn't be answered today. What was next? What was the plan for the day? Would Larson resign? Who would someone be demanding answers? Luke needed to talk with the GM and bring him up to speed on the theft of the gold. Show him the CD of Payne returning the gold bricks the same day they bought them. Show him Payne's car sitting in the driveway at Caroline Summers's house, but he could do none of it. James Bergman had instructed him not to talk with any of the principals involved in the pending hearing. Luke was stuck. He knew Dan Payne would claim he was fired for violating a policy established by Blake Mancini. The truth was much different. Payne had extorted money after Luke gave him a direct order not to. Damn, he was sorry he had ordered Pam off the property. Dan Payne had extorted money from her the night he was fired. Not likely she'd be open to being called in as a witness. Especially after he suggested she was a whore and ordered her off the property.

There was also the issue of relevancy. The hearing was the result of Dan Payne alleging he was terminated for violating a procedure established long ago by Blake Mancini. It was not about the theft of the gold. If Luke tried to make it that, he was certain both Payne and James Bergman would argue it wasn't relevant to his termination. Bergman, as the newly appointed head of human resources, was likely to want to be seen as a defender of employee rights. Hell, when Luke thought about how quickly the hearing was scheduled, coupled with being cautioned about talking to anyone involved, it became obvious where the hell Bergman's head was. Ironically, the hearing was about Dan Payne being terminated, but if he prevailed, if he got Bergman's vote and Caroline Summers's, the compass would turn and point at Luke. His brief career as the director of security would be over. How could he stay if his judgment was overruled, and a thief was reinstated? They wouldn't have to ask him to go, he'd resign.

His possible resignation brought Green Valley to mind. How the hell could he write Candice Harmond a ten-thousand-dollar check and then resign. The answer was simple. Luke's outlook was grim. Dan Payne's words when Luke fired him came haunting back. *"You're going to regret this, Mitchel."* And he was regretting it. There wasn't a hell of a lot he could say other than Payne's termination was justified. Even if Greg Larson sided with Luke, Dan Payne still had Caroline Summer's favor locked up, and Jim Bergman was on the fence because of their recent clash over homosexuality. Two out of three. Dan Payne was turning out to be a challenging opponent. It was as if they were playing a game of poker, and Dan Payne, it seemed, was holding a full house.

Luke was hoping his phone would ring and Gayle Turner would tell him the IT gang had found something else, but as morning gave way to afternoon, his telephone stayed quiet. Luke called Sergeant Stone to alert him that he was needed at Payne's hearing. "Just tell them what you saw and heard," Luke suggested. "Do you remember seeing him drop the money on the floor?"

"Yeah, I remember. He was really pissed."

"So, tomorrow you tell them about it."

"Got it. I'll be there."

"Sarg, could I have your first name?"

"Sure, it's Anakoni."

"Could you spell that for me?"

Luke read daily logs and dialed into a live video from the kitchen. The senior chef had complained about what he suspected was a low inventory of frozen shrimp. There was more shrimp missing than prepared. Luke sent an alert to his three watch commanders and surveillance. How much shrimp could you stuff in your coat pockets? A lot. Luke found he was not the only one watching when the PTZ view of the kitchen changed and zoomed in on a man preparing a shrimp salad. Luke's interest waned after five minutes of watching. How did surveillance do it? They watched people for hours. Luke wished them well and went back to his notes on Dan Payne. He found that boring, too. Boring in that if Payne prevailed at tomorrow's hearing, the gold investigation was over. Luke would brief the GM and resign. Either way, he was determined to get a piece of Dan Payne's ass.

Finding a summary of last night's sold-out show for Lady Gaga made Luke think of a woman important in his life. Barbara Nichols, the new director of food and beverage at the Wild River Casino in Alta Vista, Arizona. He tried to remember the last time they talked. Who called who. That was important. He wasn't sure why, he just knew it was important. The question followed. He knew it would. Should he call her? He tried to think of a reason for a call.

Calling simply because he missed her was a sign of weakness. Or was it? He could be calling just to see how she was. Did she like being a director? Did it fit? Had they appointed a new security director? Who was it? Why was he banned after saving a woman's life? The Mojaves were a tough bunch. Was his life easier with them than it was at The Silver Palace? It was a tough question. Luke decided he liked both. Working for the Mojaves was challenging but working at The Silver Palace was proving to be an even greater challenge. Who in their right mind would steal a gold brick weighing over two pounds. Not once, not twice, but three times. And then, the theft is reported by the head of cash operations who was likely the lover of the suspected thief. He decided calling Barbara would be much easier than thinking about the fucking hearing. He pulled his cell off his belt and punched in Barb's number.

"Hello."

"Hi, Barb. It's Luke. How are you?"

"Oh," Barb answered. "Today's been a bitch. We've got a group of two hundred and fifty hog farmers scheduled for a banquet tonight. Our chef wanted to prepare them a pork dinner. A plate with pig on it for a hog farmer."

Luke smiled. Barb was being Barb. Ask how she was and get ready for the answer because she was going to speak the truth. "So, no pork. What can you do?"

"What I did was go to every supermarket within forty miles and buy all their steaks. We only had twenty pounds of filet."

"It sounds like you may like your new job," Luke teased.

"You know, I go home at night now, but I can't sleep. I worked nights too long. Yeah, I like it. Being boss feels good."

"I'm glad."

"So, what's up?"

Luke thought about an answer. He thought about the

condo in Green Valley. The mess the GM was in, and the freaking hearing set for tomorrow. He thought about all of it but decided to push them aside and say something she could hold on to.

"I called because I miss you."

Barbara raised a hand to her heart. "I miss you too, Luke. Why don't you come home."

"The day we met, I asked you where you were from," Luke countered. "Your answer was, I'm home. Seems you were telling me the truth. You're there, with the Mojaves, and you like it, and I'm up here in Vegas, because I like it."

It was quiet for a moment. Both had found words that held the truth, but neither liked hearing it. Finally, Barbara spoke. "Luke, I appreciate your call, but I've got a lot of steaks and only a couple hours to do it."

"Remember, I like mine well-done."

"I won't forget."

Luke ended the call. He stared at the telephone after laying it on his desk. He wished he hadn't called her. Hell, he said nothing about why he really called. He loved this woman, or was it he *wanted* to love her? Maybe that was it, Luke reasoned. He wanted something different than what he had. He thought it was Barbara, but their words got in the way. She was obviously happy. He wasn't. He'd lost the woman he loved to a steak. She was going to fix dinner for a bunch of hog farmers when she could have fixed his.

TWENTY-ONE

THE TRUTH WILL SET YOU FREE

JACKIE FALLON BECAME the barrier between Greg Larson and the demanding press. She answered their calls. And there were many. She was learning what skilled liars reporters could be. *"I'm from the FCC and it's important I talk to the GM. Hello, Howard Gilman calling. I'm an attorney representing your boss. Is he in? Jack Inghram, here. I'm Greg's cousin. I need to..."*

She answered nineteen of them while Greg Larson went on with his talks with engineering and the plans for a rooftop glass pool. The engineers were followed by Tom Roberts, the card room manager, who wanted his desk in the center of the room raised on a four-foot carpeted step platform so when he sat down at his desk, he could see all of his dealers and tables, and then there was the publicist for The Silver Palace, Gary Clinger, a fifty-year-old, Larson had hired away from the Desert Sun, Las Vegas's premier daily newspaper. Jackie didn't like the man because he kept hitting on her. Her rejections were quick and firm. Dating him, Jackie thought, would be like going on a date with her uncle. She knew

Clinger was there because of the kiss heard round the world. All of Vegas wanted to see what happened, and Clinger would tell them with a press release he was already working on. He was a skilled and respected writer who knew the heart of the town. His press release, he told Jackie, would be titled *Kiss and Tell. Yesterday, he kissed her, and today we're going to tell why.* Jackie granted him a smile as he waited his turn in the Throne Room.

When morning yielded to afternoon and Greg Larson's meetings continued, Jackie ordered him lunch. "Make it for two," she told room service.

Gary Clinger was hanging on while Lesia Gardener, the head of housekeeping, awaited her turn. A VIP guest had complained about a housekeeper eating the remains of a candy bar she left unattended. Greg Larson's kiss heard around the world may have made for great gossip, but the task of running The Silver Palace was making its daily demands. At least, that's the way it appeared. In reality, Greg Larson was hiding in his office doing what he did best, running from the truth by wrapping himself in idle talk, making calls, pretending there was work that had to be done. He was right, and he was lost in it. Ignoring a world, he crowded out. He hoped Charlotte was doing the same.

————

Luke hadn't slept well. He had stayed in his office until darkness was chased away by a night not allowed beyond the fabled illuminated sign that read, *Welcome to Las Vegas.*

Instead of ordering room service, he rummaged in the fridge in his suite to find a cold bottle of Starbucks and some Orioles. Sitting on his couch, he thumbed through a thick volume of The *Silver Palace's Employee Rights and Privileges*. He read it and his six pages of notes, time and time again, while watching the CD the IT duo had prepared. Every time Dan Payne appeared, he cursed. The sonofabitch was threatening not only Luke's job but everything he loved. He had himself believing Dan Payne was responsible for Barbara's attitude. If it wasn't for him, she would be sharing his bed tonight. Luke finally fell asleep with the CD still playing its silent images.

"Holy shit," Luke said when he awoke to find the Strip basking in sunshine. He looked for a clock. "Fuck!" It was seven-twenty a.m. He wanted his morning to be leisurely. Time to think, prepare, and practice his speech. That dream was gone. He bolted from the couch, heading for the bathroom.

———

Naome Larson hadn't slept at all. She was dressed in a bathrobe and sitting at the kitchen table with the Rottweiler lying at her feet. Early in the evening, she talked to her daughter about her father's departure, and his plans for divorce. Tammy had taken it well.

"I knew it was coming," she told her mother. Naome knew Greg was an unfaithful, heartless prick. She'd known it for years. What made it different this time? Not having sex for six years was one thing, living alone was another. What would she tell her friends? Divorce. The telephone rang time and time again. Friends, the press and strangers, all wanting comment. *"How did you feel when you heard about it? Have you talked to an attorney? Did you know she's Black? Why did he kiss her in public? Sue him for his money! have you told your daughter?"*

Naome had turned the TV off at eleven when a smiling anchorman began talking about the *Winning Kiss* that took place at the Bellagio. The whole town was talking about it. Naome dug in a pocket of her robe for more Alprazolam. She took three. How long had it been since she took the Amphetamines stolen from a friend at the gym? She couldn't remember, and she didn't care. The telephone began ringing again. She hoped it wouldn't wake Tammy and then she remembered her daughter wasn't home. Naome had checked her bedroom around two a.m. The bed was untouched, and Tammy was gone. Just like her father. They could both go to hell. She decided to take two another Alprazolam.

———

GREG LARSON WAS IN EARLY. He was sitting behind his desk, telephone to his ear, talking to the rooms director when Jackie Fallon arrived. After a good morning nod to the GM through his open door, Jackie ordered him coffee and pastry. She, too, had a long night with her telephone. Finally, she took it off the hook and turned off her cell. Now, sitting at her desk, she wondered if this would be Greg Larson's last day. She was certain, although the Chinese investors were half a world away, by now they knew what was going on. Greg Lawson getting the boot meant it was the end of the road for her. No one would want to keep a know-it-all assistant. A new GM wouldn't be interested in keeping the girl whose loyalty could be—would be—an issue. Jackie Fallon was growing angry.

The morning talk shows in Las Vegas all talked about

The Kiss. There was a lot of speculation about what it was, but for the most part, without the obvious missing video, talk turned from serious misconduct to light-hearted jokes. After all, morning talk had to be light-hearted.

"Without the missing video, we have to wonder what part of her body he kissed," NBC suggested.

"The crew at Bellagio took pictures, but they claim the film is still being developed," CBS reported.

"Greg Larson, the GM of the Silver Palace, now holds the record for how many Black women you kiss before a meeting starts." FOX smiled.

"Many are claiming when the kiss ended, Larson cried out, Black is beautiful," Channel 13 claimed.

Channel 21 reported, "The GM from The Silver Palace claims he kissed her because Black Lives Matter."

"Remember," the anchor at KTNV, claimed as their show signed off, "What happens in Vegas, stays in Vegas."

TikTok stole the show on social media by airing a video of *The Big Kiss.* It had over three million views in its first three hours. Don Marandino considered launching an investigation into the leak, but after reading the online comments the kiss was drawing, he decided against it.

Greg Lawson and Charlotte Johnson both refused to take calls or watch the news. They were at work not because business demanded it, but because work helped with the agonizing waiting game. A game from which they both expected to be thrown out of. Neither would have believed the dramatic kiss that drew applause from the Big Ten at the Bellagio was now being turned into smiles, jokes, and on its way to becoming part of the Vegas legacy. Reservations at both The Silver Palace and the Bellagio showed a bump in calls. Many of the callers asked about the kiss.

James Bergman was the first to arrive for the nine o'clock meeting in the GM's office. He was followed shortly by Anakoni Stone, in civilian clothes. The two men didn't speak. Caroline Summers was next. She chose to walk through the GM's closed door without knocking or speaking to any of the others. Dan Payne, dressed in a suit and tie, wasn't far behind her. He was surprised to see Stone. He offered both men a nod before sitting down beside Bergman. Luke was next. He first said good morning to Jackie and then looked at the others, avoiding eye contact with Payne. When the minutes passed and the nine o'clock hour arrived, Jackie picked up the telephone. "Sir, everyone's here."

"Bring them in," Gerg Larson answered.

They all stood, and Luke was careful to keep his distance from Dan Payne as the four filed into the GM's office where Caroline Summers and Greg Larson waited.

Jackie followed last, after a girl from accounting arrived to cover for her as she took notes in the hearing. There were seven of them.

Housekeeping, at Jackie's direction, had arranged comfortable padded chairs in a semi-circle around a large glass console table facing a flat-screen TV that was on, playing a screensaver, depicting glamorized images from around The Silver Palace. On the glass table sat a large pitcher filled with ice. Six glasses, evenly spaced, were arranged around the pitcher of ice. The GM got up from his chair and joined the others as they selected seats. Luke was careful to stay away from Dan Payne. He chose a chair beside Anakoni Stone. Caroline Summers, no surprise to Luke, sat down beside Dan Payne.

Although he noticed they did not speak. Greg Larson sat on the end. When all were seated, the GM spoke. "Jim, this hearing was at your request," he said from his chair. "Please introduce all present and we'll get started."

Bergman, notepad in hand, stood and walked to the far side of the glass table to face the others. Luke tried his best to keep his composure. His mouth was cotton-like, and his heart pounded in his ears. He glanced at Payne. The man had his legs crossed, looking relaxed and confident. The sonofabitch.

"Good morning, everyone," Bergman said, offering a smile to the waiting faces. Anakoni Stone coughed and reached for one of the empty glasses on the table. He poured ice and then water as Bergman continued, "We're here as a result of an employee of The Silver Palace, Daniel L. Payne, filing an appeal to what he alleges was an unreasonable, unfair, and biased termination of his employment as a lieutenant in the security department."

Luke tried holding his breath. It didn't work. His heart continued pounding in his ears as Bergman went on. "Lieutenant Payne's assignment at the time of his termination was—"

Luke's limit had been reached. This wasn't a hearing. It was a fight between two men. A fight to determine truth. A fight to expose a fucking thief. He bolted to his feet, and Bergman fell silent. "I'm going to save us all valuable time," Luke said, rounding the table to stand beside the shocked Bergman.

"You'll have your turn," Bergman said, giving Luke an annoyed look.

"My turn is right now," Luke said forcefully as he reached into a jacket pocket and pulled out a CD.

Luke pointed the CD at Dan Payne who now looked worried. "Payne, you're not going to like what you see."

His look went to Caroline Summers. "Caroline, perhaps you know about this, maybe you don't, but we do know who's been sleeping in your bed." Luke stepped to a VCR beneath the flat wide-screen TV. He pushed the CD in.

"This is out of order," Bergman said, burning a look at Luke.

"Shut up," Luke barked in a challenge that could not be ignored.

The video image from the CD lit up the TV. It showed a polished sedan from The Silver Palace pulled into a parking lot. Dan Payne, in uniform and wearing a gun, stepped out of the car. Caroline Summers emerged from the passenger's side.

"Look familiar," Luke said with a look at the two. Then, to the others he added, "They were there to buy gold from the Southern Nevada Mineral Merchants. A buy approved by the general manager."

"This has nothing to do with what we're here to discuss," Bergman protested as he moved away from Luke.

"Let it play," the GM said firmly, as on-screen, Payne and Caroline returned to the car. Payne now carried a nondescript shopping bag which he placed in the trunk. They climbed into the car, and it pulled away. All watched in silence.

"Next," Luke added as he watched the images, "you'll note on-screen, it's six hours later. Watch a black BMW as it pulls in." He looked to Payne. "The car belongs to you, Dan Payne."

On the screen, the black BMW pulled into the lot and parked. Dan Payne, now dressed in civilian clothes, climbed out. He walked to the trunk of the car and lifted out a shopping bag.

"You may think this is the same shopping bag you

saw earlier with two pounds of gold in it," Luke continued, as on-screen, Payne walked toward the gold
merchant's office. "You'd be right. Why now, off duty, in
civilian clothes, why's he bringing the gold back."

"He's took the fucking gold back to sell it to them!"
Greg Larson said in disbelief.

"You bastard!" Dan Payne screamed, bolting to his
feet. He grabbed for the pitcher of ice, flipping the glass
table aside to charge at Luke. The table crashed to the
floor. The two women filled the room with screams.
Payne swung the pitcher at Luke's head. Surprised, Luke
raised an arm, but the heavy pitcher slid over his arm,
slamming against his head. Glass and ice showered
everywhere. The screams got louder. Blood sprang from
the side of Luke's head, running down his jaw and neck
as he staggered and went down on both knees.

"Die, you sonofabitch," Payne yelled, kicking Luke
hard in the ribs with a booted foot. The blow sent Luke
crashing onto his side into the mix of glass and ice on
the floor. His jacket was pushed high, exposing his
holstered pistol.

Payne grabbed for it, ripping the automatic pistol
from Luke's belt. He stood, raised the gun, and aimed at
Luke's head.

The sound of the two gunshots in the office was loud.
Again, the women screamed. The wide, scenic window
rattled. Dan Payne dropped the pistol he held and raised
a hand to a now bloody chest. He looked bewildered,
confused, as he stared at the blood squirting out between
his fingers. He opened his mouth, but there were no
words, then he fell, like the dead man he was, crashing to
the floor.

Greg Larson lowered the automatic pistol he held.
Bergman's hand was shocked. He covered his mouth.

Caroline Summers slumped in her chair as she fainted. Jackie and Anakoni Stone both went to the floor, kneeling beside the bloody Luke.

"Get me some towels, something!" Stone barked, pressing both hands over the bloody gash on Luke's skull. Jackie pushed up and went to the bar. Beneath a sink, she found a roll of paper towels.

Greg Larson shook his head. He was in shock, he laid his pistol on his desk and picked up the telephone to dial 911. "We need an ambulance. Two men. One shot. One bleeding. In the GM's office at The Silver Palace. Send the police, too."

Caroline Summers stirred and looked in shock at the two fallen men. Jackie had returned to Stone's side where they tried to slow Luke's heavy bleeding. Bergman moved to the shaken Caroline Summers, deliberately standing in front of her. "Don't look," he said, lifting her to her feet.

Loud pounding sounded on the outside of the door. "Open the door or we'll kick it in," a male voice ordered.

Larson moved to the door and opened it. Sergeant Lopez and two uniformed officers burst into the room with guns drawn. They saw the GM, the blood, and the two men on the floor.

"You all right?" Lopez questioned with a look at the shaken GM.

"Yeah, I think I killed a man."

"Where's the gun?"

"On my desk."

One of the officers went and picked up the automatic pistol from the GM's desk. He popped the magazine, worked the action to eject a live round and pushed the gun into his waistband.

As Lopez and the two officers joined Jackie and

Sergeant Stone near the two fallen men, the GM went to his bar to pour himself a drink.

"This one's dead," he heard one of the officers say.

Caroline Summers was escorted away by Bergman. She was in tears and shock.

Two LVFD paramedics were first on the scene with a stretcher and a first aid kit. After a quick exam of Daniel Payne, they turned to Luke, pushing the bloody, crying Jackie aside, along with Sergeant Stone, who went to the sink at the bar to flush blood from his hands. Both of Stone's knees were bloody from cuts where he kneeled in the shattered glass. Jackie sank into a chair and covered her face with her bloody hands. She was weeping. The paramedics started CPR on Luke. The paramedics were followed by a two-man team from the LVFD. They joined in working on Luke. More uniformed security officers arrived.

The officers paused in the open doorway, and Sergeant Lopez waved them away. "Block the door," he ordered. "Nobody gets in."

The Metropolitan police arrived. Three uniformed police officers with guns drawn, entered the room. "Everything under control?" a sergeant with a beard questioned, looking to Lopez.

"One dead, another possible," Sergeant Lopez answered soberly. The officers holstered their weapons.

"Who shot them?" the bearded sergeant asked, looking at Payne's lifeless blood-covered body lying on its back, eyes open, staring sightlessly at the ceiling.

"Only one shot," Anakoni Stone answered, wiping his wet hands on his pants. "Dead guy hit him with a glass pitcher."

"Was he the shooter?" the sergeant pressed.

"No, I am," Greg Larson volunteered, raising a hand. There was a drink glass in his other hand.

"Where's the gun?" the sergeant asked, stepping toward the GM cautiously.

"I've got it," the security officer with the GM's gun answered. He pulled the automatic from his waistband and handed it to the sergeant.

The sergeant looked at the gun, then to Larson, before glancing at one of the men close behind him. "Take him into custody."

One of the police officers stepped behind Larson, pulling out his handcuffs. Larson quickly downed the rest of his drink as a handcuff clicked onto his free wrist.

"Get him out of here. He talks to nobody."

"I've got a CCW," Larson said as he was led away.

Two of the paramedics got up from where Luke lay. One of them had Luke's gun in hand. He offered the pistol to the sergeant. The others continued taking turns with CPR. Jackie dared a look and then covered her face again. The telephone on Larson's desk rang time and time again. The sergeant took it off the hook. Two of the paramedics readied the stretcher.

One of them spoke into a radio mike pinned on his lapel. "Alert Spring Valley, we've got one on the way. Major blood loss, full cardiac arrest."

Three of the paramedics lifted the bloody Luke from the floor onto the stretcher. He was strapped in. "What about the other?" one of the paramedics questioned.

"No hurry with him."

The police sergeant keyed his radio as Luke was wheeled away. "King Sixty to control. Alert homicide, we got one down. GSW. Another on the way to Spring Valley. We're at the scene."

Jackie and Anakoni Stone were led out of the GM's office by the Metro cops. Jackie was still weeping. "Find a place to keep them until the dicks get here." When they were gone, the sergeant looked at Payne's body, then the bloody spot where Luke had fallen, the broken glass and melting ice, and the two bullet holes in the wall near the flat-screen.

The sergeant turned to his partner. "Welcome to The Silver Palace."

CPR continued as the unconscious Luke was unloaded from the ambulance at the Spring Valley Hospital ER. He was wheeled inside where a team of physicians took over. Luke was given oxygen and a shot of adrenaline directly into his heart. The two doctors and nurses stared at the monitors as the seconds ticked by. Finally, a beep sounded, followed by a weak spike on the screen. Then another.

"Okay, he's alive. Let's get some blood in him," one of the doctors ordered through his mask.

EPILOGUE

LUKE AWOKE THREE HOURS LATER. He had a serious concussion and a crack in his skull just behind his left ear. There was a nurse sitting bedside with him in his ICU. After opening his eyes, Luke looked around the room and then wiggled his toes to make sure he could. He had a headache, and he was cold. He turned his head to find the nurse beside him reading a book. Luke took in a breath before he spoke, his throat was dry. "Do you know what time it is?"

The nurse reacted to Luke's voice with a smile. She closed her book, stood, and glanced at her watch. "Three-thirty-five," she answered.

Doctors were called. They checked Luke's blood pressure, asked him what day it was, and who was the president of the United States. He got them right. They checked the staples behind his ear. "We're going to keep you overnight for observation. Maybe you'll be out of here tomorrow."

Luke was moved to a regular room. He was given a

shot for pain and then Candice Harmond and Gayle Turner arrived. They offered smiles and encouragement.

Seven thousand three hundred and twenty-seven miles away in the city of Hong Kong, it was six thirty a.m. In the International Commerce Center building at 1 Austin Road West, in Kowloon, the five members of the Star Man Wind Investment Group were meeting in an emergency session to discuss finding a new general manager for their flagship property, The Silver Palace in Las Vegas, Nevada. Word of *the Kiss* had reached them the day before. They were being laughed at in the investment world. Greg Larson would have to go. He would be fired and replaced temporarily by the rooms director until a new GM could be found. When it was time to vote for Larson's firing, Chang Ling, the chairman of Star Man Wind, asked for a show of hands.

Five hands were raised. It was unanimous. Chang Ling would be the one to call and tell Larson he was finished. He had performed well. They made money. Lots of it, but the laughter could not be tolerated. Chang was about to go to his office to make the call when Mei Kum, his young Chinese assistant, came in. The girl, looking troubled, bowed to the five men around the conference table and then asked to speak privately with Chang Ling. Chang and the girl stepped into a hallway and closed the door. Several minutes later, Chang returned, and now he was the one looking troubled.

"There is news from Las Vegas," Chang said, standing at the head of the table. "Greg Larson has shot and killed a man in his office. The man attacked another employee after it was discovered he stole some of our gold from The Silver Palace."

"What does that have to do with Larson being fired?" one of the Chinese investors at the table asked.

Chang Ling leaned both of his hands onto the polished table. "Mei Kum saw this on CNN as breaking news just a few minutes ago. Greg Larson is now being called a hero by the press, social media, as well as the Las Vegas Police. If we fire him, we will be the ones laughed at. If we keep him, maybe we can have the last laugh."

———

AT THE SPRING VALLEY HOSPITAL, Candice Harmond dangled a set of keys in front of Luke Mitchel's face as she and Gayle stood bedside. "Guess what, dude," she said to the weary-looking bandaged Luke. "While you were playing *taking one for the Palace*, I talked to the realtor who listed the condo in Green Valley."

"And?" Luke questioned, from where he lay in the raised hospital bed, then reaching with a hand and a finger, he touched the bandage behind his ear.

"And they accepted your offer."

Two sober men wearing jackets and ties came into the room. One wore sunglasses. All knew they were police officers. "We need a couple minutes with him," the older of the two detectives said.

Candice pocketed the keys and looked to Gayle. Gayle, in turn, looked to Luke. "We won't go far."

When the two women were gone, the detectives looked to Luke. "I'm Sergeant Hanson. This is my partner, John Mattingly. We're doing the follow-up on the incident in the GM's office. So, someone hit you with a glass pitcher," Det. Hanson questioned. "Do you know who it was?"

"Yeah," Luke answered, "his name is Dan Payne. I fired him a couple days ago. We were holding a hearing because he appealed my decision. Is he under arrest?"

The two detectives exchanged a look. Mattingly lifted off his sunglasses before he spoke. "Dan Payne is dead."

"Dead! Who did it? How?" Luke was shocked,

Sergeant Hanson took the lead. "The witnesses in the room tell us Payne knocked you down with a glass pitcher. After you were on the floor, he tried to take your gun, saying he was going to kill you."

Luke's heart raced. "I don't remember shooting him. I can't…"

"No, no, you didn't," Mattingly said, "the GM shot him, twice, when Payne aimed your gun at you."

Luke's face showed his disbelief. "The GM! And Payne is dead?"

"Very," Hanson added, "and you didn't know that?"

"No, I didn't know. How is Larson, the GM?"

"Rattled," Sergeant Hanson explained. "We took a formal statement prior to his release. He has a valid CCW. It looks like he saved your life."

"So, the shooting was justified?"

"You're breathing, aren't you?" Mattingly suggested.

The two detectives spent nearly an hour with Luke as he laid out the investigation leading to his suspicion that Dan Payne was the thief.

"Won't be hard, looking at what kind of money he had," Sergeant Hanson assured. "We'll need copies of the video you have. Looks like The Southern Nevada Mining Merchant might have some dirt on them too."

"What do you think of Caroline Summers's, involvement?" Mattingly asked.

"I told you about Payne's BMW being at her house."

"Was he doing her?"

"Why else was he there?"

"With shots fired," Sergeant Hanson concluded, "you know you're done with this. It now belongs to us."

Luke nodded agreement. He was glad that the Metro cops were taking over the case.

"You were a cop with the LAPD," Mattingly questioned as the interview wound down.

"Once upon a time," Luke answered.

"And you gave it up for this?"

"My base pay is probably four times bigger than the two of yours, combined. I don't get insults, or callouts, or worry about how much of a raise the city might give me next year. I've got an office, a small army to support me, and I still carry a gun."

"Where can I apply?" Mattingly smiled.

Sergeant Hanson wrapped it up by asking Luke for help. "Listen, there is one more thing."

"Do what I can," Luke promised.

"When we came in, there must have been six, eight reporters out in the waiting room, along with camera crews. They know you're here. Get the story, get a statement."

"Got it," Luke assured.

———

Charlotte Johnson was in her office at the Cosmo when an assistant stuck her head in the open door. "Aren't you a refugee from The Silver Palace?"

"Yes, why?"

"Been a shooting over there. In the GM's office."

Charlotte was shocked. Her hands trembled as she tried calling Greg Larson's private cell number. No answer. She tried Jackie Fallon. Again, no answer. Finally, Jim Bergman did answer. He knew why Charlotte was calling. "He's fine, Charlotte. He's probably still talking to the cops."

———

Lopez, Stone, and KC King all came in for a quick visit with Luke. Gayle and Candice stayed through the dinner hour and ate most of what he didn't. Gayle promised him she'd get the cops the CD they needed for follow-up.

Along with darkness, came quiet. Luke was relieved. He was weary and in pain. He complained but the nurse told him the on-duty physician said it was too early. He could have more pain drugs after two a.m. Luke wasn't happy with the answer, but he reasoned his anger was deeper than a doctor stalling on a pain med. Once again, death had found its way into his life. This time, some of the blood spilled was his own, but nonetheless, death was back, and it was haunting him. Was Dan Payne's life worth more than three bars of gold? Any life was, but he once again saw himself setting it in motion. A dead Marine, a dead cop, and now Dan Payne. He was surrounded by them. The pebble in the pound. The ripples stretched far and wide. Luke saw himself as the one responsible for the death of others. It was chilling and painful. The ICU nurse returned, but she didn't say anything. She simply sat quietly, reading, occasionally checking the instruments wired to him.

Finally, after several hours, Luke broke the silence in the quiet room. "As a nurse, how do you deal with death."

The nurse closed her book. She was quiet for a moment. "That's a very big question."

"Life is a big question," Luke suggested.

"I know what you're feeling," the nurse suggested. "I couldn't help but hear what the police were talking about, and all the press that's out there."

"Everything has a starting point," Luke added.

"And you think you started this."

"I don't think it. I know it."

The nurse noticed as Luke talked his blood pressure was climbing and his pulse rate was up. "The man that was shot was the man that hurt you?"

"But he's dead and I'm not."

"I used to blame myself for what others did, but then I learned I'm not the one responsible for them. I can only hope that now and then I can help, but how someone lives or dies is seldom anyone's fault but their own."

"You're talking like a nurse."

"And you're talking like I used to."

"I don't understand?"

"Okay, I'll bare my soul, but you promise it stays in this room?"

"Yes, it stays."

"You work at The Silver Palace?"

"Yes."

"I may be telling you something you already know," the nurse said, sitting down to clasp her hands together. "In the not-too-distant past, I stayed at The Silver Palace. My then-husband and I had just got married. We argued over something, not much. It wasn't my first marriage. It was my third. He left me in the room. I called my son. That didn't go well. I knew it was all my fault. I thought of ways to punish him. Jump off the balcony and die came to mind. He'd be sorry I got nude and went out on the balcony."

Luke's pulse raced higher as he listened.

"I was going to jump but this guy came from some-where and somehow saved me," she sniffed. "I never even saw his face. I heard his name later on the news, but I didn't really listen. In the weeks to follow, I realized he did what he had to do. He saved me. He didn't know me. I didn't know him, but our lives crossed, and I'm alive.

"My point is," the nurse continued, without looking at Luke, "I'm not in charge of my life. Something, someone who is much bigger, someone who knows it all, is in charge. All I can hope is I get it right, along the way. Do my best. Do what's right. The man who saved me did his best and I'm alive because of it. After he saved me, I quit my job in San Diego, got a divorce, and moved up here. I hoped moving here, where my life really started over, would help someone with their life. I know I've done what's best. That's all any of us can do."

Luke nodded silent agreement.

It was nearly midnight when the GM and Charlotte came in. Greg Lawson had to shake Luke awake. They shook hands, hugged, and laughed. Luke was truly glad to see them. He told them he was worried. "Hell, we were worried," Greg Larson confessed.

After the hugs, tears were wiped away and the laughs ended. The GM then looked to Charlotte. "Babe, give us a couple minutes for some man-talk."

Charlotte kissed Luke's hand and left.

"You okay?" Larson asked soberly after Charlotte was gone.

Luke reached and took Larson's hand in his. "I'm good. How about you? I'm told you saved my life."

"So now you owe me one," Larson answered, pulling his hand from Luke's. He looked embarrassed. "The press has been a pain in the ass," Larson added, trying to move the conversation in a different direction.

"I'm glad they're after you and not me," Luke suggested.

"Any idea how long you're going to be in here," Larson questioned.

"Maybe tomorrow. Just a concussion. I should be back in a day couple days."

Larson looked awkward. Luke saw it. Finally, their eyes met. "I can't let you come back as director, Luke. I'm giving security to Gayle Turner."

"What!" Luke was shocked.

"You heard me." the GM smiled. "Gayle Turner's getting security, so you're moving up to become our director of integrity. Yeah, okay, I'll make security subordinate to you. You're going to find out why we're short three hundred pounds of shrimp, and forty-six steaks, who's been resetting payouts in slots, where did two hundred and six digital lights go, and why aren't we catching all the counterfeit tokens coming into the cage, who do we buy our cardstock from? In other words, you're going to make sure integrity knows no compromise at The Silver Palace."

"Holy crap," Luke whispered.

"Okay, okay, so, we'll factor in a raise too."

A LOOK AT: VEGAS SKIN (THE VEGAS TRILOGY BOOK 2)

Beneath the glamour of Las Vegas lies a darker reality—a world where sex and money collide, and the line between survival and crime is razor thin.

Luke Mitchell, Director of Security for the Silver Palace Resort & Casino, is no stranger to this reality. Every night, he and his team are responsible for keeping thousands of guests—and millions in cash—safe from the dangers lurking in the shadows of Sin City.

In *Vegas Skin*, the second installment of the *Vegas Trilogy*, Luke faces his toughest challenge yet: battling the rampant prostitution that threatens to overrun his casino. Everyone wants a piece of the Silver Palace's wealth, and when a Hip Hop Legend's after-hours debauchery puts Luke in conflict with the casino's powerful GM, the stakes become personal.

As Luke fights to maintain control, secrets surface that could destroy everything he's worked for. And as if that weren't enough, his personal life takes a hit when his long-time girlfriend, Barbara, takes a questionable job at a local gentleman's club.

Sex, lies, and betrayal threaten to unravel the world Luke thought he knew. In a city where everyone has something to hide, can Luke keep the Silver Palace—and his own life—intact?

In *Vegas Skin*, what happens in Vegas may not stay there for long.

AVAILABLE FEBRUARY 2025

ABOUT THE AUTHOR

Dallas Barnes, a former Director of Security & Surveillance in Las Vegas as well as a Los Angeles Police Homicide Detective, is the author of twelve novels. Vegas Gold is the first novel in the series based on his experiences while serving as Director of Security & Surveillance in Resort & Casino environments, including those listed below…

MGM Grand Signature—Las Vegas, NV
Hyatt Regency Resort & Casino—Lake Las Vegas, NV
Fantasy Springs Resort & Casino—Cabazon, CA
Agua Caliente Casino & Resort—Palm Springs, CA
Augustine Casino—Coachella, CA
Morongo Resort & Casino—Cabazon, CA
Blue Water Resort & Casino—Parker, AZ

Made in the USA
Las Vegas, NV
01 March 2025

18906934R00198